The Current

Yannick Thoraval

Publisher: Furber
Postal: 7/700 Riversdale Rd, Camberwell, VIC 3124
Tel: +61 03 0414 399 218
Email: yannickthoraval@yahoo.com
Website: www.yannickthoraval.com

First published in Australia 2014
Copyright © Yannick Thoraval 2014
Cover design: Zero21
Illustrations: Tauseef Ahmed

National Library of Australia Cataloguing –in –
Publication entry
Thoraval, Yannick
THE CURRENT
ISBN: 978-0-9925916-0-1
Cover layout and design by Zero21
Illustrations by Tauseef Ahmed
Printed by IngramSpark
Typeset in Palatino 11pt on 12.5pt

Disclaimer
All care has been taken in the preparation of the information herein, but no responsibility can be accepted by the publisher or author for any damages resulting from the misinterpretation of this work.

For all who have lost, or found, or are still searching for their home.

L'Eden Sur Mer

No Man is an Island

No man is an island entire of itself; every man
is a piece of the continent, a part of the main;
if a clod be washed away by the sea, Europe
is the less, as well as if a promontory were, as
well as any manner of thy friends or of thine
own were; any man's death diminishes me,
because I am involved in mankind.
And therefore never send to know for whom
the bell tolls; it tolls for thee.

—John Donne, from Meditation XVII Devotions Upon Emergent Occasions, 1624

This Be the Verse

They fuck you up, your mum and dad.
    They may not mean to, but they do.
They fill you with the faults they had
    And add some extra, just for you.

But they were fucked up in their turn
    By fools in old-style hats and coats,
Who half the time were soppy-stern
    And half at one another's throats.

Man hands on misery to man.
    It deepens like a coastal shelf.
Get out as early as you can,
    And don't have any kids yourself.

—Philip Larkin, 1974

Chapter One

Peter slid the invitation into the pouch of his seat. It had been in his breast pocket all day.

He was a radar blip somewhere 30,000 feet over the North Atlantic, and he was about to eat salmon mousse. Everyone complained about airplane food. He loved it; the little trays that portioned everything equally and separated the salad from the bread, from the mousse, from the fruit cup—it appealed to his appreciation for logistics and process. It was good.

The portions were weighed, balanced, packed and stored with consideration for everything from the food's aesthetic, nutritional, and market value, right down to the meal's drain on the plane's fuel consumption. It was perfect. *It's not so much food as a project in diplomacy.* The salmon mousse was the end result of meetings and memos and reports about branding, due diligence and business process.

This tray of bland salmon mousse was part of a long chain of events entirely lost on the remaining fish, still floating around some 30,000-plus feet below him in the murky waters off the coast of Dover. Below the fish, the seabed was littered with Spanish galleons, German U-boats and British Destroyers. But above it all, in no man's land, Peter ate his salmon mousse and thought how privileged was his current position. He understood how acutely his situation demonstrated the importance of embracing what was modern.

Peter had come to think of modernity as a litmus test for old age. Now approaching sixty, there were men among his peers who no longer wished to learn, no longer absorbed the information that surrounded them—convinced the best of everything had already come and gone. These men drew their cultural references from a reservoir of past experiences. Their allusions were archaic and their comfortable, sentimental remembrances prevented them from truly relating to the present.

His father had been that way, and it had cost him dearly as a businessman. Peter recalled how Roland had offered to ferry his clients across town when he was making deliveries in the company truck.

"Business is about building relationships," he would say, seeing no shame in making just enough to survive.

When Peter had pushed his father to expand the business, Roland had refused, saying he didn't want to jeopardize the service he had always provided.

Peter had developed a plan to introduce a VIP program to the family delivery service—it had sent his father into an inexplicable rage.

"Why is someone having to pay double to get the job done right!" he said.

Roland Van Dooren was old-fashioned – charming, but doomed to fail. To the end, Peter had never understood why his father had insisted on being at home for the last few months of his life (pride he supposed) but Peter had always resented his father's heavy presence in the house, propped up on that hospital bed in the living room. The thing had looked clumsy and out of place, and its bulky, industrial frame had made the room feel sinister and uncomfortable.

Peter had felt sorry for Roland, of course, but he also hated his father for taking over the house those last six months. The old man should have spent his last days in the hospital, where the family could have regulated its exposure to the daily shock of his deteriorating condition.

Peter liked hospitals; they were monuments to the contemporary;

filled with people suffering from diseases that would have long killed them were it not for medical intervention. Hospital, not a church, is where people go when they discover something is seriously wrong with them; they might surrender their fate to a god, but where there is hope, there are hedged bets, and a growing faith in the value of qualified medical advice. God is no oncologist, and home is no place for the dying.

It wasn't just his father's bed, it was all the medical equipment strewn around the house: IV stands in the hallway, boxes of medication and little vials of liquid in the fridge; those handle bars over the toilet. What really haunted him was that yellow container in the bathroom in which to dispose of Dad's needles. It was a bright, almost cheerful box that his mother had placed casually next to the toothbrushes and the soap dish, as if it belonged there. The instruction: "INCINERATE CONTAINER & CONTENTS" was printed on the side in a sober, uncompromising font. Peter had read those words over and over while sitting on the toilet. That container would one day burn anonymously among other refuse in some routine, clinical inferno. What would he be doing that day? Probably nothing special.

He would not go out that way. *He* was a modern man. *He* had kept abreast of emerging trends and technologies, had grown his father's humble delivery service from two trucks and a shuttle bus into an international shipping conglomerate.

Peter Van Dooren was at the forefront of the industry, thanks to his enviable knack for spotting emerging markets. Years before South Korea's export potential had been clear, had been much less viable, Peter's bilateral commercial agreements with several Korean manufacturers had already been negotiated.

He had quickly appreciated the business potential for following seasonal produce: apples ripen in the fall, strawberries in the summer. In that sense not much had changed since the agricultural revolution ten thousand years ago. But technology, mobility, connectivity, they made it possible to follow the seasons wherever they might be. If Chinese wheat and Iranian apple flakes made their way into American cereal boxes, Peter

Van Dooren had helped to get the raw materials to the manufacturer.

His ancestors, toiling in the seventeenth-century port of Rotterdam, could never have dreamed that the Van Dooren name—their name—would one day be plastered on shipping containers that circled the globe in a multi-billion dollar industry. Peter had made that happen. Him. It was a legacy of which he was proud.

The proof was in that invitation. It had arrived a month ago:

DEMOCRATIC REPUBLIC OF L'EDEN SUR MER

Office of the President

Kai e ko toomo ike namoi

Mr Peter Van Dooren
Founder
Van Dooren International
225 Eddington St, Boston, MA 02108
United States of America

Dear Estimable Mr Peter Van Dooren,

On behalf of my Government and the people of the Independent Republic of L'Eden Sur Mer, I invite you to attend a summit of your peers. It is my hope that your ingenuity will succeed where the world's governments have failed.

It is my wish that you agree to attend this vital conference and my honor should you accept.

With deepest respect and admiration,

His Excellency, Mohala Koyl
President
Independent Republic of L'Eden Sur Mer

Office of the President, Parliament of L'Eden Sur Mer
P.O. Box 2690 — 9846

Peter liked it when people said they wanted to do something meaningful with their lives. He already did. He had personally created one hundred and fourteen thousand jobs. People depended on him for their future, their livelihood. Modern shipping made it possible to bring anything anywhere. Directly and indirectly, he had played a part in lifting the standard of living to the highest levels in human history.

Mohala Koyl had managed to strike the right balance between flattery and solicitation. The nebulous 'summit of your peers' was bound to pique his interest, if only to discover who else had received this decidedly odd invitation. 'Where world governments had failed', aligned with Peter's long-held view that industry shaped the world, while governments only managed access to it.

Peter leafed through the briefing notes the Van Dooren Research Department had prepared for him. They knew he liked thinking things through, in numbers where possible. *If there was such a thing as an absolute truth, a god, then it/he was probably an equation.*

The island was sinking. Without a doubt.

Data from satellite imagery, tide gauges and GPS confirmed the sea level was rising at about 0.7 millimeters per year. At this rate, the islanders had between 15 and 25 years before L'Eden Sur Mer was completely uninhabitable, with most of its land-mass submerged beneath the waves.

Peter pored over the data, mentally calculating the sea's encroachment on the topographical map in front of him.

He flicked the plastic tabs in the binder with his thumb as he read. It made a hollow snapping sound.

He flipped to the section marked Media and skimmed over some newspaper clippings from *The Herald*, *The Bugle*, *The Sun*. Puff pieces, mostly. Sentimental human-interest stories focusing on a handful of island families building rock walls to protect their wooden shacks from the incoming sea. There were pictures of them, the Sur Merians, white teeth on brown faces. *Why were they smiling? Didn't they realize their efforts were futile?*

Flip.

Here was something interesting. A Canadian communications student had earned his PhD by helping the islanders blog their experiences through a purpose-built website. Visitors could send messages of hope and make cash donations to those affected by the rising tide. At least this plan made some money, which was more than could be said about most PhDs.

Flip.

A Danish film crew had recently completed a feature-length documentary comparing L'Eden Sur Mer with the fabled disappearance of Atlantis. Pseudo-intellectual melodrama. *How Danish.*

Flip.

Peter flicked past the media section of his briefing notes. He knew there was more to this place than sentimental rubbish. He turned to the section on Economy and Transnational Issues. *Here we go.* Fifteen years earlier, the Australian government had whipped up international indignation by offering to construct a processing center for asylum seekers on L'Eden Sur Mer, in which to temporarily house Australia-bound refugees. While debates had raged elsewhere about the moral rectitude of offshore processing for refugees, the Sur Merian islanders themselves had welcomed the center as an opportunity to improve the economy and, more importantly, their personal living standards. With unemployment historically steady at seventy per cent, the refugee-processing center had promised local jobs, a proposition that was too good to pass up.

Peter liked doing his homework. He didn't like surprises. He liked to be prepared. Peter noted the island was labeled as disadvantaged. The International Monetary Fund had recently estimated that L'Eden Sur Mer's GDP had experienced zero growth for the last eleven consecutive years. Poor soil quality made industrial agriculture unviable. The island's remoteness and the absence of a deep-sea port killed the possibility of any meaningful export business; large ships just could not come in close enough to anchor near shore. Things looked grim.

Public sector workers accounted for more than half of Sur-Merians who were formally employed. Able-bodied males with a sense of adventure found work as crewmen aboard foreign-owned merchant ships. Many left behind families, only to return with drug addictions and gambling debts, becoming indentured servants to the shipping companies that became their personal supply line. While the remittances of merchant seamen made an important contribution to the local economy, their absence from island life was blamed for the wayward behavior of a lost generation of youths who had no father figures to look up to.

The asylum seeker processing center was a step forward for the islanders. At least it was a kind of local enterprise. Surely the legions of roustabouts and seasonal public servants turned full-time cooks, cleaners and security guards, saw the asylum center as a gift, offering them a standard of living previously glimpsed in television commercials and the glossy magazines left behind by the occasional tourist.

The rising sea level doomed everything. That much was clear. There was no higher ground.

Peter reread the invitation, caressing the coarse, grey paper with his thumb. So this was President Koyl's plan: invite some of the world's finest business minds to his country and challenge *them* to solve his nation's problem. *How can I refuse?*

Peter sat back, content in the limited options afforded by his current surroundings. He always felt comfortable in the air. He liked the feeling of being definitely out of range, and had long taken pleasure in imagining all the steps that someone might have to take to get a hold of him. How many phone calls would it take? How many plane trips and cab rides? How far was the separation between him and someone he knew? Hours? Days? He had read somewhere that, today, you can get virtually anywhere on the planet within 24 hours. But here, on this plane, for a short while anyway, he was nowhere. He was at peace.

Peter studied his fellow passengers. Most were business travelers grown accustomed to the relative luxury offered in first class, their minimal luggage efficiently stowed in their seat pods, as they busied themselves reading newspapers and fiddling with computers. Things were calm, neat and orderly.

This was in sharp contrast to the chaos of economy—where the tourists were. There, people travelled with their worldly possessions jammed into overstuffed bags, often dressed in sweat pants, hunkered down for a journey into the unknown. A starched blue curtain separated him from their misery.

Peter sat back, half-heartedly flicking channels on the entertainment system until he came across a vintage boxing match. While he didn't recognize the two fighters, the grainy, sepia footage placed the bout somewhere in the late 1970s, maybe the early 80s. *It's from the corner, between rounds, that boxing truly makes sense.* From the corner the brutality of the fight is offset by the tenderness and respect shown the boxer by his support team, who rub his shoulders, mist water in his face, and reassure their warrior that everything will be okay. Time in the corner is what makes the fight worthwhile.

This was *his* corner. Right here, on this plane.

A baritone voice cut through the hum of the jet engine.

"Ladies and gentlemen, this is your captain speaking …"

The captain now offered a long pause, allowing the promise of his coming announcement to sink in for the weary passengers aboard his aircraft. Captain's voices always sounded so languid and reassuring. *Was it something they were taught in pilot school?*

"On behalf of myself and the flight crew I'd like to thank you for travelling with us this evening on flight BA1031 to Fiji. We will be making a scheduled stop in Singapore to pick up some additional supplies. It, ah … looks like we'll have fine conditions for most of the way. We might, ah … get a few bumps later on, but I'll keep you updated as the flight progresses. For now, I thank you for travelling with us and trust you'll have a pleasant flight."

The pilot's smooth voice cut out with a little puff of radio static. It was nice to have heard his voice from inside that locked cabin at the front of the plane. Up there, the man was in charge.

Everyone could respect that. The plane swept above the face of the water. Peter stared at the ocean below and could almost make out the little waves.

15

Chapter Two

Water poured from the oversized showerhead. Gracie tested the temperature with her hand, then her forearm. It was hot, but not too hot. Stepping into the shower stall, she looked down at herself, at the three deep cuts just below her elbow. She foamed a bit of soap in her hands and smeared it over the top of those symmetrical lines; winced at the sting of it. It felt like a kind of justice, a release. Now she was clean.

At nineteen, Gracie was certain she had already seen more of life than she was ready for. Everything seemed to move too fast: technology, fashions, language itself seemed to morph and change at an uncomfortable pace. The whole world was forcing her to grow up faster than she wanted to.

Blame, she knew, fell squarely on her parents for failing to raise her and Stephen in a more supportive environment. Peter and Alma's time was taken up with company dinners and business trips, leaving their children to a parade of nannies and babysitters.

More recently, television bore the brunt of her blame—any form of popular entertainment, really. It was all a distraction. Trivial things were made important; important things trivial. It was dangerous.

The only thing she hated more than TV was secular, self-help books—the ones her mother read then left lying around on the coffee table: *Will Your Way to Wellness, Claim Your Karma, The Dying Art of Living.* It was all an attempt to reassure ageing baby boomers that their lives could hold meaning if they turned inward; these books spoke the language boomers understood best: me, me, me. They, too, were dangerous.

Most of all, though, Gracie blamed sex for competing with everything. It was everywhere: movies, magazines, billboards, and in conversational innuendo. It was all so easy and boring.

Now in her first year of university, most of her peers had had experience with the opposite sex; kissing and groping, a casual hook up, many had already had actual relationships.

Gracie had never so much as kissed a boy, and from what she saw there was no reason to rush things. The guys she knew were immature. Not because they were childish, more that they seemed to prematurely embrace the trappings of adulthood: buying cars, having relationships, desperate for sex—these things didn't interest her in the slightest. In fact, they seemed to invite complication into what could otherwise be such an enjoyably simple life.

Without a trace of irony, she still slept with a teddy bear.

Despite her best efforts, Gracie was desirable. Boys, and, more worryingly, men, found her attractive. It scared her. Her beauty was naive, effortless, and it defied her every attempt to suppress it beneath baggy corduroys and pilly, animal-patterned sweatshirts. The way men looked at her, smiled at her, made her want to hide at home. Gracie often wore a bored, distracted expression to deflect men's wandering, prying eyes—they interpreted the slightest hint of civility as a personal invitation to impress her. She ignored them the best she could, but did they really think she wouldn't notice their eyes sweeping up her legs like prison searchlights?

After her shower, Gracie stood a moment at the mirror, her skin flushed from the heat. Bobby pins in her mouth, she twisted her curly blonde hair into a tight bun and pinned it. A few stubborn curls wandered loose at her temples and at the base of her neck. She hid her body beneath a tee-shirt, the dun folds of a long and heavy dress, then shrouded herself in a thick cardigan.

Her dress scraped the carpet as she made her way down the staircase. Her lips were dry and cracked from the constant licking and biting; a nervous habit she had picked up since giving up lip balm a year ago, even the kind that professed not to be tested on animals. She didn't want to get addicted to the stuff.

Men are stupid. She had come to think of them as lumbering animals that poisoned everything with their lust for power and control. Gracie had decided that without the moderating influence of women, men invariably over-indulged their vices. Her own father would sit and drink whisky in his study when her mother was out of the house. *Was he an alcoholic?* She wasn't sure. One thing she was sure of, though, was that he would drink more if she weren't around. He would sit at his desk with that stupid crystal decanter, probably imagining himself to be some great statesman, a general, or something.

For Gracie, the unspeakable cruelty and debauchery of past civilizations was directly proportionate to the relative influence and power women were granted in those societies. For their part, women stupidly relied on men for a sense of security; a strong and confident man at her side assuaged a woman's tendency to indulge feelings of insecurity and self-doubt. It was a pathetic foundation for a relationship, and Gracie had no time for such nonsense.

The kitchen cupboard was full of the usual crap her mother and brother liked to eat: sugary breakfast cereals and fruit salad cups, individually wrapped in plastic. *Shouldn't those be in the fridge?* She parted the colorful boxes of cereal lined up on the shelf and reached for her tub of untoasted muesli, gave it a shake to mix up the nuts and seeds and poured herself a bowl. *Need more soy milk.*

Gracie closed her eyes; a quick prayer before breakfast.

At school, most of the boys left her alone, and that was thanks to Jesus. Gracie spent most of her time with her friends, Lucy and Joanne, and the three of them, the 'Jesus Freaks', the 'dykes' or 'missionaries' (depending on who you asked), were mostly untroubled by the taunts thrown at them.

Faith mattered. If people were offended when reproached for living sinful, empty, hell-bound lives, they were simply acting out their self-loathing for not living up to God's standards. Offence was proof of depravity. Gracie, Lucy, and Joanne spread *God's* Word, not their own. Why was that so hard to understand? If others couldn't accept the word, it was *their* problem, and the trio was content to leave them with their insults. What *they* thought didn't matter. *Their* judgment was irrelevant. Only God's judgment mattered.

Gracie opened her eyes as soon as she heard her mother rattling jars in the fridge behind her. Her mother was so noisy; a plodding, fumbly person, nervous and accident-prone. Gracie picked up her spoon and lowered it into the bowl of muesli that sat before her.

Alma had watched her daughter from the kitchen doorway. *Praying again?* To let Gracie know she was there she had noisily rattled bottles and jars in the fridge.

"Good sleep?" said Alma, shaking cereal into a large bowl.

"It was okay." Gracie didn't turn around.

Peter and Alma weren't particularly religious; had consciously raised their children to make up their own minds about that sort of thing. Both of them had felt a little out of their depth when, a few years ago, Gracie had asked to attend mass at the local Catholic church one Sunday morning.

Alma had sat nervously through the experience, surprised to discover Gracie capable of making recitations without referring to the text. It was the first time she had really understood that her daughter was a completely separate person, moving independently through the world. Alma had briefly resented Gracie's freedom; her daughter's piety offended her. This church, this scene, these people wearing hats and singing silly songs—all of it was an insult directed at her. This was not about God or faith, or brotherly love; this whole place was about one-upmanship. It was not Gracie's assertion of belief or devotion; it was Gracie's way of criticizing her upbringing. Alma was sure of it. This was Gracie's way of saying that her mother lacked spiritual depth. This praying business was more of the same.

What did Gracie know? It was easy, at her age, to think in idealistic terms. Good and evil were distinct. She wanted to skip forward twenty years, after Gracie had felt fear and remorse, after she had tasted failure and loss. Alma wanted to stand there, at that moment, and remind Gracie of the ludicrous commitment she had once shown to what she would then admit was little more than a distraction, a parlor game. This religion business was a hoax. Gracie would see. *Poor thing.*

Alma resisted the urge to stroke her daughter s hair; she imagined Gracie recoiling, and couldn't have handled her pulling away. She became aware of Gracie as someone neutral, saw her—fleetingly—as she might have appeared to someone who didn't know her. She looked … small, sitting there at the kitchen table, covered in dense layers of clothing.

"I slept great," said Alma. Gracie nodded, apparently absorbed by whatever she was reading. "Yes, I think it's the temperature," Alma continued. "The nights are becoming cooler now and I think it helps you sleep better."

"Yeah, it probably helps," said Gracie absently.

She was growing up, Gracie. But she was still fragile. Had Alma really done all the things she remembered doing at Gracie's age? Life was short and long all at once. Alma filled with a sense of dread that something awful would befall her daughter. So much could still go wrong. It was natural to think that way, wasn't it? It was nothing more than a mother's protective instinct, even though it was always better to prepare for the worst. Wasn't it? Why wouldn't the car get a flat tire? Why wouldn't the bridge collapse or the airplane fall from the sky? Why wouldn't the doctor confirm that the mole on her shoulder was the beginning of the end?

Try as she did to shield her children from these anxieties, Alma accepted that Gracie and Stephen were probably well aware of her restlessness, had probably found ways to work around it, the way one might avoid someone's obvious physical defect such as a palsied limb or a lazy eye, or an uncomfortable subject with a sensitive dinner guest. No matter how hard Alma worked to exert the appearance of strength and confidence, her nervous habits would eventually betray her: the nail biting, the hair twirling. She needed these things. But she didn't like the idea of being someone who had to be endured.

The kids could not appreciate how composed she really was. There were things they did not know, things they could not know—things she had to keep locked inside her.

Like the child that had been torn from me. My first child. Peter's insistence she undergo a number of ultrasound tests—a procedure then considered to be at the forefront of obstetric medicine—had thrown up a number of 'sonographic flags'. The series of blobs and splotches on the printout had indicated to the physician the presence of certain possible abnormalities. Words had been shot past her: fetal foot length, ear length, potential chromosomal problems, full-term risk ... termination.

Termination. A decision was made. Had she been a part of that decision? Sort of. Peter's insistence and the doctor's caution had convinced her, confused her, worn her down. The decision was made.

Her son had been fine. Alma was certain of it. But what value was certainty in the face of medical evidence to the contrary? Perhaps she could have been stronger. Maybe. It didn't matter now. The ensuing years of reflection, the counseling, the pathological exercise and random medications, had her accepting it was unfair to hold her present self accountable for past decisions. It had to be enough.

Alma's cereal bowl made a heavy clunk as she put it down on the kitchen table. *Is the glass chipped? Relax. I see my thoughts. They are just thoughts. I am not my thoughts.* From under raised eyebrows Gracie looked and returned to her paper.

It was predictable that Gracie sought an outlet through religion—her daughter had always been idealistic.

Even the tidy sum they'd invested from Gracie's three years as a child model, their daughter was intending to donate it to victims of female circumcision.

Gracie ate her muesli in slow, rhythmic mouthfuls. "What are you reading?" said Alma.

"Nothing," said Gracie, folding the newspaper over. "Just the local paper."

"Oh. Any news?" said Alma leaning forward.

"Not in here, anyway." Gracie pushed the folded newspaper away from herself. Alma took the paper and scanned the back pages, the ad section: plumbers, electricians and brothels.

Alma looked out the kitchen window at the pool house down near the back of the grounds. "Is your brother awake yet? It's almost nine o clock." A light was on in there. At least Stephen was awake, even if he was going to be late for school.

Chapter Three

Stephen locked the sliding glass door. That would be enough to keep anyone from bursting in unannounced. He dropped his pants to his ankles then sat in the office chair in front of the computer.

The Internet was a source of comfort for many. It was a salt lick for retail addicts; a refuge for queers living in theocratic states; for people craving sex with children, or animals, or buildings.

Stephen's personal niche in this storeroom of human compulsion was home-made pornography. The authenticity of watching ordinary people reach beyond their comfort zone, the awkwardness of it, was what drew him in. Some were clearly doing it to impress whoever was behind the camera, someone who had probably reassured them the footage would go no further than the bedroom. Others had shot the footage themselves, alone in their bedrooms, cars or workplaces, posting it for the world to see, as if their moment of defiance confirmed their own existence. There was honesty in the home-made stuff, a vulnerability that made it all the more alluring.

Most of his school peers just streamed pornography—watched it then discarded it. *Crass.* Moving from one image to the next without commitment seemed like an empty pleasure. Stephen saved his files; had amassed a sizeable cache of his favorite images and videos, squirreling them away on his hard drive under the uninviting file name: 'server protocols'. Among his collection were biblets and teens, flabby housewives jiggling their breasts while wearing their daughters' clothes, and slim schoolgirls flashing their underpants to cell-phone cameras on the bus home from school.

There was something tender in this perversion, as if this fantasy world was made more accessible by the ordinariness of the subjects. These were not actors. Their faces registered real human emotions: shame, fear, discomfort, determination and bashfulness. Stephen had grown quite attached to a few of the girls in his collection. Among his favorites was the young blonde in the black cocktail dress. It was an unusually long video of exceedingly good quality. She had set the camera up herself in her family's sunken living room and performed a slow striptease to some instrumental samba music. She was not a great dancer. Her movements were unrehearsed; she paused every once in a while to ponder what she would do next and then settled, self-consciously, on her next position. It was adorable.

Extensive reviewing had allowed Stephen to note and take pleasure in the details of the video: the way the girl's movements left footprints in the thick, beige carpet (2:27); the long, smooth gesture she used to remove a wisp of hair that got caught in her mouth (4:17); the tacky nouveau-riche chairs that were clustered around a heavy dining room table in the unlit background.

Stephen used these details to flesh out the scene and extend the fantasy well beyond the eight minutes and seventeen seconds that had been filmed. In his mind, he had come over to this girl's house—he thought of her as Emma—to help her with her math homework and she had made him an iced tea. This was her way of saying thank you. Sometimes he would take 'Emma' to the movies or out to dinner as a prelude to sex. The vibrancy of these fantasies could sometimes rival genuine memories.

He abhorred the glossiness of commercial pornography. That was just about power. Those people had robbed sex of its humanity and their 'work' offered nothing more than the erotic equivalent of a theme park. He had once downloaded a computer virus from a site purportedly hosted by a celebrity porn star. Who was she to have garnered such attention? Why had someone seen fit to protect her intellectual property by setting up a dummy site where a nasty virus lay in wait for its horny prey?

Stephen scrolled down his list of files.

The Internet was a dangerous place and he had found refuge in a handful of trusted sites that delivered what he expected. Here, too, the Internet had succeeded in loosening the corporations' grip on the entertainment industry. The web had enabled real people to control and express their sexuality.

There was a new girl at school—Sara—and she was the stuff of pure fantasy. On her first day of school Sara had worn black leggings and a long, white hoodie. When she slung her bag over her shoulder, it lifted her top just enough to reveal one cheek of her round behind.

He flicked through some familiar thumbnails, half looking for someone whose butt resembled the glimpse, the impression he had of Sara's as he lazily tugged himself. His first real erection had been in his dad's office of all places, and in the presence of his father's ancient secretary whose recent stroke had left one eye in a permanent, sinister wink. Stephen had become aware of the pulsing throb between his legs as his penis had stood to attention. He had adjusted his jacket to cover the conspicuous bulge that felt like it threatened to tear open the crotch of his trousers.

He had found a disabled toilet and unzipped his pants to let himself breathe. Stephen stared down at that innocent little appendage, previously known by a handful of childish euphemisms: willy, noodle, and so forth. How inaccurate those terms now sounded in the presence of this organism that clearly fed on altogether darker, more profound impulses than those silly names acknowledged. It demanded attention like the outstretched neck of some ghastly, flightless bird hungry for a feed.

He didn't really know what to do and stumbled around the sterile environment of the bathroom looking for ways to pacify his arousal. He dragged his penis against various textured surfaces in the bathroom. He tried the tiles, but they felt cold and inflexible; slapped his dick against the countertop, but that did little. He shuffled around the handicapped bathroom like a horny penguin as he waited for the feeling of urgency to subside. The idea of some poor cripple patiently wheeling their chair back and forth in the hallway outside, bursting to urinate, or empty their colostomy bag, did nothing to curb his arousal.

Surely his absence had been noticed by now. The secretary would know what he was up to, or she might suspect he was taking a shit. Stephen couldn't decide which was more embarrassing. The erection eventually choked and went limp, and he carefully raised his trousers, sure that the slightest provocation would stir the creature back to life.

Stephen had since become a diligent student of the art of masturbation. He had experimented with various techniques. He used one finger or two, he palmed it, reverse-palmed it, he dry-humped mattresses and dipped his penis into jars of lukewarm water to replicate what he imagined the moist interior of a woman's vagina might feel like. When he learned to stroke himself, Stephen, who had never really excelled in sports or academics, believed he had found something that he was truly good at. The momentary weightlessness of orgasm redeemed the enduring burden of his life.

Sara was out of his league. He knew that. But in his world beneath the covers of his bed, or in front of his computer, she would do anything he asked of her. There was a certain satisfaction when he saw her holding court at her locker the next day. Sara's pliable body, her moist kisses and smooth flesh remained safely locked inside the prison of his mind.

Stephen scrolled through a list of videos and settled on the short-haired blonde in the spandex shorts, shot from behind on the exercise bike. He rubbed himself through his trousers as he watched. He switched to the up-skirt of a plump, red-headed girl in a bookstore, then to the hip hop dancer ... the blonde in a football uniform, before finishing on the beach-volleyball team.

It had been a logical and rewarding progression of videos.

Stephen sat for a moment, breathing through his mouth. His cock was still throbbing. The office chair squeaked beneath him as he adjusted himself in the seat. He leaned back, settling into his ritual of reading the newspaper to help draw down his erection.

From the banner he could see that 953 people were on line. *Does that include me?*

Police investigators say the 61-year-old cyclist was struck by a mini-van on the south-east corner of Cooper Street and Highway 7—Kim Jong-un visits Pyongyang school, click to view video—Drivers in the area have been advised to allow extra time or take an alternative route—163 people are reading this right now—Paramedics arrived at the scene but were unable to revive the cyclist—Childless Couples Have Fatter Pets—Wanted, Development Manager for Leading Edge Research Company $100,000-150,000 click for job description—The 27-year-old truck driver was not injured.

Stephen's hard-on subsided. He dabbed the head of his penis with a crusty sports sock and hit the 'sleep' button on the computer. Time for breakfast.

Chapter Four

Alma caught a glimpse of herself in the reflective glass of the security window and instinctively looked away. These few moments before passing through the main gate always felt the most intense. It didn't matter how many times she entered a prison, she had never grown accustomed to it. Even though her anxiety never really went away, she had become a lot better at hiding it.

The gate didn't buzz open like it did in the movies. In fact, it was more of a door than a gate, a heavy door that unlocked with a loud metallic click when operated from a remote location. When the pneumatic hinge swung the door shut behind her, the artificial silence filled the place. There was no echo, no commotion, just an eerie vacuum that sealed prisoners in from the very ambience of the world outside. Even traffic noise from the adjacent highway could not slip inside the penitentiary walls.

Alma was hit with the sickly smell of body odor and stale cigarette smoke. It lingered that ghost smell of decay. It seemed to sweat out of the walls. She could almost taste it.

A prisoner, escorted by a guard, passed her in the unventilated corridor. The prisoner smiled and nodded his head.

"Good morning, Miss," he said. Prisoners were always so polite.

As they passed each other, Alma could feel him turn around to look at her backside. She always wore baggy clothes and long jackets to prison. She quickened her pace, footsteps muffled by yards of blotchy red carpet.

Even incarcerated, these men were proof that brute strength still counted for something in this world. No matter how much she earned, no matter how much she knew, no matter how much influence she might have elsewhere, she would always have to look over her shoulder because of men like these. It was unfair, but that was just the way it was.

She consulted her files on Ahmed Elwi Saif. They did not specify his crimes, but he was being held in D block—protective custody. Alma knew that classified Saif as either a sex offender or some kind of police informant; either one made him a trophy to other inmates. Between that and his medical profile, Ahmed Elwi Saif did not have long to live. It was sad, but Alma had seen his kind before.

She arrived in the medical ward, where she was surprised to find a gaunt and elderly man, presumably Saif, sitting on a grimy, green vinyl hospital gurney. The doctor had already begun his examination. Technically, it was against regulations for the doctor to begin his examination before the interpreter was present, but Alma knew well enough to stay on the right side of the physician in these situations.

She introduced herself to the doctor and to Saif, whose spindly legs dangled over the edge of the bed. The wheels of the gurney were unlocked, so the bed rolled forward and back with a squeak as the doctor circled his patient with a stethoscope.

"This man, he wears too much perfume," said Saif. His Arabic was soft, almost melancholy. "Too much," he repeated. Alma did not pass along the interpretation.

She enjoyed watching the doctor work. He moved his hands gingerly over the patient, like a man examining a piece of antique porcelain, conscious that in all its years of existence, he dared not be the first to break it. The inmate's face was pockmarked and his torso was scarred. Some of the wounds were fresh and self-inflicted. Other, older scars were buried deeper beneath the surface.

Alma focused on the individual sounds that broke the silence of the room: the hum of the fluorescent lights; the rustle of hospital-bed paper as Saif shifted on the gurney; the squeaky wheel; and the whistling that filled the space between them as the doctor drew breath through unclipped nose hairs. A pleasant shiver ran through Alma. The whistling seemed to fill the hollow room, and its rhythmic presence helped her to focus on the space between the present moment and her anticipation of the next.

"Well," said the doctor taking off his stethoscope. "The patient should already know he has diabetes and glaucoma. He's also showing signs of loss of cognitive function. This may be the onset of dementia, or early Alzheimer's, maybe. It's hard to know for sure."

The doctor was supposed to address the patient, not her. That's how this interpreting thing was supposed to work. But things didn't always work like they were supposed to. Alma looked at Saif. He looked back, frowning. Alma tried to keep her face neutral. Brow soft, mouth straight. That's how it was supposed to be.

"Look," the doctor continued. He removed his gloves and tossed them in a plastic bucket. "These diseases are progressing pretty much as I would expect them to." He scribbled things, ticked boxes on a form attached to a clipboard. "Honestly, his condition does not warrant permanent transfer to a medical facility. Not yet. Maybe in six months or so, but for now he's well enough to stay here. I'm sorry," said the doctor, finally looking at Saif.

Alma relayed this information to Saif. It felt good to speak Arabic. Now she was useful. Saif just sat there looking at the floor, nodding from time to time.

The doctor picked up his satchel.

"Do you have any questions for the doctor," she asked Saif, but the man just shook his head.

Seeing this, the doctor left the examination room. It was against regulations for him to leave Alma with a prisoner, even with an armed guard posted outside the door. She spent an awkward moment in the room as Saif put on his prison greens. Part of her had already left the building, was imagining the individual steps she would soon take to get out of here: the walk down the corridor, the click of the pneumatic hinge, the sunlight outside, her footsteps on the gravel …

Saif sniffed, breaking the spell, and Alma found herself wondering if he was crying or just had a cold. She said nothing.

The prison guard entered the room.

"Hands down front," said the guard. Saif got off the gurney, lowered his hands then brought his wrists together. The guard handcuffed Saif, ready for the march back to D Block.

"*Allah yasalmik,*" said Saif as he passed Alma on his way out the door. *God keep you safe.*

Alma felt certain she would not see him again.

Alma's new earrings came in a crisp, white box. It had felt cleansing to buy something new. The buzz of Westgate Mall offered a refreshing change from the vacuum of the prison compound. She deserved to treat herself.

Westgate Mall was *her* place. She felt comfortable there. It was warm in winter and cool in summer. You could stroll down its wide, gleaming avenues without having to worry about streetlights and traffic, vagrants or buskers. Alma's doctor was here, and so was her dentist; it was where she got her nails done and the salon had one of the best colorists she'd ever had. Westgate had grocery shops and department stores, it had biodynamic butchers, wholemeal bakers and organic vegetable stalls. The mall held concerts, hosted book launches and art exhibits, cooking demonstrations and fashion shows. There was an ornamental Japanese garden where Alma liked to sit with a chai latté and watch the giant goldfish pucker their mouths at the surface of the pond. This climate-controlled oasis offered the additional benefit of private security guards and closed circuit TV.

Here things were unblemished, unused and full of promise. A thing in a store was as perfect a thing as a thing could be. Alma enjoyed the attention she received from the shop attendants, and looked forward to their offers of tea and coffee, as well as their unsolicited but no less friendly advice. To know she could afford to buy virtually anything in the shops made her feel accomplished, special.

Her spending had never been an issue, not really. Peter had playfully reproached her for this indulgence once or twice, but his disapproval was more patronizing than sincere. Peter was naturally more frugal than she, but she always got the sense that he liked to be able to talk about his wife's shopping as a socially acceptable character flaw. After all, her purchases underlined his ability to afford them and, in that sense, the arrangement was mutually beneficial. *Besides, Peter's not here. Again. Still.*

So Alma continued to buy things. She bought shoes and handbags, coats and hats. She bought shampoos infused with almond oil and watercress. She bought blouses and scarves made of Persian silk and Nepalese yak wool. She bought teak patio furniture, small appliances and hand-painted collectable plates.

It calmed her.

Special occasions allowed her to buy with impunity. It was easy to get carried away on birthdays and holidays. It would be insulting not to. Her excess was a cultural expectation at Christmas, and she dutifully filled the house with ribbons and wreaths and garlands, all in a blaze of light that twinkled off gilded angel figurines and a crystal nativity scene imported from Austria.

On advice from her personal trainer, she bought herself a treadmill, a bike and a rowing machine. Delivery? Yes. Installation? Yes. Extended warranty? You bet. She bought sneakers and cross trainers and hiking boots; a watch fitted with a heart monitor and a GPS to track her progress. Each purchase reinforced her commitment to getting fit and living healthy.

Once removed from their wrapping, though, most of these things lost that special glow they had inside the store. Shopping bags accumulated and deliverymen piled new boxes on top of old, unopened merchandise that stacked up in the cellar and garage.

Alma would occasionally sift through the bags. She had come

across leopard-pattern silk shawls, and knee-high leather boots in black and red and brown, and couldn't remember if she had intended them as gifts or for herself. She would smell the leather and run the delicate silk across her cheek, but she was unable to rekindle the kinetic joy she had felt for these objects at the original point of purchase.

Alma had started to give away some of the old stuff. One of her hand-me-downs had created a bit of a family rift. Peter's sister had been annoyed when Alma had given their daughter a Tiffany bracelet for her fourteenth birthday. She had assumed the gift was a demonstration of Alma and Peter's wealth, and had resented the game of one-upmanship she presumed Alma's gift was aiming to start.

To avoid future conflict, Alma stopped gifting her purchases, and now donated to worthy causes. A good many school raffles received the small appliances and cookware, and power tools. Second-hand-shopping connoisseurs knew of a particular Salvation Army outlet where you could find brand-name shoes and designer handbags, sometimes with the original price tag still attached. It was all a symbiotic relationship, Alma reasoned. Everybody got something out of her hobby. In the scheme of things, what did her little indulgence really matter?

Alma sat down on a lounge chair next to the ornamental fishpond. It was a vinyl chair, not leather, and the air hissed out of the cheap cushioning as the seat took her weight. It felt good to be off her feet. She nibbled some nougat and brushed the crumbs off her knees.

She watched as a woman beside her unloaded a burden of satchels and shoulder bags, sat down on a bench near the fishpond, and set about breastfeeding a child who looked to be almost four years old. The grubby-looking kid straddled the woman's knee, ruddy hair covering the woman's breast as he hungrily swallowed his mother's nipple while she fiddled with her phone over his shoulder. The scene made Alma uncomfortable. How were children ever supposed to become self-reliant adults if parents were going to treat them like that? A person had to know when to let go.

Alma had wanted her children to be resilient, and had decided not to shield Gracie and Stephen from every ugliness they might encounter in life. She had been careful not to coddle the kids too much, especially Stephen, whom she had encouraged to self-soothe when he cried in his cot at night. She refused to pick him up when he was clingy and did not intervene when he had trouble climbing rope ladders at the playground or making friends at school.

Alma winced when she saw other mothers rush over and gather their children in their arms to console them after the slightest fall or bump on the head. Alma forced herself to remain calm when Stephen and Gracie suffered some minor injury at school or in the playground: a scraped knee, a bruised elbow, a tumble off the swings. When they complained that another kid had pushed or hit them, Alma assumed her children shared the blame, and that it was altogether right that her kids understand there were consequences to their wrongdoing. She taught herself to react to these incidents with an air of distraction, indifference even, to teach her children some self-reliance. It was better for them to learn firsthand that not every experience would be pleasurable and that not every curiosity would be rewarded.

You're so calm, other mothers would say, *your kids are so independent.* But Alma battled a deep wellspring of anxiety that bubbled in the pit of her stomach. Any attempt to control the feeling—whole foods, jogging, massage, warm baths—only resulted in more stress. Shopping seemed to calm that urgent fluttering of moth wings inside her. At least for a little while.

A doctor had once suggested an anti-anxiety medication, but she had dismissed the suggestion on principle; 'anxiety' was the affliction of the moment and she would not be conscripted into the latest medicinal fad. She would strive to control her own feelings, no matter how difficult that proved to be.

A friend suggested yoga. Alma had wanted to try the yogic stretches and transcendental meditation, but she never took her friend up on the offer; never quite got around to prioritizing it.

Between the kids' judo classes and swimming lessons, and Peter's work functions, Alma always put off the yoga for another day.

But those women were right about something: her kids were independent, and Alma could congratulate herself that her regimen of tough love had achieved the desired results. Stephen had never wet the bed; had stopped being clingy. The kids never made a habit of wandering into her bed at night the way other mothers had complained their children did. Both kids were popular, doing well at school and Gracie was now attending university. Yes, they had their issues, their vulnerabilities, but that was only human.

Her kids were well adjusted, even though she often felt she had muddled through as a mother. Her maternal instinct was not well formed, but her children had turned out all right.

This mother by the fishpond was suckling a man-child, condemning him to a kamikaze mission his ego would never survive. It was irresponsible.

The phone in her purse buzzed and vibrated. Whoever it was could wait. This was her time.

Chapter Five

Peter stood on the landing of his rustic beach yurt, waiting to leave a message for Alma.

"Just calling to touch base. Reception's terrible here, so I might cut out. It's also why you might not get through if you call. Signal here is probably best after the sun goes down, so that would be … nine … eight … somewhere between 8:30 and maybe 11:00am, your time. Anyway, hopefully everything is okay. I will try to call again in a few days."

Peter switched off the phone and leaned heavily on the balcony railing, breathing in the sea air as he squinted at the morning sun. The sea was flat and featureless.

The 'purpose-built conference and luxury spa' was really just a humble construction of windowless, thatched palm cabins. It was crude, but quaint—a place where plump, white cushions offset the rustic charm of roughly hewn wood beams. The complex looked a bit like a series of tree houses with elevated walkways between individual huts and linked by communal lavatories. There was a massage parlor and a bar in which delegates were encouraged to unwind at the end of the day. The parlor was entirely staffed by men, which Peter had thought peculiar. Some of the male delegates had already grumbled about the idea of being massaged by men, but Peter intended to use the facility to help him recover from the morning runs he intended to do around the island's coastline. He had always been a runner.

Peter stepped down onto the network of slatted wood paths that connected the beach yurts. He walked slowly, examining their construction underfoot. Many of the boards were not parallel and their haphazard placement had created irregular angles in the spaces between them. *Shoddy workmanship.* Around him, the other conference delegates busied themselves in their cabins, deep into the various stages of their morning routines. A man in a bathrobe was brushing his teeth on the balcony of his cabin. He waved. Peter nodded. Another man was perched on the landing, looking out to sea. Someone else, unseen, coughed loudly. A new day.

The conference sessions were to be held in an open-air pavilion. Dozens of plastic lawn chairs had been placed, theatre style, atop AstroTurf matting. It was cool enough under the canvas sails, but by ten o'clock on the first morning, Peter sweated steadily. Most of the men had already abandoned their jackets and loosened their ties.

Peter poured himself some fruit juice laid out on a trestle table. It was dark red, this concoction. *Dragon fruit?*

The conference sessions could have been held inside the air-conditioned Parliament buildings, but it was clear that President Koyl had wanted the delegates to have an unobstructed view of the ocean. The President probably wanted nature to be a guest at the conference; wanted them all to feel the heat of the sun and hear the roar of the ocean to underline the reason they had all been summoned. Clever move.

Peter nodded, acknowledging the few unfamiliar faces that searched for his attention. He took a seat near the front of the pavilion and sipped his dragon fruit. It was too sweet and he put it under his chair. There was a conference brochure under there. It was a simple little booklet—photocopied pages, staples off center, probably put together by hand. *Quaint.* Peter leafed through the booklet, thankful for the distraction.

The President of this impoverished little island had managed to assemble an eclectic cast of characters for his conference. There was the expected collection of academics, lawyers, and philanthropists, but there were also some genuine talents from the international business community.

Among them was oil magnate Holden Nash, whose Aquarius deep-sea drilling projects had tapped some of the deepest oil reserves yet found.

Francois La Larc was a freestyle diving champion and marine engineer who had developed one of the world's most efficient hydro-electric power turbines.

Satoshi Utitsu, a horticulturalist and botanist, had spent nearly two decades developing sustainable agriculture projects for the Japanese space program.

Peter shifted around in his plastic chair, the humidity building in the seat of his trousers—it had been a long time since he'd had to sit on plastic.

A frail little man took the stage, accompanied by weak applause. Those people still standing found their seats. The little man said a few things in Kwitsa, a language that sounded to Peter like whispering with a lot of Ps and Ks.

"Welcome," he finally said in English. His voice was soft, brittle. "I give you a traditional welcome to this place. Our home. Please now welcome His Excellency, President Mohala Koyl." The little man stepped back from the podium, beaming and applauding.

Mohala Koyl trotted up the side steps of the platform and strode across the stage to rapturous applause. The President patted the frail little man on the shoulder, whispered something in his ear and took his place at the podium. He raised the microphone to his level and stood a while longer, absorbing the applause. Koyl finally raised his hand to subdue the clapping. People fell quiet. There was some rustling of paper. A few people coughed. You could still hear the roar of the ocean in the distance. Steady as a metronome.

President Koyl rested his hands on the podium. He leaned across it, scanning his audience. Left. Then right. Then left again.

"Welcome," he said. His voice was low and soft. "You know why you are here?" Koyl scanned his audience again, a slight curl growing on his upper lip. "You know why you are here. You are here because you are the finest business minds of our time."

In his peripheral vision, Peter saw people turning and fidgeting as if taking stock, only now, of who else was there. Peter kept his own eyes fixed on President Koyl.

"I'm not here to give a big speech," said Koyl. "I don't have time." He bowed his head. "You know my island is sinking. Soon it will be gone. Unless," he said, looking up. Koyl let the word hang in the air where it floated around like a speck of dust on a breeze. "Unless *you* can help. Unless *you* have an idea." He scanned the room again, searching for his savior. "I have some money," he said, looking out beyond the canvas sails towards the horizon. "It's not much. But I am prepared to spend it. For the right idea." Koyl gestured to the audience. "You are all rich," he said, smiling. "Rich because of good ideas." A sympathetic chuckle rippled through the audience. "So you can help us," said Koyl. The smile disappeared. "You must help us. This nation. These people depend on your help. I have asked governments. But they have bad ideas. No solutions. So I invited you because I want to hear your ideas. No matter how unconventional. No matter how crazy. Because this is how we change the course of history. And this is why you are here. I have built small homes for you. It is not much, I know. You are used to better. But you are welcome to stay here as long as you want. All I ask in return is your help. Thank you." The audience clapped, more slowly than before. Koyl nodded and walked off the stage.

He was bold, this President Koyl, thought Peter. That's what you sounded like after being in power for thirty years. Self-confident. Brazen. The President had put forth an entertaining challenge, but surely not a serious one. This was all part of a media stunt. Surely it was.

A pair of dull if well-meaning academics took to the stage next. Their slides were neat and well presented, but the presentation was filled with academic clichés: *Now if you'll turn your attention to this chart, graph, table, what this data set is telling us is.* The presentation was competent. Artless, but informative. And their dithering all but erased Koyl's energetic challenge issued only moments before.

According to the researchers, sea-level rises had implications for the establishment of future maritime borders, international trade routes, the migration of contagious diseases and, with some generous interpretation, could threaten existing compliance with international treaties on human rights. They spoke of the United Nations Convention on the Law of the Sea, of the importance of maintaining the legal status of the territorial sea, of the air space over the territorial sea, and of its bed and subsoil.

Peter moved around in his seat; he was already bored. *Why the hell am I here?* He dragged his foot along a patch of the artificial grass beneath him, cleaning the sand dust off the soles of his shoes. He imagined the stiff little bristles would be pleasant to walk on barefoot. He forced his attention back towards the podium.

A mousey little woman was now laying the historical and environmental groundwork for the conference. Hadn't anyone else done their homework?

"The first recorded European sighting of the island was an entry dated 11 March 1788 in the log of the French navy vessel, *Tourville*, commanded by Admiral Francois de Bascard," said the woman. She was obviously reading, sticking to her script. "The entry could so easily have been written into the log of the British vessel HMS *Supply* commanded by British naval officer Lieutenant Henry Lidgbird Ball, who had been in the area exactly a month earlier," said the woman. She was smiling and seemed genuinely bemused by the near coincidence of it all, the great explorers passing each other, ships in the night.

For some reason there was an image of Lieutenant Ball up on the screen; his droopy face looked back at them. What a stuck-up old codger he must have been. The mousey little woman pressed on.

"Ball had noted on 8 February 1788 that his ship had been surrounded by innumerable seabirds, which made him suspect that he was close to an uncharted island or reef. He also noted the waters at that location were streaked with strong and dangerous currents but, seeing nothing further, wrote down the coordinates and continued, on course, for Botany Bay." She seemed saddened by this, the little woman, as if Lieutenant Ball had missed a turning point in his life. "And so it was that the French had arrived first," she added with a touch of melancholy. "A month later, Admiral Bascard sighted the island and circumnavigated it, looking for an adequate port to moor his vessel. Finding none, he noted the island's coordinates and continued, on course, for the New Hebrides, that's modern day Vanuatu," she said, departing from her script.

The woman sighed. "The *Tourville* disappeared on a journey the following year, prompting calls for a search mission; but the political upheavals in France drowned out the story of the *Tourville*, whatever it may have been, and the whole affair was quickly forgotten as France descended into its revolution. But that is another story."

Yes it is. Peter looked to the front row where Koyl was seated. The President was openly conversing with the little frail man who had introduced him. If the woman was bothered by their conversation, she showed no sign of it.

"It would be another half-century before Europeans set foot on the island," she said. "Landing here in 1841, just beyond that ridge there," she said, pointing out towards the back of the seating area. People turned. "That's where the French naturalist, Georges Marelles, noted in his diary that he thought the island: 'small, low, with little shade or fertile soil, and covered in profoundly unremarkable vegetation.' And so it was with more than a little irony and colonial smugness that he dubbed the Island *L'Eden Sur Mer* before departing the place, only to die of malaria a few months later."

The woman looked down at President Koyl seated below her and blushed slightly.

"During his brief stay on L'Eden Sur Mer," she continued, "Marelles gathered some crude oceanographic data that we today use as a point of comparison for the rising sea, which now well covers the narrow peninsula where Marelles landed, just behind you, more than a hundred and fifty years ago."

The woman looked down at Koyl again. She smiled politely, no blushing. "President Mohala Koyl has been the head of state of L'Eden Sur Mer for more than thirty years, and has been championing this issue for a long time."

A weak rumble of applause interrupted the woman. She leaned back on her heels and shuffled her papers, managing the unscheduled reaction.

"The transition to self-government has been relatively smooth," she said before applause had completely died out. "The move from colonial outpost to a presidential republic recognizing traditional chieftains was made possible by this country's unique history." A black and white picture of American soldiers sitting on a beach, palm trees in the background, went up on the screen.

"L'Eden Sur Mer was almost entirely overlooked during the geopolitical upheavals of World War Two," said the woman, gesturing at the image behind her. "The Japanese briefly carved an airstrip at the west end of the island," she pointed off to her side, "only to abandon the place entirely a few months later when it was clear the island offered no strategic advantage. There is no record of advancing American forces having ever stepped ashore."

The woman scanned the audience from behind her glasses.

"And so it was," she continued, "that L'Eden Sur Mer's traditional political structure of four regional chieftains loosely representing the north, south, east, and west of the island remains culturally intact." She turned slightly towards the screen behind her where a map of the island was now projected. Peter wondered how long it would take to run around the whole island? *Two hours? Maybe three? No more than four.*

"This traditional council of elders—'Gray Hairs' in Kwitsa, the local tongue—exercise informal authority at the local level, and their influence is largely based on long-standing family ties and personal reputations within the community. This political system is unique, and it too needs preserving. Thank you." The woman looked down at Koyl, seeking … what? Approval? Koyl just nodded slowly. She seemed satisfied.

The woman gathered her papers from the podium. She was grinning, willing applause. The map of the island stayed up on the screen behind her.

Peter's head felt fuzzy, his thoughts seemed distant, irretrievable as the very air around him seemed to thicken with the heat of the day. Overhead the limp canvas sails were no match for the sun. Polite applause mercifully shifted Peter's attention to the next item on the day's agenda: morning tea followed by a tour of the island.

The tour began at the harbor. President Koyl himself led the group of delegates to the water's edge where a dozen small wooden boats bumped against the pylons of a concrete pier that seemed unnecessarily large and industrial. Koyl was solemn, almost accusing, as he pointed out white lines on the pylons that marked the rising water level.

"Faster than a growing child," he said, miming the rise with his hands. "Come this way. Please."

Koyl spoke slowly, a man unafraid of interruption, a man used to being heard. In the distance, yellow and red buoys bobbed on the light swell marking out important fishing grounds near the port.

The delegation dutifully shuffled along behind Koyl as he presented his battered lands. The delegation visited a breadfruit orchard tended by people who lived in the surrounding village. The villagers themselves were nowhere to be seen.

Further inland they visited an abandoned coffee plantation. "Our climate for growing coffee is ideal," said Koyl.

Peter knew the soil was not. He'd read the mining test reports and the coffee project, like so many others, had floundered because resources, natural and man-made, were in short supply on L'Eden Sur Mer. Even the promising opportunity of strip mining the island's rich guano deposits had failed because the rights could not be secured. In the end, only a handful of families had built substantial personal wealth from the short-term promises made to the mining consortia. The Koyl family was the greatest beneficiary of the scheme. But nothing had come of it.

L'Eden Sur Mer was no land of opportunity. This plantation, which looked more like a small airplane hangar with some concrete outbuildings, now stripped of any useable materials, was a cautionary tale for anyone thinking of doing business here. A rusted door hung heavy on its hinges. Small shrubs and palms sprouted through cracks in the flooring of a concrete bunker. How quickly nature reclaimed its space.

Koyl walked ahead of the group in slow, deliberate steps, a man unhurried by schedules or prior commitments. When he spoke, he searched your face for what it might reveal, and tethered his gaze to your head movements. Even when you looked away, you could feel him tugging at your peripheral vision. When spoken to, Koyl seemed distracted, and would gaze beyond the horizon as if the subject of conversation or the answer to a question naturally resided there.

"Mr President," said a plump, fair-skinned woman dressed in blue linen. Koyl turned, slowly. "How responsible are the local chiefs for maintaining these commercial projects?"

Koyl smiled. He seemed amused. "They are not responsible," he said.

The woman's eyes were hidden behind enormous sunglasses. "Forgive me for not understanding, then, but under a local government model, wouldn't it be—"

"There is no local government model," said Koyl. "There are chiefs, yes. Regional chiefs. But they have no resources. Theirs is like a … social power. But resourcing, infrastructure … this is all centrally planned." Koyl turned around and walked on, ending the conversation.

Peter had been on a thousand tours like this, where various chairmen or CEOs showed him around their factories, their assembly plants, their call centers. He had seen in those leaders the same self-assuredness he now recognized in President Koyl.

Koyl showed them a paved road submerged beneath a few feet of water. "Three years ago," he said, standing beside the road, "this one paved road serviced the whole island. Sometimes it would flood. Maybe three or four times a year." Koyl surveyed his audience. "Now." He knelt beside the submerged road. "Well, you can see." Water covered the asphalt completely. Peter noticed small fish swimming between the dotted white lines that ran the center of the road.

"Come," said Koyl, turning his back on the road. The group made its way down to the shoreline, where a pontoon boat was waiting. "Please," said Koyl motioning to the ramp. "There's something I want to show you."

People shuffled onto the flat deck of the boat, again covered with synthetic grass matting. A skinny kid unhooked the ramp and tossed it on the shore where it rumbled like thunder. He gathered ropes and pushed the boat out, wading until the water was up to his waist before climbing aboard and taking the steering wheel.

Anticipating the movement, the ocean swell, Peter spread his legs for balance and held on to the railing. A few people gasped and reached for it as the motor propelled them forward, throwing them off balance. Peter smirked.

The pontoon boat churned through the water, choppy waves banging hollow against its aluminum hull. The water was blue and clear, and the flat seabed was visible beneath the surface, interrupted by the occasional patch of coral. Peter felt the cool salt spray on his hands and face and he breathed in deeply.

The boat rounded the island's rough, pebbled shoreline.

President Koyl's diplomatic efforts to contain the rising sea level had not been entirely in vain. A few small-scale projects stood as evidence of the international community's involvement on L'Eden Sur Mer.

Small, individual sea walls had been built to protect homes along the beach. The walls had gone up, separating neighbors into little concrete pens along the foreshore.

But the walls hadn't been strong enough. One by one, the sea had breached them and concrete slabs now littered the beach like an aborted game of giant dominoes.

Peter watched smoke rise from behind the little houses, the only sign that anyone was home.

Past a shallow reef system the wind picked up suddenly. The sea was darker here. It looked bluer, deeper, and colder. The motor revved higher but they moved no faster through the water. They must be fighting the same currents that droopy-faced Lieutenant Ball had noted in his logbook.

Peter squinted at a silhouette in the distance. Not a mountain. Not even a hill. It was more of a mound. Curly white waves broke against its steep shore.

The motor quieted and the boat circled the little island. Shards of broken glass and twisted metal from a collection of crumbling buildings glinted in the sun.

"This is the Peak," said Koyl gravely. "People used to be able to walk to the mainland from here."

The shoreline of L'Eden Sur Mer was only a few yards away.

"Six years ago," said Koyl, "we used a giant machine, a dredger, to bring sand and rock from the bottom of the sea and put it on the surface. This was already the highland, you see. So we made it higher." Koyl's turned to the sandy, rocky formation outside the boat. His audience did the same. "Locals call it the Peak," he added quietly.

A dredger. Cunning, thought Peter. All of this sand, these rocks and boulders had just been lying, useless, on the seabed. For how long? Centuries? Millennia? Now they'd been brought to the surface to do something useful.

The flood-resistant island within the island had been the brainchild of the Öersk Development Corporation, a Danish company that had been contracted by the government of L'Eden Sur Mer to build and settle the new housing project. It was to be Öersk's expansion project and serve as an alternative model for international development.

"It was a good idea," said Koyl. "But it didn't work."

Some three hundred families had been persuaded to relocate

to the Peak, lured by the promise of new, two-bedroom apartments, complete with air conditioning, double glazing and European appliances.

The boat circled the Peak a second time. A bent and rusting metal sign said something aspirational. The writing was barely legible: *new, proud, construction, home.* Only the top of the government crest remained to be eaten by the rust. Whatever the sign said was unimportant now. The experiment had failed. The relocation had muddled the islanders' traditional social ties, which had long been based on their regional identity and their connection to ancestral land holdings. On the Peak, people from the east of the island had been lumped in with those from the west and it wasn't long before in-fighting between families over meaningless domestic issues assumed religious proportions.

A series of arson attacks within the development had sparked an exodus, led by people with young children who felt they had too much to lose by remaining at the Peak. A band of youths had briefly taken over the burnt-out buildings but had been 'moved on'.

The apartments lay vacant and served as giant nesting boxes for the Pacific gulls that squawked as the boat passed by. Fittings and fixtures had been torn out. Mounds of sand had blown in through shattered glass patio doors. The wind whistled around the sharp and broken edges of the Peak.

No one spoke.

"The Peak has become a cursed place," said Koyl. "Most people dare not come here at all. Some have started to speak of it as an omen about the coming end of time."

Chapter Six

Stephen looked up at a picture of a tropical island that hung on the wall of his math class. It was a cardboard poster, the kind of thing he had seen on display in a travel agency. The image was yellowing and the corners were curling inwards. Stephen wondered if that poster had any special significance for the math teacher. Had he taken a trip there? Or was it just part of an old daydream? The bell rang, sending teenagers pouring out of classrooms and into the hallway.

The first day back at school after the summer holidays was always a time of high excitement. Confusion collided with expectation as hundreds of students paraded the halls with untested bravado for the year ahead. There were people everywhere. Mostly it was the same group of faces from the previous year. Some had grown taller over the summer, others fatter. The break had seen acne clear for some; for others it now covered their face and neck like smallpox. Puberty was unkind.

Stephen was flushed down the hallway with the rest of the stream. Students backed up, clogging the school's designated open spaces. The veterans among them spread out on the floor, comparing timetables or strumming acoustic guitars. The new crop of kids fresh out of primary school were instantly recognizable by their brand new clothes. It would take them a few months to fit in. For now they separated the herd.

Stephen opened his new locker, 171b, and read the graffiti scribbled on the inside of the door:

I love Pud
never wipe
I took your stuff. Ha ha.
تخخريال
war for peace
Satin rules!

Words of wisdom past. Where were the locker's previous owners now? It didn't matter. For the next ten months this little rectangle in the wall was his docking station, a home coordinate in the vast indifference of space and time.

He would soon add to the locker's secret history—pin notes and hang pictures in its interior. For now, though, Stephen appreciated the new beginning its emptiness represented.

"You cock!" The locker slammed shut. "Who did you suck off to score this address?"

Talysn had an energy all his own. Some called it charisma, others arrogance, but when Tal entered a room, you were sure to know it.

They had met two years earlier. Tal had called Stephen a poser for wearing a Led Zeppelin tee-shirt and had challenged Stephen to name even one album the band had recorded. Stephen had named them all, plus the known bootleg concert recordings in circulation.

The two shared little in common. Stephen's parents were married and rich, and lived in a big house in a nice part of town. Tal lived in a social housing duplex with his mother. There was something real and honest about Tal, though, which reassured Stephen, as if his crassness prohibited duplicity of character.

Peter had once counseled Stephen to be wary of people who might try to befriend him for the "wrong reasons," for "who he was," and "what he had," whatever that meant. The warning had seemed absurd to Stephen, whose weekly allowance was a pittance when compared to what many of his peers received from their parents. Rather than taking his father's advice as a general caution, Stephen heard it as a specific criticism of his relationship with Tal, whom his father just didn't like. Peter's disapproval of Tal only strengthened Stephen's resolve to forgive his friend's shortcomings.

"What?" asked Stephen.

"The locker, Man. Sweet spot, right outside the girls' can."

Tal danced around in one spot, ducking and weaving like a shadow boxer.

"Oh," said Stephen.

"Oh, he says, what a dick … Hey, have you lost weight? Just kidding, you're still a porker."

Stephen instinctively shielded his belly. His weight had somehow become an acceptable topic for family discussion. Peter, who ran at least three times a week and boasted that he could still swim thirty-five straight laps of the local pool, couldn't understand why his son refused to take pride in his appearance. He blamed Alma for spoiling the boy with food.

"It's just baby fat," she would say. "He'll grow out of it."

The Van Doorens seldom ate together. Other things always seemed to get in the way: a late meeting or an overseas trip, Gracie's tap lessons or horseback riding. But when the family did sit down for a meal, his father would study the contents of Stephen's plate. A heaviness then descended around the dinner table, more so when Stephen took a second helping. Dessert was always tense; Stephen often refused a serving of cake or ice-cream, only to eat a stashed bag of cookies in the privacy of his own room.

Stephen had grown fat—his mother called him heavy—and it left him feeling vulnerable and self-conscious, and he had entered high school like a wounded wildebeest approaching a pride of lions.

Gym class was the worst part of his week, especially basketball, when coach McGregor separated the teams by shirts and skins. Stephen always ended up on the skins side of the court. He would spend the weekend anticipating the moment of shame when he would be forced to remove his shirt, revealing his curtains of flab to the guys in his class. He was especially ashamed of his nipples. They weren't small and tight like the other guys'. His nipples were fat, with large areolae like a woman's. He was embarrassed of those nipples and was forever pulling at the top of his shirts to keep the fabric from gathering in a way that would outline the contour of his chest. Stephen never showered after gym class. He just changed back into his regular clothes and sat for the remainder of his classes, feeling the trickles of sweat travel down his back and soak into his trousers. Shirts and skins left no place to hide. The guys were cruel, especially Ethan Decker, the skateboard prodigy who was rumored to have been near to signing a sponsorship deal with a top-tier skate brand.

"Holy man-boobs!" Ethan had said one day as Stephen peeled off his shirt for a game of basketball.

It was the inevitable comment. But the group cackle that usually followed an insult like that was cut short. In what seemed like a moment of fast-forward, Stephen noticed that Ethan was on the ground, bleeding from his bottom lip. He looked up to see Tal in a shoving match with another kid before coach McGregor stepped in to separate them.

Tal got a week's suspension for the assault, and the Decker family had threatened legal action if Ethan's cosmetic injuries caused any disruption to his imminent sponsorship deal.

"Thanks," Stephen had said to Tal when he saw him a few days later.

"I didn't do it for you, you fat fucker. That guy's just a cunt."

They never mentioned the incident again. But they both knew it was there.

The bell sounded, dismantling the little groups that had formed in the hallway. Without saying a word, Tal gripped Stephen's hand. They twisted their hands from side to side and then knocked their elbows together. It was a little ritual Tal had created—more intimate than a handshake, not as lame as a high five. He felt a bit stupid doing it, but it was their thing. Stephen shut his locker and joined the current of students making its way down the hallway.

Chapter Seven

The door of the change room opened suddenly. Alma stood there in her bra, completely unprepared for the sales girl. Why did she think she could just open the door like that? Wasn't it reasonable to assume privacy would be respected in here?

"Oh," said Alma to the sales assistant. "You scared me."

"Oh did I? Sorry about that. I knocked but maybe you didn't hear me. I just thought I'd bring you a couple of other things you might like. There's this one," said the salesgirl, holding up a pair of sequined jackets and a pencil skirt. "It's more of a cream color, and this skirt I just got in."

The sales assistant handed the hangers to Alma, who was still shielding herself with the blouse she had been trying on.

"Thanks," she said and closed the door of the change room.

"No problem, just gimme a yell if you need anything."

God these rooms were small; like changing in a pantry. And these mirrors were unforgiving. Alma got one arm through the blouse, bumped her elbow against the door. The latch rattled. She twisted it to make sure it was fully locked before peeling off her trousers.

Alma's phone rang. She had never really got used to the idea of a cell phone; she preferred the freedom of making calls when she wanted and resented the assumption of availability that having a mobile phone invited. Knowing the device could go off at any moment prevented her from truly committing to any one activity. One of the benefits of working in prisons was that cell phones were strictly prohibited. She only agreed to carry a phone because of the children, but even then she usually turned the ringer down so low she often missed incoming calls.

Stephen teased her about the amount of time it took her to respond to messages. Alma was also terrified of carcinogens—another reason not to carry a cell phone. Now her phone was ringing. Loudly. Ringing and vibrating, the trill of it rippling through the thin walls of the change room, her phone the epicenter of a miniature earthquake. All of the other shoppers, the half-naked women in the surrounding booths, would be rolling their eyes. Alma fished around in her bag. *Of course it is buried at the very bottom.* The number was unfamiliar. She answered, instantly aware of the other shoppers now feeling entitled to eavesdrop on her conversation.

There was a delay on the line and Alma heard her own voice echo back "Hello" as the word reached its destination across the ether. She braced herself. This was a familiar scenario, Peter's call from some remote location: an Icelandic fjord, a canal lock, a customs office on the north island of New Zealand.

"A-m-a." Peter's voice was muffled and broken.

She was glad to hear his voice and at the same time wary of the communication problems of these long-distance calls. Peter had once put the children to bed via CB radio: "Good night. Over."

These conversations accentuated the distance between them and left her yearning for real communication. It was almost better for generations past, she thought. At least for them, when people went abroad, they were definitively absent, their memory preserved, intact, to be reanimated upon their return. These modern devices reduced communication to chatter, glorifying the needless transmission of superficial details. Alma had long ago learned to keep her sentences short or risk the frustration of being misunderstood.

"Things are fine … "

"The kids are fine … "

"A bit warm today, but it's supposed to rain later … "

"No, I'm okay, just a bit tired."

Peter sounded preoccupied and hinted at having many things to discuss upon his return. As she listened, Alma grew annoyed. She was half naked and her legs were cold. What was the point of calling only to say you would soon have much to say?

She had been very supportive during Peter's building of his career. The Van Doorens had moved a lot, a different port city every two to four years: Le Havre, Rotterdam, San Francisco, Portland, Hong Kong, Kuwait City, Cape Town, Vancouver. With each move, Peter reassured Alma he was drawing ever closer to his professional goals, but each relocation presented fresh opportunities and new leads to pursue. She and Peter had moved around so often that Alma came to think of people anthropologically: as sources of local knowledge that could help them all fit in with the ever-changing cultural milieu. What were the right clothes to wear at school? The right lunches to pack? The right toys to play with?

Every relocation, with its attendant farewells and awkward introductions to new social groups, had worn at Alma's patience, adding to a mental tally of what she was owed. Even if she didn't consciously identify the currency in which the debt would be or could be repaid, it just seemed unfair not to be aware of the sacrifices she had made for the family, especially when Peter often seemed to take them for granted.

The daughter of a French diplomat, Alma's greatest misfortune in life—after having never known her mother—was having been born in Iraq while her father had been posted at the French embassy in Baghdad, long before it existed on the fringes of the hippie trail. Though a French citizen, Alma's birthplace forever tainted her credibility, and complicated every administrative process that later required her to present official documents. It was exhausting. Passport applications, security clearance forms, a wedding license—Alma's request for these documents was regarded with a degree of suspicion the moment she produced her Iraqi birth certificate, a card-table-sized, hand-written scroll, in Arabic, accompanied by a notarized official translation of the document that required updating every two years. The thing looked dubious and improvised, and Alma had, at times, cursed it and her father for not having lived a more tranquil, suburban life somewhere less complicated.

She learned to speak French, Arabic, English and Italian. The accumulation of those languages had convinced Alma that studying a language is one thing but living it was quite another. To get angry in a language, to shout and swear in it, to fight and dream in it, these were the experiences that bound a language to one's soul.

She had not learned Arabic. She had lived it. Her relationship with that language had grown parallel to the adolescent experiences of her life. It had developed with her over time and been continuously refined: through the slang she picked up from friends at school; through the twangs and local dialects she absorbed from street vendors and market bazaars; through the neighborhood squabbles she helped to mediate, as well as a hard-lived experience with a Moroccan boyfriend. It was her language. Not her mother tongue, but the one she had chosen, the one that brought her ever closer to articulating the essential human experiences that language itself had been invented to communicate.

She had met Peter in Le Havre while he was working with a French shipping agency as part of an international placement. Alma had found work transcribing and translating documents at a regional customs bureau. Though unglamorous, the job was a formal government role, vital experience for an aspirant to the United Nations, where Alma one day hoped to work as an interpreter.

Peter was the only man in the office who hadn't assumed she was the receptionist. He was always deferent and seemed to take a genuine interest in learning more about her role within the organization. He asked for her opinions on how processes could be improved. When the rest of the office would clear out for the evening to resume the mayhem of family life elsewhere, the two of them had often stayed back, working well into the night. It was on these occasions that Peter and Alma had allowed themselves some friendly conversation.

Over the months these conversations grew less formal. Alma told Peter about losing her mother to a brain hemorrhage as a child and Peter sympathized. They began to share their hopes and dreams, and Alma was surprised to discover that she was beginning to feel a strong desire to kiss Peter. She had taken an instant liking to him, but had not been physically attracted to him. As the months wore on, she had found comfort in the regularity of his company. His low, deep voice and slow, but deliberate movements added to Peter's reassuring self-confidence. He put people at ease. He seemed ... harmless. Alma wanted him, and felt certain that she had seen him watching her with increasing interest as she got up to move about the office. She let herself act coyly, lingered at work stations with her back turned to him longer than was necessary. She wanted him to want her. She wanted to open herself to him, if he would only let her in. He didn't, and Alma found herself growing annoyed by the very qualities that had attracted her; Peter's deference now seemed cold, his tactfulness prudish.

It was on one of their evenings back at the office that Peter received a phone call offering him a position in Rotterdam. Surmising the gist of the conversation, Alma had been surprised at how instantly disappointed she had felt at the prospect of losing Peter's company. He was given only five hours to accept the job.

That night they celebrated. Emboldened by the champagne, they found themselves back at Alma's flat, where Peter had groped her awkwardly, pawing at her breasts like an untrained puppy. After her previous experiences, Alma had thought Peter's inexperience with women sweet and endearing.

During the ensuing elixir of relief and euphoria he suggested Alma come with him. The offer had seemed impulsive, but safe. Peter was a good man. Someone she could depend on. He was kind and thoughtful. He was motivated. She agreed to go with him for fear of losing what might be if she refused.

A light rapping of knuckles, more of a scratching sound at the change-room door lifted Alma out of her present daydream.

"You doing okay in there," said the sales girl, sounding like she was still smiling, all teeth, from behind the closed door.

"I'm good," said Alma automatically.

"Do you need me to get you any more sizes or anything?"

"No. Thank you. Sorry, I am on the phone."

The salesgirl responded sympathetically, as if it was perfectly normal to hold a three-way, international conversation from inside a tiny cubicle in a department store. How quickly the world had changed and how quickly people had adapted.

"Oh, okay, sorry about that, you just let me know if you need anything." The sales girl left Alma to Peter's disembodied voice.

"Oh, nothing," said Alma into the phone, "just the sales girl from the shop."

"Oh," said Peter. "Well don't go too crazy in there."

"I'm not," said Alma, coyly. "Just a few little presents."

In the full-length mirror of the change room, Alma's bare legs were dimpled with cellulite. She pulled the skin tight around her thighs. Pencil skirts were not for her. Had the salesgirl suggested it to make that point? She probably had, the skinny little bitch. Alma listened to Peter as she collected clothes from the change-room floor with her one free hand. The conference was going well. L'Eden Sur Mer was an interesting place. Peter would spend another week there, at least.

"I love you too," she said, and let Peter hang up the phone.

Alma dressed quickly. The change room felt claustrophobic. She handed a pile of unwanted clothes back to the sales girl, but did end up buying the pencil skirt; the salesgirl had been so helpful, it wouldn't have been right to deny her the commission, the little twerp. Besides, Gracie might like to have the skirt one day.

Peter lay in bed holding the phone across his chest as he stared at the ceiling of his little wooden yurt and listened to the muted crashing of the waves outside. He swung his legs to the side of the bed and searched with his feet for his running shoes. This was how he forced himself out the door: committed, feet first, to the run before his mind and the rest of his body could protest.

Peter stretched, dressed only in boxer shorts and a pair of laced up running shoes. It had been a long, sticky night and his body was already moist. He picked through the contents of his suitcase and unfolded one of the synthetic running shirts that absorbed the sweat, then pulled on a pair of running shorts. It had just gone 5.00 am, but already the sun was sharpening the visible details inside his dingy little cabin.

When Peter stepped outside, the surf slapped against the shoreline loud and heavy. He looked over the ocean towards the horizon; one could be forgiven for believing the world was flat. Had Alma sounded distant? Remote? She was always so damned uncomfortable talking on cell phones.

His feet felt heavy and awkward as he set off, clumsy strides that worked out the little kinks in his joints until he found a rhythm.

Urban development spread from the center of L'Eden Sur Mer like ripples in a pond. The central capital, such as it was, held a Lego set of concrete government buildings and cinder-block houses with tin roofs and lockable aluminum doors. These were the footprints of international aid.

Sur Merian 'city' dwellers surprised Peter's expectations of Pacific Islanders. They were enormous and waddled around with their arms held at a distance from their sides, further exaggerating their heavy frames. Everywhere Peter went, young men, fat and sullen looking, herded together in groups of three or four. They eyed him as he ran past, sneering, but saying nothing.

The rising sea level had changed the Sur Merian diet. Subsistence agriculture was threatened when seawater started bubbling up through freshwater swamps and arable land, poisoning staple crops like cucumber, sweet potato and banana.

The islanders had become increasingly reliant on donations of imported food. Increased consumption of processed foods had spiked incidents of previously unknown conditions like obesity, diabetes and heart disease. People were generally pretty heavy set, their bellies hanging out of absurdly undersized tee-shirts that had arrived on the island from God-knew-where, printed with fading images of yesterday's heroes: Mickey Mouse, Astro Boy, Michael Jordan. In the main street, Peter ran past an enormous man struggling to wash his dusty feet with a garden hose. 'University of Kansas' was emblazoned across the front of his tee-shirt.

Along every trail and behind every house lay the same disintegrating mound of plastic bottles and aluminum soda-pop cans, labels bleached by the sun. Scrawny dogs nosed through the piles of rubbish, looking up briefly as Peter ran past. Some of the trash heaps had been set alight and the dark smoke of smoldering plastic rose high into the sky. Peter's head spun.

His legs wobbled underneath him as his feet shifted from running on pavement to sand. He felt different muscles take over, adjusting to control his balance on the unstable ground. There, in the distance, halfway between the beach and the water line, lay another one of those familiar mounds of garbage. He pulled to a stop, panting, and inspected a few of the items tucked away in the heap. There were torn plastic bags; empty cans of vegetables and ready-made soup; ripped sacks of rice and beans, and lentils; discarded jars of preserved tropical fruit; cartons of flavored condensed milk, and iced coffee. He pulled out a can of something that had Asian writing on it. *Korean*. Peter recognized the word for pears. He turned the can over in his hands, squinted as the sun glinted off the metal, and tossed the can back on the heap.

Peter knew he was supposed to feel this load of trash was a blight on the landscape, a stain on paradise—it was not a pretty sight. The mounds of trash should be disposed of, but the feeling that most overcame Peter as his eyes wandered over the individual components in that great mound of junk was a sense of admiration, a sense of triumph at what the human spirit had managed to accomplish. Each can and glass jar, each wrapper and plastic bottle cap, registered a threshold of human ingenuity. Minerals had been buried, hidden deep beneath the ground, and man—yes man—had found a way to extract them and put them to use. It was man who had understood the fabric of the universe, teased it out into its elementary particles and used them for his own designs.

Who else but human beings could have co-opted the world's resources in this way and shaped their own destinies by imposing their will on nature's initial design? Peter was proud of that mound of garbage, the way he imagined a boxer might feel gratified standing over a vanquished foe; you didn't gloat over it, but you had proven yourself smarter and stronger than your adversary. You won. He won. Nature could be tamed.

He trudged on through the sand, legs aching as he shifted his weight from side to side, avoiding the larger rocks and pebbles along the shoreline. From here, he could see a fuzzy crop of green scrub that lay inland beyond the palm trees, the tops of which were haloed by the rising sun. He moved further inland until his legs welcomed firmer ground.

Away from the developed center of the island, most Sur Merians lived in clustered shanty shacks facing away from the water. It was like traveling back in time. These temporary dwellings were put together with lashed palm fronds or long grass, driftwood and whatever detritus found its way to shore. Though crude, these constructions struck Peter as more pleasant to live in than the cinder-block huts with no ventilation at all.

Still early morning, the sun was already heavy with heat. Humidity would soon cling to everything.

These outer villages were not on the beach as Peter had expected. Most of the villages were inland, under the speckled shade of the scrub brush. Here, a dozen or so huts were arranged in a roughly circular shape. Between them, a permanent haze of campfire smoke hung low to the ground in the airless gloom of the dry and salt-encrusted brush. Each house had a patch that grew yams and beans. A few scrawny, black-haired pigs paced nervously inside makeshift pens. They cowered as Peter ran past.

People here seemed to get on with things, to busy themselves with the various labors of the day. Absent was the feeling of listlessness Peter had felt wafting from those groups of young men slumming around the center of town, thumbing old-model cell phones with their chubby hands. The villagers lived in a different country altogether, a different century. They were thinner and darker, and some even waved when they saw him. How much did they have to do with the conference? Did they even know about it? Would they care?

His pace quickened as he set off towards a low canopy of dusty bushes and spindly trees. He came upon a kind of path, a vague trail among the shrubs, and ran to the sound of his legs swishing through tall grass and the snapping of twigs under foot. Willing himself to keep running, his heart pounded in his chest as he ducked low-hanging branches and sprang over the brackish pools of water that occasionally barred his way along the narrow path. His lungs burned.

Peter emerged from the scrub into a misty, sodden clearing that looked to have been hacked from the surrounding brush. He drew to a slow stop and sucked oxygen, palms pressed tightly against his knees. His chest hurt and his head tingled. The saliva was thick and pasty in his mouth. He spat and panted, recovering his breath. It had been a long time since he had run off-road. He smelled the smoke before he saw it. The bitter, acrid smell of burning green, sappy wood hung heavy on the thin morning air; Peter's stomach churned. A wisp of smoke rose from the grubby trees beyond the clearing.

Peter stretched his calves as he traipsed toward the smell.

Voices drifted to him as he approached the edge of the thicket. He climbed a gentle slope and into a tangle of wood and bamboo. The sun-dappled canopy of gnarled branches and palm leaves closed in around him. He could make out two figures perched on a mound, silhouettes that came into focus as his eyes adjusted to the darkness of the grove. As their contours sharpened, he realized they were women, naked from the waist down, and squatting on top of a nest of twigs.

"*Maht, Maht*," they said, noticing Peter, and wiggled their bare bottoms from side to side.

Peter froze, unsure of what he had stumbled upon. He turned away from the women and took shelter behind a bush. The women called out.

In his haste to retreat, he backed himself into a pocket of dense and brambly bush that cut him off from the beach. The other voices grew louder as they approached, the voices of women and children, following him. Peter could now hear the snapping of twigs underfoot as the group made its way down the hill towards him.

This hiding was absurd. Peter stormed out of the thicket to face a group of eight or so women and children standing above him halfway up the embankment. They grinned and turned to one another, whispering things that further broadened their smiling faces. One of the women pointed at Peter and said something to her companions that drew hearty laughter. From the base of the embankment, he waved meekly at the small crowd.

Peter struggled up the embankment. "What's so funny?" he muttered.

The women covered their mouths to stifle their laughter, but their amusement grew as Peter clamored up the slope to meet them.

"You are in a toilet," said a boy, standing beside the group of women.

Peter stopped dead; looked down. He was ankle deep in the soggy mess. How had he not noticed the smell? Had he been panting that hard? He was aware of it now, though. The stench of human excrement wafted up around him, sticking to his skin.

"You must go out and around," said the boy, gesturing with his hands. "The beach is there."

Peter steadied himself against a tree to get his bearings. The way out was over there. He waded his way towards the bushes, the muck sucking at his shoes as he struggled through. He stumbled, and one of his shoes was sucked under.

"Fuck."

He scrambled to his feet. The onlookers and the smell and the color of that sock drove him to thrash his way through the brambles and onto the beach.

"Fuck," he said, hopping around on the sand.

Peter dropped to the ground and yanked off his remaining shoe then peeled off both socks before dashing to the ocean to wash himself. He washed his hands and feet in the shallows, scrubbing them with handfuls of sand. He walked further out, feeling the water gradually lifting the weight of his body off his feet. He stood there, looking out to the horizon, feeling the current push against him.

Laughter made him turn. Three boys darted back into the bushes. The bushes rustled and three heads popped up. The boys then mimed Peter's running, flailing their arms and legs as they laughed.

"Yeah, yeah." Peter faced the horizon. It felt good just to stand in the water and have the pulse of the ocean soothe his tired legs.

Seated next to Koyl at dinner that evening, Peter asked the President why so many islanders seemed determined to avoid him, explaining that on his walk back to town after the incident in the clearing, people ignored him, and when he had approached a group of women skinning coconuts, they had retreated to their homes. Aloof, not hostile.

"Avoidance is a sign of respect," said Koyl. "They don't disturb you because they assume your business is more important than theirs."

Peter buttered a piece of bread. "Is it a kind of caste system, then?" He thought of those young people in the town center who carried cell phones and wore western clothes; they had seemed to be living an entirely different life from those he had seen on the outer fringes of the island.

"It's not a caste system, no," said Koyl. "It's part of what we call *Pwaanhashaay*. It literally means, 'path of the wind'. You cannot change the direction of the wind. So it's better to just get out of its way. It's a simple solution." He seemed satisfied with his somewhat cryptic reply, munching contentedly on little pieces of bread he had torn from the roll in front of him. His jaw muscles bulged as he chewed.

"So what do the Sur Merians think about all this, then?" asked Peter, gesturing to the group gathered in the resort's dining hall.

Koyl's semi-permanent smile broadened. It was an expression that lay somewhere between a smirk and a grin. "In some ways they are like children," he said between chewing. "They are stubborn. Some are amused by what we're doing here. For others, the rising water is just *Pwaanhashaay*. The people, they are very attached to the land. It is their home."

Koyl broke off another piece of bread and turned to answer a question whispered to him by one of his attendants, a frail older man who never seemed to stray far from the President's side. Koyl nodded, silently, dismissing the little man with a flick of the wrist.

The President of this impoverished island really had managed to assemble some legitimate talent for this conference.

Without her glasses and blue linen on, Peter now recognized the dumpy, fair-skinned woman as Jancis Sloverband. She had championed a new model of international development where corporations financed civic works in impoverished nations in exchange for bilateral agreements that guaranteed territorial exclusivity for sale of their products and services. Her brand of feudalism had drawn fierce criticism from both sides of the political spectrum, but she pointed to the results in sub-Saharan Africa as evidence of the model's success. For Sloverband, the drop in crime and infant mortality rates in countries like Angola and Tanzania spoke for itself. The free market worked better than charity. Give people something to do with a machete and they were less likely to use it on each other.

At a different point in history, under different conditions, these people might have been great statesmen. They might have been lords and generals, emperors and kings. Rightly or wrongly, each age had its heroes, people whose life's works and ambition captured the ethos of their time. The past had seen Confucius and Aristotle, Christ and Muhammad; it had embraced the likes of Da Vinci and Newton, Darwin and Einstein. This age, too, had its champions. It had Rockefeller and Ford; it had Gates, Buffet and Branson. A global hunger to taste their success would ensure the twenty-first century saw wealth's apotheosis.

Despite its potential, the conference had so far explored few real solutions to the island's predicament. Much time had been spent bemoaning the rising sea level and quarreling about its potential causes. An unspoken consensus favored the evacuation of the island.

It was the younger generation of those more urban Sur Merians, explained Koyl, the ones with cell phones, who preferred this plan. Removed from the traditions and culture of their elders, gods and ancestral lands seemed like quaint relics of a time they had never known. Many young Sur Merians were intrigued by the idea of going abroad. They knew almost nothing of places like New Zealand or Australia. These places were no more than words, impressions formed by random photographs they had seen, yet they captivated the imagination; they were fantasy landscapes where dreams of affluence and independence came true. Younger Sur Merians looked around them and found little to celebrate in their degraded land. Their parents' stories of better days were behind them. Life would be better beyond this starving landscape.

Did the Sur Merians have enough drive, enough guts, and enough self-determination to free themselves from their current situation? Peter dared not pose that question to Koyl.

"What is the political influence of these tribal chieftains?" said Peter. "On the beach you said they had no power, so what is their purpose?"

Koyl shook his head quickly from side to side. He was still chewing. He waved his index finger. "I said they have no resources," said the President, swallowing a pasty mouthful. He sat back in his chair, hands folded in his lap, as if reconsidering the question. He picked his teeth with his tongue. "The people of this country are spiritual. Superstitious. The Grey Hairs are like what is, for you, a clergy. They are the people's conscience. You can choose to listen or ignore." Satisfied with his answer, Koyl leaned forward and tore off another bite-sized piece of bread with his long fingers.

Peter too reached for his piece of bread. "And what do *they* think of all of this?" said Peter, gesturing towards the room of delegates.

Koyl chuckled to himself and stifled a burp. "They only have one question about this," said the President, wiping his mouth with a colorful napkin. "Why?" Koyl searched Peter's face, watching how the word settled in. "They want to know why companies like yours would help us when governments do not. They don't trust you. But then, they don't trust anybody."

The little man returned to whisper in Koyl's ear. The President frowned as he listened. "Excuse me," he said to Peter. "I must go." Peter half rose from his seat to honor the President's departure. He sat back down and pondered the question.

Why would companies help?

The question bothered Peter. *Why wouldn't they?* Companies were in the business of improving things, of making them better, faster, safer, cheaper, and more accessible. Because the market could solve big problems. At its heart, Peter's life quest was a democratic objective. More people today ate better, dressed better, lived better and longer than they previously had, thanks to people like him. Here was an opportunity to develop something novel; to get the world's attention and remind it that technology and innovation were solid foundations upon which to build a civilization. Here was a chance to remind people that knowledge wasn't just power; it was God.

Later that evening, in the spa lounge, Peter sat alone at a table, catching up on work. The volatile foreign currency market was clouding his financial projections for the upcoming quarter. He mused at how much worse the situation could have been had he accepted the advice to list Van Dooren International as a public company. He congratulated himself on having refused. Why shoulder the burden of stockholders? People couldn't be trusted to ignore their instincts and superstitions; their behavior on the share market was proof of their fickleness.

Peter rarely permitted himself a drink, but he had one now. The alcohol felt warm in his mouth. It flushed his cheeks. The feeling reminded him that he was just a man, a ball of matter, responding to a biochemical reaction, no different to the photosynthesis of a plant. It was a pleasant feeling.

Uninvited and unannounced, Holden Nash pulled out the chair opposite and sat. "You're working too hard, Van Dooren. It's wind-down time. A man's got to know when to quit."

Peter smiled awkwardly. He didn't like being disturbed. "Just working on a few things," he said.

"I can see that," said Nash. "I know you've got a CEO in that company of yours, Van Dooren. Let him do the work. You ought to learn to hang back a little. Be an ideas man. Behind the scenes. You might live longer." Nash slapped the table playfully.

Holding his empty tumbler to the barman, Nash rattled the ice inside the glass. The barman dutifully set about preparing him another drink—the two of them had worked out a tidy little routine. Nash turned back to Peter and grinned. "Kid's been a bartender about ten minutes. He's getting the hang of it, though. What are you working on there, Van Dooren? A plan to save the world?"

Peter realized he was still perched over his notebook. He had a tendency to freeze in position when disturbed, as if waiting to resume his activities the moment the interruption passed. Alma hated that habit; said it made her feel like she was an annoyance. Peter had never understood her irritation. After all, she had been the one to interrupt him. He caught himself with Nash, closed the notebook and offered a gesture of conversation.

"How do you think things are going so far?"

Nash downed the last of his drink and exhaled slowly through moist lips. "They're not."

Peter was surprised by the shortness of Nash's response. He had expected a more diplomatic answer. "Well, it's still early days, I guess."

Nash sucked on a piece of ice and squinted one eye. "Well I don't know about you, but I don't make my living making guesses. I make bets, and I'm willing to bet this dog and pony show ends up where it started which, frankly, is nowhere."

The bartender—a tall, slender fellow of indecipherable age—arrived with Nash's drink. Most of the islanders confused the physical cues Peter normally used to determine a person's age and social status: hair style, the quality and number of teeth, clarity of the skin. Many looked older than their years. They had dry, creased skin from a lifetime spent in the sun. Their teeth were stained and invariably crooked, or at least awkwardly spaced.

All of these abnormalities (at least by familiar, western standards) made Peter recognize how normal, how conventional, it was to see people wearing make-up, or with straight white teeth. It had not always been this way. He had understood it in the abstract, of course, but here they were, people who, he was sure, resembled human beings of the past. The modern aesthetic Peter had grown accustomed to was very new indeed. L'Eden Sur Mer was a kind of time machine.

Nash handed a small fold of bills to the young bartender, winked, and watched the man as he walked back to his post behind the bar. Delegates had been asked not to tip the service staff at the resort for fear of corrupting them. Nash was clearly flouting the rule. Holden Nash slurped a mouthful of drink and munched on his piece of ice.

"What do you think of the Sur Merians?" said Nash.

Peter thought of the young, obese men he had seen loafing around in the city center wearing faded LA Lakers and Chicago Bulls jerseys; he thought of the villagers who seemed to largely ignore him as he passed.

"Is it just me or are they kind of rude?" said Peter. He didn't dare bring up his having wandered into a village toilet, but it was on his mind. No one had offered to help him.

"Ha," said Nash, still smiling.

"It's like they look right through you," said Peter, "like they don't really have any interest. It's weird; it's almost like they don't even notice you're there. "

Nash took another sip, then dabbed his forehead with a moist handkerchief. "Oh they're looking," he said. "They just look at you sideways is all. They see plenty, believe me; they just don't want you to know they're watching."

Chuckling to himself, Nash sniffed trickles of perspiration back up his nostrils.

"People paint us as the bad guys," he said, presumably referring to himself as an ambassador for the energy companies. "That gets to me. You see, we turn the lights on. We keep you warm in winter, cool in summer and we take you on your vacation when life gets too much for you to handle. I don't like what comes out of an exhaust pipe either, but it sure is nice to be able to get from A to B, isn't it?" He took a long drink. "Well at least the whisky works in this place, eh? That's a relief."

Nash exhaled slowly, as if blowing out a stream of cigarette smoke. The candlelight cast double shadows against the bamboo walls. "You having a good time, Van Dooren?"

Peter smiled, sharing Nash's appreciation of the absurdity of their situation. "It's been an interesting day," said Peter, smiling.

"That's one way of putting it."

The tension the conversation had started under eased. Nash dabbed his top lip and forehead with the handkerchief. His face was red and swollen. He stirred the ice in his drink with his index finger. "I've never been real good with the heat," he said. "It's not getting any easier as I get older."

He wiped the back of his neck and stuffed the hanky into the pocket of his pants. He took a sip of his drink, sighed as he scanned the lounge. A few people were milling about, talking in hushed tones in the unlit corners of the room.

"How long you going to stick around for?" said Nash.

Peter flicked some crumbs off the table. "Don't know. Few weeks, maybe. You?"

"Long as I have to," said Nash, picking at the outside of his nostril. "Say, what do you make of our host?" he said abruptly.

"Koyl? I don't know," said Peter. "He seems … sincere. You?"

Nash turned his drink in the pool of condensation that had collected on the table under the glass. He pursed his lips. "I've known Koyl for a while. He's got balls, I can tell you that."

Peter wasn't sure what Nash was referring to. Did he mean the President's decision to hold the conference was a bold one? If so, he agreed. "He's introduced some good initiatives," said Peter.

Nash smiled to himself. "You're talking about that Australian half-way house there?"

"That's one of them," said Peter. "You can think what you like about mandatory detention for asylum seekers but it was a shrewd move for Koyl. I mean you've got to put those people somewhere. Koyl just had the courage to say, 'Put them here'."

"It's just a prison though, really, isn't it."

Nash took a long drink, put the glass down on the table and leaned forward. "You know something, Van Dooren."

Having noticed that Nash had finished his drink, the bartender crossed the floor with a fresh one. Nash waved him away impatiently before leaning toward Peter. "You mentioned courage, right? Your word, not mine. Well … I'm not in the business of importing people, thank Christ," Nash wiped the top of his lip. "But if I were … I'd want the people who stayed behind. The ones with the courage and the conviction, the guts to stay behind and fight, to endure whatever shit those people in that lock-up couldn't face. You know what I mean? I'd want the winners."

Nash grinned. Peter couldn't tell if the man was trying to provoke. He tested him. "What do you make of this place, then?"

"What? L'Eden Sur Mer? Lost cause. You and I both know better than to stick our necks out for lost causes."

Peter grinned in turn. "So better to abandon it then?"

"I like you, Van Dooren; don't go spoiling it for me now. I see the little trap you're setting for me, but you can't compare the two situations and you only look dumb trying." Nash cleared his throat and smacked his lips together as if tasting something unseen. "Look," he continued, "when your house burns down, you get a new one. It's sad, but that's the way it is. You cut your losses." Nash leaned back in his chair, as if he'd finished, then he shot forward again. "You can't live in what's not there, you follow me? And this place … it isn't really here, you know what I mean? Might as well be imaginary," he waved his hands around, and wiggled his fingers. "Hell, it will be in a few years. It'll be a story. A place you tell kids about when you tuck 'em in at night. The Island of the Drowned King. Atlantis part deux."

Nash hiccupped. "Fuck it, he said. "Koyl ought to take his people and move them the hell off this place. Like I said, a man's got to know when to quit."

"Why did you come down here, then?"

"Same reason you did," said Nash, bracing the table to get to his feet. "You see a car crash on the highway, you slow down to take a closer look." Nash brushed his chair aside. "See you in the morning for the traffic report, Van Dooren. Don't stay up too late."

Nash slapped Peter on the shoulder and waved to the bartender as he stumbled out of the lounge.

That night, Peter lay awake in his cabin. Mosquitoes buzzed around his head like thought clouds as the wind hissed through the narrow slats of the hut. The weight of nature pressed down against the bungalow's thin walls. The wind, the rain and the sun conspired to slowly and patiently gnaw at this hut. He thought of the frigate birds that ripped twigs and mortar from the structure to build their nests. He thought of the termites, the fire ants and Loma beetles that consumed his thatched, palm roof. Nature was designed to invade the fragile sanctuary of his little home. Out there, beyond the horizon, the sea was plotting to drown them all.

Peter got up and paced the room. Where was that mosquito buzzing around in the dark? The spark of an idea was upon him, growing, glowing, then receding with the buzzing of those mosquito wings. He slapped the back of his neck.

Got him.

Chapter Eight

The university chapel was a bright, sky-lighted place. Home-made tapestries looked down on Gracie with their cheerful, non-denominational images: sun, trees, clouds, and children. It was an open, multi-faith prayer space, which Gracie avoided when the Muslims occupied it—shoes piled at the entrance, puddles of water splashed all over the bathroom tiles from washing their feet in the sinks. Why was their devotion so messy?

It was quiet now.

No shoes at the door.

Gracie stopped at the font of holy water. It seemed a silly ritual. Still, she liked to imagine the holy water as having a kind of power that could burn the impure. She dipped her finger in it, briefly expecting something other than for it to feel … wet.

Her parents didn't go to church. There wasn't even a Bible in the house. For whatever reason, Gracie felt that God had given her the gift of faith, despite her upbringing. Gracie just knew that God existed and that they were friends. She had always prayed to Him, even when she was little, before she knew what prayer was. No one told her to. She didn't learn it from a relative, in school or from TV. She just spoke to Him as if they had a personal relationship and Gracie knew that He understood. None of her family knew that she prayed every day of her life, mostly for them. She had prayed that Stephen's arm got better when he broke it rollerblading one summer; she had prayed that Alma found the favorite necklace she lost—it turned up inside the sofa; she had prayed that her father got home safe.

Where was her father just now? What did he see? She imagined him on a beach, his feet buried in sand. *Such big feet.*

Chatter broke the meditative silence of the room as two women in headscarves came in. They were talking loudly, but their voices dropped to a whisper when they saw they were not alone. Gracie watched the two women as they set about washing their hands with bottled water, spilling it all over the floor near the back of the church. *Disgusting.* Gracie left before the women started praying.

Looking out at the view from her apartment, Gracie wondered if it was windy outside. There was no way of knowing. No trees to sway, no corn or wheat fields to ripple in the breeze.

To save Gracie the four-hour commute between campus and the Van Dooren estate, her father had sub-let this one-bedroom apartment in a luxury condominium complex in the city. The place belonged to one of her dad's colleagues, who used it as standby accommodation for overseas clients and guests, so it came fully furnished. Her father reassured her that having her own place would also help her make the transition to adulthood and self-reliance.

The intercom sounded.

"Ms Van Dooren, there are some young ladies here to see you." It was the concierge, the man who seemed to live in the little glass booth in the lobby downstairs.

"Okay. Let them up," said Gracie. *Young ladies. What a creep.* Gracie released the intercom and stood by her front door, waiting for Lucy and Joanne to make their way. It wouldn't take them long; that elevator shot up so fast it always made her ears pop. Gracie waited until she heard the ping of the elevator, the sound of the doors opening, Joanne's and Lucy's muffled voices in the corridor, then she opened the door.

"Hi," said Gracie. "Over here," she said, motioning.

"The place is a bit of a maze."

"It's nice," said Lucy, looking down the long, dimly lit corridor with its deep wool carpet. "Real nice," she repeated, hugging Gracie before stepping inside the apartment.

"Yeah, awesome place," said Joanne, brushing her fingers across the marble counter top of the breakfast bar.

Joanne and Lucy had found accommodation in the campus dorms. This was definitely a step up.

"Swish," said Lucy, taking in the city view.

"Yeah. I don't know," sighed Gracie. "It all feels a bit ... " she scrunched up her nose.

"What? No way," said Joanne, cutting her off. "This place is sweet. I'll totally change places with you if you don't want it."

"Definitely," added Lucy, plopping down on the leather sofa.

"You guys, it's not like I'm trying to be all spoiled and bratty about it or anything. It's just ... it's a bit much, don't you think. I mean, everyone who lives in this building is, like, fifty."

"So?"

"Well it's just a bit weird. I'm all, like, Rapunzel up in the tower."

"Yeah, except that you've got a dishwasher and a spa bath," said Lucy, picking up one of the sofa cushions and putting it on her lap.

"Yeah. Seriously, Grace, get over it," said Joanne, folding one leg under herself as she joined Lucy on the sofa.

"Okay, let's just shut up about it then." Gracie had expected Lucy and Joanne to be more sympathetic about her discomfort, her moral opposition to the building; its ostentatiousness, its phallic insistence on being the biggest, tallest, and brightest thing on the skyline.

The three of them sat on the sofa and took in the view; the cocktail mix of night and day had turned the sky pink. *I should chill out.* Tonight was about celebrating their new-found independence.

"Well I want you guys to come over all the time," said Gracie. "There's a pool and stuff downstairs."

Gracie felt blessed to have such friends.

Chapter Nine

Mohala Koyl stood at the sink. He couldn't sleep. An easterly was howling outside. The President knew what that meant: western Sur Merians would be all right. They were far enough inland and would be tucked in bed waiting out the gale. Those in the north would be thinking of their breadfruit trees, straining to stay upright against the wind. Southerners would worry about their boats as they lashed their double-hulled canoes to posts along the shore. They would be considering the conditions, weighing up the risk of leaving their vessels to battle the waves alone in the shallow waters of the port where they might be shattered against the rocks, or setting out for the relative safety of the open ocean where they could steer their boats away from the reefs and stones that threatened their livelihood. He knew some would risk their lives to save their boats—it was honorable to die at sea. Pride did nothing to soothe the grieving widows and feed the children that the honorable left behind.

Koyl thought most about the people of the east. The wind would hit them hardest. They would huddle together with their families in the trembling walls of their shacks, like he had as a child. He looked at his watch; the tide was still rising. It wouldn't peak for another hour and he knew his people would patrol the exposed shoreline, monitoring the advancing waves, watching as the wind blew those salty crests ashore.

The tide would have advanced past the mangroves to the palms that lined the shore. An hour from now it would spill over the sand dunes and curdle what remained of the freshwater lagoon. Once freshwater fish had swum in that lagoon—catfish so fat and lazy it almost seemed unfair to catch them. Things would get worse if it rained. Flooding would channel the swell further inland and wash out the unpaved access roads, which would hamper transport and supply lines. If that happened, eastern Sur Merians might be cut off from the rest of the island for days. Koyl listened, but heard no rain. If he wished hard enough, maybe the rain would keep away.

Koyl stepped out onto the balcony into the wind. He grasped the railing with both hands and squared his broad shoulders to face the wind.

The President's vision of true reform had cost him social and political capital. It wasn't just the inherited blame of his father's dealings with the mining consortia, even though that legacy had caused many among the ruling elite to think of Koyl as something of a traitor. Koyl knew that his foreign education, too, was considered by some as a forfeit on his claim of being a true Sur Merian. Koyl's absence from island life as he studied abroad, followed by his triumphant return, had left the more conservative political factions wary and uncertain about the principles that underpinned his decisions.

Koyl's insistence on gender equality was a particular source of anxiety for the Gray Hairs. To his critics, Koyl's stance was evidence of his essentially foreign nature. He knew that, behind closed doors, he was said to be the product of a European education and was not attuned to local sensibilities. Koyl was an islander, yes, but his values were sometimes at odds with traditional culture.

He did not let his people do as they had always done because he knew best. He got things done. He won them independence. He had built the asylum center. And now he had brought together this conference. He had done all of this. Mohala Koyl, father of the nation. He would know what to do.

His eyes watered as he squinted in the wind. Lightning flashed in the distance.

Koyl paced the balcony. He shot a glance inside at the phone on his desk. There was no one to call. Not now. The storm was already upon them. No more could be done tonight. He had to trust his people. There was nothing to do but wait.

The island's independence—a day Koyl thought of with great pride—also marked the start of his social isolation. He had shaken off the vestiges of empire. But freeing the country of its colonial past also meant losing a convenient nexus of blame that had previously helped Koyl unite the country. L'Eden Sur Mer was now free. The country's problems were now *his* problems, and he would have to shoulder them without the brace of history to support his discomfort.

It had been possible, at least for a while, to unify the country on the strength of people's residual animosity of their colonial masters. But it wasn't long before cracks began to appear in the foundation of the island's social cohesion. Koyl's decisions about which families had been allowed to work in the asylum-processing center had created social divisions. Koyl's critics observed that only those loyal to the President had received the sought-after jobs. He had brushed aside these criticisms as inconsequential. After all, the detention center couldn't have employed the whole country. Some were bound to be upset. And why should he not reward loyalty? Though he never faced real dissent, Koyl found it was easy enough to dissuade would-be detractors from publicly opposing his will. The threat of sentencing people to a life's labor on a merchant ship was usually enough to diffuse contrary opinion. Differing views were an important part of a democracy, but there had to be limits.

The weather was different. He couldn't reason with it. He couldn't threaten it. It had no master.

President Koyl had been a fixture in the geopolitics of the South Pacific for decades. Elsewhere, he had seen statesmen come and go, pushed out by the fickle whims of the people. He was philosophical about the ebb and flow of political time, and had studied history well enough to believe that most people eventually got what they deserved. Koyl understood that many of his neighbors saw their best interests were in keeping their traditional partners such as the United States and Australia.

L'Eden Sur Mer was his home, not the next Guantanamo Bay. He'd struggled to free it, now to preserve it, and these people, these children, wanted to leave it all behind. Yet there was nothing out there but disappointment. Young people wouldn't understand that until after they left. Koyl had to save them from themselves. *Father of the nation.*

Things had changed in the Pacific since Koyl's unilateral victory against the French. Strategic partnership was the *mot du jour*, and the currency of international diplomacy. The world was no longer held to ransom by two bloated superpowers, and the world had got bigger and smaller at the same time. Australia, the United States, China, Russia, Indonesia, India, Taiwan, Japan, and the European Union were now all part of the contest. This was the Asia-Pacific Century and it was anybody's game. Not since World War Two had the region hosted the world stage. It was a time of new alliances, new opportunities and new fault lines. There was money to be made. It was *Pẁaanhashaay*, the grass bending to make way for the wind. *I am the wind.*

But he had to be careful. A Chinese radar station on L'Eden Sur Mer could mean nothing more than a bargaining chip, something with which to oppose an American economic sanction or complicate a South Korean military exercise four thousand miles away. Koyl rejected the idea of L'Eden Sur Mer being a square—not even a pawn—in a geopolitical chess game. He was more important than that.

He didn't need foreign aid. He needed investment. Companies, not governments, were his natural allies. In a moment of weakness he had agreed to let the Australians have their processing center. The President needed the votes at home, but deals with countries meant compromise and oversight, and he was not about to repeat that mistake.

He didn't trust his peers. Koyl had outlasted them all. He felt like a mountain climber who had scaled a lone peak and now had the privilege of looking down on the valley below. There had been times when he had felt too weak to maintain the load. He sometimes wished he had a mentor, a trusted confidante in whom to find refuge and understanding. *What source of strength had the great leaders of history drawn on?* And was it not from that same reservoir that he too must drink to find the energy, the courage that his struggle demanded? He had to find a way. His people needed him, now more than ever.

The answer was here. Somewhere. Someone in that conference could help him. They would help him. It had to be.

Standing on that balcony, braced against the weather … he hated that wind, hated it as if it were some beast awakened from an invisible dimension that had come screaming, clawing, scratching, biting its way into his world in search of him. He shouted, raged back. The wind carried his voice towards the deep, black sea.

Chapter Ten

Alma slipped the remote control off its wall mount and pointed it at the fireplace. With a beep, the flickering blue flame of the pilot light blossomed into the solid glow of manicured flames. She sat on the sofa and nestled under a blanket. Her hands, which itched incessantly, felt tight and dry as she scratched them. Alma had moisturizers stashed all over the house, and the pot of moisturizing cream nearby released the scents of lime, ginger, and lemon grass—the aromas of her favorite day spa. But it didn't matter how often she used them, her skin still felt like an onion's: thin and papery.

She picked up the novel she had put down a week ago, skimming a few sentences to reorient herself in the story. A fisherman, yes … his wife and daughter were in some kind of plot against him … something about a mistress and buried treasure—it was coming back to her now. She read a page, a long description of grey sky on water, then put the book down again. She couldn't concentrate; couldn't remember the last time she had been able to read a book from cover to cover.

Alma breathed in deeply. Peter's smell, that woody, perfumed soap he used, had evaporated from the house. She missed the aroma now that it was gone. It smelled masculine. Reassuring.

Alma turned on the TV and began flipping through the channels, pausing just long enough to hear snippets of dialogue:

"We just haven't known how to get—"

"… he did tell him, in fact I heard him say it several times—"

"… up to seventy-five per cent—"

"… of its kind. Like most lemurs—"

"… looking at a few degrees cooler tomorrow with a little morning cloud that should burn off by about mid-afternoon."

Keys jangled at the front door. She turned off the TV, picked up the novel and cracked the book to a page at random as she settled back into her cushions. Footsteps echoed in the hallway.

"Stephen?"

"Hey," he said.

Alma slowly folded the book onto her lap.

"Hi," she said. "You okay?"

Stephen shrugged his shoulders. "Fine."

Alma slid her glasses up to her head. "Come talk to me," she said, patting the sofa.

"Mom, it's late. I kind of just want to go to bed."

"Oh come on, you have a few minutes to say hello to me."

He sat in one of the high-backed chairs across from Alma, his hands held tight in his lap. He sighed. "What are you reading?" he finally said.

"Oh, it's nothing. It's stupid," said Alma turning the book over on her lap. "How was your day?"

"Okay." He shrugged. "Yours?"

"Mine was okay too."

Stephen fiddled with the string on the blinds beside him. He'd always been fidgety. "Did you work today?" he said without turning around.

"No. I've not been for a few days."

"Oh." Stephen turned to look at the hearth. "How come you've got the fire going? It's really not that cold outside."

"I like it. It's pretty."

Stephen nodded.

"Are you hungry?" she said. "There are some leftovers in the fridge if you want."

"Thanks, I already ate."

Alma nodded, studying her son. He needed a haircut, but … he was a good boy. She watched as his eyes searched the room, his gaze settling on nothing in particular. "Oh, go," she said.

"Sorry," said Stephen, rising from the chair. "I just kind of want to get to bed."

Alma waved away his apology. "Kiss," she said turning her cheek. "You can give one little kiss to me before you go disappearing again."

As Stephen bent down, she breathed in deep, searching for the odor of anything peculiar but smelled nothing out of the ordinary. He was a good boy. "Good night," she said.

"Night," said Stephen.

Alma listened to his footsteps traipse up the staircase. They were slow and heavy, comforting. She was glad he was sleeping in his room tonight and not in that pool house. She shifted her glasses back and flicked on the TV.

Peter sighed. It was Jancis Sloverband's turn to present. Her credentials and international reputation made her something of an unofficial keynote speaker at the conference and there had been much speculation about her presentation. Sloverband's belief in the synergy between capitalism and international development was clear from the outset. Her proposition was based on a single premise: fish and cash. Sloverband was adamant that L'Eden Sur Mer needed to produce more revenue if it had any hope of a future.

"Tuna has proven commercial potential," she began. "A state-of–the-art tuna cannery, if designed and managed properly, can be highly profitable."

Behind her, a pie chart divided per-annum yields of the fish, broken down by countries that officially fished the region.

"Korean, Taiwanese, Filipino, and American vessels have joined Japanese tuna fleets that have been fishing this region since the 1980s. The idea is a simple one. Build a cannery. Seek foreign partners to help develop your tuna fisheries and processing facility. Other Pacific island governments have done this and have vastly improved their people's standard of living."

True, thought Peter; the tuna canning industry was a highly successful enterprise in the South Pacific, as well as in South-East Asia. Low labor rates, raw tuna supply, low overheads, and low freight rates had kept things that way. It was a market he had failed to tap and he had been angry with himself ever since. There was nothing wrong with Sloverband's reasoning—this was all appealing from a commercial perspective. Yet there was something artless about this proposition. It lacked vision.

"And if your people don't want to work the factory it may even be possible to get Chinese or North Korean labor, depending on what can be negotiated. The details can be for you to decide, but this could be a win-win situation across the board," said Sloverband.

Nash shot up from his seat.

"Mr President," said Nash, half-turning to Koyl while addressing Sloverband. "You don't want the Chinese poking around in your affairs. And just about the only thing you want less is to go into business with North Korea. You must remain adamant about keeping more international interests out of L'Eden Sur Mer."

Koyl, eyes half closed, offered Nash nothing more than a nod, reassuring him that his comments had been taken on board.

Sloverband leaned over the podium with a smirk. "I understand your squeamishness, Mr Nash. I do," she said, "but this country needs capital revenue. Unemployment's, what? Seventy per cent! There's got to be a more commercial approach to creating economic stability here. This country's economy has been constrained by its remoteness from the international marketplace. An industrial cannery will employ some twelve hundred to two thousand cannery workers. It could be one of the largest employers in the country. Revenue can be invested in trust funds to help cushion whatever future transitions are necessary for this nation and provide for the island's economic future. You've got to sink before you can swim, if you'll pardon the pun."

Nash, still standing, was unconvinced. "Oversight is not what this country needs, Ms Sloverband. It does not need red tape."

Sloverband rolled her eyes ever so slightly. "Look, a cannery is basically a license to print money. A commercial cannery means more shipping lines to and from here to other countries. That means collateral business; that means demand for a retail and service sector. That means jobs, and *that* means a higher standard of living. In money terms, this is nothing less than a revolution for L'Eden Sur Mer."

Eyes moved to the President, who had sat virtually motionless throughout the mini-debate. Nash scratched his head nervously.

"These are short-term solutions," said Koyl, finally. His expression was pained, his wrinkles more pronounced. "I appreciate your proposal, but you seem to forget that we have a future of about fifteen years, maybe thirty at most."

"That's a generation, Mr President," said Sloverband immediately. "Maybe by then there'll be something else your people can try." Her doughy arms hung limp at her sides. "At least this plan gives them something to work with in the here and now."

That evening Peter excused himself from the usual gathering at the bar. He felt listless, and had never been much of a drinker. He headed to the beach, knowing it would be deserted—the perfect place to consider the details of his idea. He didn't want to appear foolish; he had a reputation to protect.

The ocean lapped gently against the shore as if soothing the broken stones that littered the beach. The sky over L'Eden Sur Mer was a sparkling dome of stars, a twinkling, fizzing champagne canvas of light—greater and more sacred than any cathedral. Here it was easy to imagine that each fiery orb had sparked myths and legends that were passed down through generations, that those who gazed skywards retrieved the collected wisdom of the ages. This ocean of light above was made all the more dazzling, more alive, by the black and featureless desert of the sea that now spread out below it on this infinite night.

Long ago, Polynesian sailors had found their way to these

far-away lands, navigating by these very stars. They had dared to cross vast oceans in their tiny craft, while Europeans still clung to the shores, afraid of their own shadows. They must have felt like gods, those Polynesian sailors—no obstacle, no force too big for them to overcome. There was greatness in them, and Peter could feel it stirring just below their surface.

It had been years since Peter had allowed himself to appreciate one of nature's daily dramas. He saw wondrous things in that deep sky. Beauty that defied his imagination. He saw constellations and oceans of light, swirling and spinning on worlds of gas and cosmic dust. He saw new worlds created in the heavens just beyond the reach of his outstretched fingers. Peter could believe, if only for a moment, that he was at the center of the Universe, and that he, too, was a god.

It could work. Technical advances in biomaterials and nanotechnology, in buoyancy and flotation, made it possible to rebuild L'Eden Sur Mer; to rebuild it better and stronger. It could 'float' in its current location. It wouldn't be a boat. It wouldn't be a pontoon. It would be an island. It would be *the* island, built to scale and identical in every detail. It could be moored to the seabed for stability, or fixed in place by solar-powered propellers that kept the structure locked in to a coordinate on the global positioning system. With the right anchor points and ballast there would be *some* movement, yes, perhaps during rough seas, but most of the time it would feel like a solid land mass. On telescopic moorings, the island would rise and fall with the tides, and the sea could rise as much as it liked. It wouldn't bother L'Eden Sur Mer.

He was an engineer, and it could work. It *had* to work.

It was man's duty to deliver himself from the indifference of nature and triumph over calamity. That was Peter's calling. Peter smiled. *Louis Pasteur, Norman Borlaug, Peter Van Dooren.*

Chapter Eleven

Gracie had come home for Thanksgiving weekend, and Alma was determined to send her back with a carload of groceries.

They walked along the supermarket aisles as if pushing the cart along a pleasant country lane. The shelves held a dizzying array of products and urged the idle shopper to buy in bulk. Who needed that much cheese? Twenty cents off butter! $1.30 off Rice Krispy squares! How much had they cost yesterday?

"How's it all going?" said Alma, wanting the question to sound as harmless as possible.

"Pretty good." Gracie didn't look up from a pack of organic lentils.

"What about Lucy and Joanne? How are they adjusting to everything?"

"Adjusting?"

"Do they like this new experience of university life?"

"Oh, they're all right. Say, do you know if you have to soak these?" she asked, holding up the lentils.

"Yes, or they are too hard to eat. Or you can get canned ones if you don't want to wait so long."

"Nah, I'll just get these," said Gracie, dropping the bag into the cart.

"Well that's good," said Alma. "I was worried you wouldn't see them as much, you know, with them living on campus and you in the apartment."

"No, it's okay. I end up spending a lot of time at their place and we just kind of use the apartment as a crash pad, you know, when we just want to get away from everyone and relax."

They strolled past the magazine aisle, absently browsing the covers. The whole of western culture was distilled onto those racks in aisle nine:

Air Force, Homes and Gardens, Cooking Light, Sports Digest, Cosmopolitan, Hustler, Forbes, Car and Driver, TV Guide, Time.

Magazines gave way to stationery and miscellaneous household goods: hooks with suction cups, cheap Teflon pans. Beyond them stood racks of personal hygiene products: whitening, sensitive and medicated toothpastes, face creams laced with papaya and cherry blossom, anti-bacterial gels infused with aloe vera, and chocolate-flavored condoms.

Gracie bought some beeswax lip balm while Alma put two jars of eye cream on the child seat of the cart next to the bananas and the eggs. She wasn't convinced they would clear those dark circles as they claimed, but it wouldn't hurt to try. One jar was a day cream, the other a night version reinforced with antioxidants and vitamin K.

Gracie picked up the night cream and looked at Alma with mock reproach. "Mom."

"What?"

"You know this stuff doesn't work, right?"

"How do you know? You're a dermatologist?"

"Because, this stuff is just junk. It's in that category of stuff you don't really need."

Gracie went to put the night cream back on the shelf and Alma held out her hand. "Excuse me? Can I have my cream back, please?"

Gracie smiled and held the cream behind her back. "No."

Alma put her hand on her hip. "Please put the cream back in the basket."

"What for?"

Alma looked down the aisle; a few shoppers were approaching

and Alma was starting to feel this little stand-off looked a bit silly. "Can I have my cream back, please?"

"It's not yours yet, it belongs to the store."

Alma avoided looking at a middle-aged man who walked past. "You're being ridiculous, you know. There's a whole shelf of that cream just behind you. If you don't put that one back, I will just take another."

"Fine," said Gracie, dropping the jar back into the basket. "I'm just kidding, anyway. Relax."

Alma led them down the baby aisle. A wall of diapers greeted them. Various brands and sizes offered parents the peace of mind to let their children crawl, toddle and walk with confidence. Gracie had been cuter than the babies looking down at them from the packaging. It was a shame her daughter had shown no interest in pursuing modeling further. It would have been something they could have done together.

Alma remembered those evenings, boiling glass baby bottles and laying them out to dry, anticipating the long night ahead.

Alma had known mothers who made it look easy, women who baked cakes from family recipes and sang lullabies from memory; women who made their own stuffed toys and sewed animal costumes without a pattern. Alma had done those things too, but she had drawn less on talent than on her sense of duty. When she baked, she followed recipes to the letter. She hadn't known you could use dates as a substitute for sugar, or that bananas could replace butter; she didn't know to keep old socks and egg cartons to make puppets. These things she learned through embarrassment when other, more capable mothers pointed them out. Alma loathed crafts for the chaos they wrought in the house. On more than one occasion she had bought ready-made children's costumes to which she added personal flourishes to make them look home-made.

Alma sensed that motherhood clashed with her temperament. She didn't really know how to play; it felt unnatural. Alma would sit on the floor and observe the children, coaxing them to strum, beat and blow into the band of instruments they had been given by well-wishers who had long stopped coming around to see if she needed any help. She didn't enjoy it, not really.

To cope, she had over-scheduled herself with play dates and swimming lessons, went for long walks with the stroller, shopped at markets not convenience stores, and did household chores while the children busied themselves or watched TV. Late afternoons were hardest, sitting on the floor watching the clock, waiting for Peter to come home, waiting for the kids' TV shows to come on to help run out the clock until bedtime. She would play hide and seek, then check the pot on the stove; she would make Plasticine animals while writing out that week's grocery list. She built towers of blocks and Stephen would knock them down. She knew children instinctively destroyed things before they learned to construct them. Each time he knocked a tower down she rebuilt it; her only choice was to keep going.

Gracie and Alma walked down the cookie aisle.

"Do you want any of these?" Alma held a bag of double fudge baby brownies.

"Mom! Do you know what's in those?"

"Do you know how awesome these are?"

Gracie laughed.

"What?"

"Nothing," said Gracie with a smile. "You're cute."

Alma felt encouraged by whatever she had done. "Why? What did I say?"

"No one says awesome anymore, Mom, that's all. So it's just kind of cute to see you trying to keep up with kids today."

Alma flicked her hair in mock indignation. "Well," she imitated a huffy teenager. "I think these brownies are, like, totally, like awesome and I totally think we should get, like, two bags and veg out—can I say veg out?—in front of the TV and savor our awesomeness."

Gracie laughed. "You're a dork."

"An awesome dork," Alma corrected.

"You're awesomely dorky, I'll give you that."

Chapter Twelve

Tal's mother, Carol, kept the house neurotically clean. She followed her son with a dustpan, would wipe rings of condensation from the Formica kitchen table before the mess could "settle in", as she put it. A lit cigarette smoldering in an ashtray was never far from Carol's reach, so while the house was always neat and tidy, the dingy odor of stale cigarette smoke permeated everything in the duplex.

Stephen didn't know much about Tal's father, Dave, though Carol seemed to scrub the countertop just a little more vigorously at the mention of his name. It was Tal's birthday and Dave had dropped by that morning to deliver his gift: a video game console that Carol knew her son had wanted but she hadn't been able to afford. Tal had immediately taken the PlayStation down to the basement suite that was all his, and had spent the afternoon shooting unarmed pedestrians at point-blank range. Stephen had the same game at home and had become more adept than Tal at handling the controls, but he held back, letting his friend get the upper hand.

Celebrating later that night, Carol, Tal and Stephen ate out at the Golden Dragon, an ancient Chinese restaurant that had a large fish tank at the entrance and faded wood paneling on the interior walls. Tal loved the sweet and sour pork. Carol loved that the Golden Dragon was one of the few remaining restaurants that let her smoke inside, a gesture the establishment's chain-smoking owner offered his patrons in open defiance of the law … so long as the place wasn't too crowded.

Stephen peeled open the sticky menu and perused its offerings. He was conscious that Carol would probably insist on paying for dinner and scanned the price column first, looking for modestly priced items to order. The contents of the fish tank out front were strictly off limits, so he settled on a lemon chicken stir-fry, no appetizer. If he were still hungry afterward, he would nibble on something at home.

They ordered, and Carol snapped her menu shut, surveying the two boys with pride. She triumphantly lit a cigarette. "So tell me about this game you guys have been playing all afternoon."

"It's a shooter game," said Tal. "You just go around blowing stuff up."

"Oh. Okay. So it's not that great, huh?"

"It's not the best game ever or anything, but it's pretty cool," said Tal.

"I always thought you said video games were sort of for geeks," said Carol. She twirled her cigarette butt on the inside of the ashtray, shaping the ash and the cherry to a sharp, glowing point.

"Nah, they're pretty good," said Tal. "Plus Dave says it's important to get along with geeks."

"Oh yeah, why's that?" asked Carol, taking a long pull of her smoke.

"Because nerds are people too?" ventured Stephen, in a lame attempt to diffuse the tension building now that Dave, the absent father, had officially been brought into the conversation. No one laughed.

"Well you've got to be nice to nerds," said Tal, "because who do you think's going to be sitting on the other side of the desk when you'll be asking for a raise."

What Tal said came as a shock to Stephen. The statement contradicted everything he had been taught to value in life: education, security, upward mobility. In a word: options.

At sixteen Tal was resigned to an adult life of subservience to some future boss in some future job. His personal forecast ran against Stephen's inherited worldview that adolescence was about creating the opportunities of tomorrow. Stephen now understood that Tal's boisterous irreverence had a purpose. To Stephen, high school promised to be nothing more than a blip in the radar of his life. For Tal, high school was a brief and treasured period of freedom, a temporary state of exhilaration before the inevitable obedience of adulthood. Tal felt he could dismiss teachers because they held no real power over him. But he was ready to obey a boss because later, in fact all too soon, that boss would hold the purse strings to his life.

Stephen picked at a hangnail, a little jealous of his friend. Tal seemed to approach his life with genuine confidence and acceptance, almost as if he regarded its future events as predetermined. It was a maturity Stephen seemed to lack. Tal was more of a man for having a clear view, an understanding of his place in the world, where Stephen saw nothing but confusion. It granted Tal a measure of independence.

Tal was only a few months older than Stephen, but he looked more mature. He was taller and thinner, had already started shaving regularly and could even grow a beard if he so desired. Hadn't the waiter addressed him as sir throughout the meal?

In comparison Stephen felt like a boy in his smooth skin and round body. There had been no sir for him. It all felt a bit like last summer when he and Tal had gone out and bought Chicago Bulls hats and jerseys because it was the done thing. Tal made it all look cool; the branded jersey hung perfectly from his thin, muscular frame, and the Bulls logo on Tal looked like the mark of a proud warrior, a valued member of the team. On Stephen's jersey, that same logo bulged out, making a mockery of that bull's flaming nostrils.

Where Carol and Tal were chummy and regarded each other as equals, there was a formality to Stephen's home life. He didn't share his parents' cultural background, and their European heritage placed a premium on observing a family hierarchy based on age and experience. Respect your elders. Peter and Alma had travelled more, had seen more, were more educated than their children, and they used their lives to carve a trough of experience that separated the adults from the children. To them, university, marriage, career and children were the rightful measures of adulthood. To Stephen, these were rites of passage that seemed so far into the future that his parents could only treat him as a child. For Carol, her son's sixteenth birthday brought him one step closer to adulthood, to parity. For Stephen, it would be just another number.

"He'll soon be the man of the house," said Carol after the waiter had served the food.

Tal also paid his mother a small amount of rent from his job as a dishwasher at Motel 6 on Wedgewood Avenue. He only worked the dinner shift three nights a week, but it was still a grown-up thing to do. Tal had encouraged Stephen to apply for a job as a kitchen hand, but Alma and Peter had refused, fearing the late hours would interfere with his schoolwork. Instead, they offered Stephen odd jobs to do around the house to earn extra pocket money.

"There'll be plenty of time to work," Peter had said. "For now, just focus on your studies so you can get into a good university."

Stephen wasn't even sure he wanted to go to university and he resented how his parents just assumed he would.

He was conscious of having withdrawn from the celebratory atmosphere around the table, even though no one had seemed to notice, and now he felt conspicuous using chopsticks while the others used forks. He thought about switching, but dismissed the idea as ridiculous. Before they had finished their mains, the waiter brought out deep-fried ice-cream with a single candle to a chorus of *Happy Birthday*. Everyone in the restaurant clapped.

When the bill came, Stephen felt uncomfortable watching Carol dig into her purse and then shuffle a wad of crinkled five and ten dollar bills to cover the tab. He offered to pay for himself but Carol refused.

"It's my treat," she said. "It's just nice not to have to do the dishes. You can leave the tip, if you like."

As they filed out of the restaurant, Stephen made sure to be last in line out the door. He handed the waiter a twenty-dollar bill. The gesture made him feel like a man. Stephen left the restaurant determined to get a job.

Back at home, he pulled a plate of nachos out of the microwave. The cheese had bubbled nicely and was now oozing down the pyramid of corn chips. *Time to add the hot sauce and the sour cream.* His phone rang.

"Oh, hey, Dad …"

He put down the plate of nachos.

"Good …"

Stephen eyed his food. The cheese was hardening. A good plate of nachos was all about timing. He swirled a chip around in a blob of sour cream. He didn't dare pop it into his mouth. Not yet.

"She's out …

"I don't know, just out …

"Uh huh. Yep, okay, I'll tell her … okay. Bye."

He folded his mouth around the chip, the black olive and sour cream squirted out their gooey goodness. It was good to have had Dad on the phone like that. Fuck him. *You can't be away for weeks and still expect to command things from … wherever.*

Chapter Thirteen

Alma and the decorator, Justine—whom the neighbors had highly recommended—sat at the breakfast bar sipping chai lattés and flipping through the paint and fabric samples that Justine had brought.

Alma flipped through a ring binder of color samples. How was she supposed to decide anything from these postage stamp sized examples of paint and fabric?

Peter had called earlier. He was staying on the island a few more weeks. Fine. It was time to redo the kitchen. A renovation was long overdue. The kitchen's pink marble bench tops and ruffled cream curtains felt too pretentious. Who did they think they were, living with brass taps and a black and white tile splashback? The whole thing was due for a makeover, something less ostentatious. The baroque fussiness of the enamel-plated knobs of the gas cooking range just offended her.

"I'm just trying to get a sense of the color palette you're after, Alma," said Justine, touching Alma's arm. She was a toucher, Justine, with long French-manicured nails. "We're not deciding anything now, just getting a feel for what you like."

Justine agreed that the ornamental fixtures in the kitchen were passé and that a modern look would "refresh" the kitchen, making the space "more agreeable." Alma took an instant liking to Justine, who seemed genuinely comfortable sitting there talking to her. It was as if they had known each other for years. There was something charming, reassuring about Justine's self-confidence. Even the rattling of Justine's gold bracelets sent pleasant goose bumps down Alma's spine.

"You guys been living in this house a long time?" said Justine.

Alma looked around the kitchen. "No, not really. A few years."

Justine took a long drink. She wiped the froth off her lip with the top of her hand. "Well, anyway," she said, "it's nice to spruce the place up." Justine pushed her latté aside, as if she'd had enough. "I have a lot of clients who do over their whole place once their kids leave home," she said.

"Oh, my son still lives here," said Alma. Did Justine think her older than she really was? "He stays mostly out in the pool house, though," she added. "You know how teenagers like to have their own space."

"Tell me about it," said Justine, leaning in. "I don't think mine will ever leave. I guess that's why clients wait until the kids are gone to finally do up their dream home—they don't want to make it too comfortable or the kids'll never leave."

The heartiness with which Justine laughed at her own joke compelled Alma to laugh as well. Justine struck Alma as a woman who had long abandoned social pretenses, if she'd ever had any. Alma liked her.

"So," said Justine, reaching for one of her colorful binders. "What's your husband's name again?"

"Peter," said Alma and took a long drink.

"Peter, right." Justine opened the binder, revealing some forms. "So do we want to involve Peter in this project or is it okay if we just go ahead without him?" Justine picked up a pen and started to fill in some details on the form.

Alma looked over at a family photo hanging askew on the door of the fridge. "He's away," said Alma, elbows propped up on the counter.

Justine put down her pen and turned towards Alma. "Business?" she said. Alma nodded.

"Does he travel a lot?" said Justine.

Alma nodded. "He does," she said.

Justine swiveled on her stool. Her gold bracelets jangled. "Well I had the opposite problem," she said, touching Alma's arm. "My first husband, he never left the house."

Alma chuckled.

"Seriously," said Justine. "Said he wanted to retire early and I'm thinking, what for?' It's not like you do much of anything now!"

Justine laughed, picked up her latté and just held it. "They'll drive you nuts," she said, lips poised over her cup. "They really will." Justine sipped her drink.

They talked about the places they had lived, about the houses they had lived in and the people they had lived in them with. *So many kitchens.* Alma felt oddly comforted by Justine's candor; the woman talked openly, disclosing the kind of personal details Alma usually kept to herself. This divulging didn't seem needy or gratuitous. It seemed … honest. Justine had come from a large family and had tried (and failed) to replicate her past with a guy she only too late discovered was more of a child himself than a father. The experience had left her to raise three boys on her own.

Alma had never really experienced a dedicated family home, a place that had absorbed generations of collected memories and family traditions. It seemed like a nice legacy to leave behind.

"You ever wonder where you might have ended up if you'd made some different choices?" said Justine. "I don't mean in a bad way or anything," she added. "I mean just, like, if you changed a couple of small things in your past, how much other stuff would it change?"

Alma looked at the color swatches and tile samples, the binders and brochures, and paperwork. *There's a lot of work to do.*

"I try not to," said Alma. "You can't change the past."

She and Peter had been living in a rented apartment in Hong Kong at the time Gracie was born. Alma had never felt so foreign, alien. When the nurse had handed her a baby, it had taken Alma a few moments to connect with the idea that this was her baby, that this was what had been moving around inside her all that time. Looking at that baby, her baby, all balled up in its blanket, Alma had been surprised by how odd it felt to hold someone so close while meeting them for the first time. It felt awkward to shower affection on someone she hardly knew. It had taken nearly a month to really connect with Gracie; her affection for her daughter was powerful but had to be rediscovered as if pulling it from memory.

While feeding or changing, an urgent sadness would sometimes well up inside her. The feelings persisted. In later years, Alma took to locking herself in the bathroom so the kids would not see her crying. Sometimes the tears would come easily, and she would sob quietly, turn on the shower or flush the toilet to drown out the noise. The more she cried, the guiltier she felt. She understood that she was lucky, privileged, and that if anyone should be happy it was her. But those thoughts only deepened her sadness and brought her clawing and scratching at something below it, something bigger and darker still. Alma despaired at knowing that nothing would ever be good enough, that nothing would ever amuse or satisfy or give her comfort the way that it was supposed to. Not even the children. Other times, she might strain but no tears would come. Those times were even harder: the wringing, prying, stubborn sadness that would not let go. Try as she did to dismiss these feelings as a childish indulgence, dark thoughts slowly percolated back into her mind.

Where would she be when she died? In the car? Here? In this kitchen? Would it hurt? Should she be buried or cremated? What if she could still feel her body after she died? Better to be cremated, then. Surely that was better than feeling decades of slow decay. Worms. Just burning. A lot of pain and then … nothing. Surely ash couldn't feel anything.

Alma learned to distract herself from these thoughts when she felt the heaviness of their presence. She learned to entertain herself with unadulterated fantasies, like the silly daydream of relocating to some pretty seaside town that might appeal while on vacation. Of course, the town might be lovely and gentle at first, but would she feel the same if she lived there? What would it be like most of the time? When winter came and it rained, and the vacationers returned to the real world of work and children, and responsibility, would it be the same?

Alma accepted that love was a textured emotion, bumped and bruised and scarred. She was unsure if she had ever really loved Peter, at least in the way she imagined she was supposed to. He had always been guarded, obtuse even, but they had built a life together, they had made a commitment to honor and respect one another and that vow was manifest in their children. Stephen and Gracie were the fusion of her life with Peter's. Nothing could break that bond and no one could eclipse the personal galaxy of her children.

Peter was part of that family and that would continue to bind them no matter what they did. The grazed knees and hospital visits, the family holidays in the mountains and by the sea. Those scenes were the canvas of their lives together, and remembering those scenes brought on guilt and a feeling of weakness for not being able to draw from the experiences all of the spiritual nourishment and wonder that she felt she was supposed to. Alma weighed her anxiety, her restlessness, against the greater uncertainty of changing her life. For all of its imperfections it was hers; she had lived it and felt reassured that it would remain there for her as long as she wanted—no needed—it to be.

Now, after the exigencies of raising young children, the daily grind of it had slowly, imperceptibly subsided. Even though she imagined the children still demanded a great deal of her attention, the reality was that there had been a slow but cumulative increase in her free time. The years had gone so quickly.

"Hey where are you from anyway?" asked Justine.

Alma blushed. Her accent. It would betray her forever.

"I mean originally," added Justine, perhaps sensing she had caused offense.

"Because of my accent?" said Alma pulling back.

"Oh, sorry," said Justine leaning in, touching Alma's arm again. "I like it. I think it's a beautiful accent. I'm just always curious about where people are from, you know, because I haven't really been anywhere. Born and raised right here, so ... Pretty boring, right?" Justine ran her fingers through her hair. The bracelets jangled pleasantly.

Alma hadn't lived in France for decades, and her experiences of the country, of the culture, drew on a different time. She was a human time capsule. Her references, the words she used, were part of a culture that had long since evolved her into extinction. When she watched French films, she felt the draw of the subtitles and used them as footnotes to make sure she had understood the spoken phrases correctly. She was out of touch and felt no culture embraced her as one of its own.

Alma sipped her drink. "Where do you think it's from?" she said.

Justine squinted and looked at Alma's face as if the answer may have been printed there. "Is it ... Germany? No?" Justine bit her lip. "I'm sorry, I really don't have a clue. I'm super bad with accents."

"It's French," said Alma and hid her face in her mug. The tea was getting cold.

"Oh, French. Duh," said Justine. "I've always wanted to go to France. So pretty." Justine sipped her latté. "I can see why you want to redo this place then," said Justine, looking around. "From what I've seen—only from pictures mind you—modern French design is really minimalist, you know, nothing's too fussy. Is that the kind of thing you're after?"

Alma looked at the color swatches and the tile samples. She didn't feel like she was from anywhere, and couldn't really imagine what it would be like to feel connected to any one place, or be moved by and feel part of anything so abstract an idea as a nation, a people; maybe others did.

Alma had always dismissed nationalists, political separatists or jihadists as nothing more than angry mobs of individuals who channeled their collected personal frustrations against any visible opposition. These people she saw on the news, the ones on dusty streets shooting guns and hurling rocks and bottles at each other, these people were just ready to interpret every personal grievance as evidence of systemic oppression. Alma had encountered men like that in prison; men who believed they were being punished not for their crimes, but for their beliefs; men who believed their offences went some way to correcting the malevolent episteme of western liberal democracy; men who considered the atrocities they committed in adherence to those beliefs exempt from civil authority, from earthbound laws. They were swimming upstream. Hopefully they died before they could spawn.

But what if—it occurred to Alma for the first time—what if such people were not motivated by personal ambition alone? What if they were moved by a deep sense of commitment, a duty to uphold something greater than themselves? If they felt about *their* country, *their* king or *their* god the way *she* felt about *her* children … What would that mean? The idea left Alma feeling like a ghost who did not fully understand the world she haunted. She felt lost and unable to touch the present she observed. She was from everywhere. She was from nowhere, invisible to all but herself. That image, too, was fading.

"It's all going," Alma told Justine. "I just want something simple. Just a kitchen, you know, something more plain."

"Clean and simple," said Justine. "That's all you really need in a kitchen. It's all about turning a house into a home, isn't it?"

Chapter Fourteen

Peter gagged at the smell. It was a thick, musty, consuming odor that invaded his whole body. He could taste it, too: a bitter, coppery flavor that latched onto his tongue. His stomach tightened; acid bubbling deep in his gut. He could imagine nothing that could rival the smell of burning human flesh.

Pyami had died. Peter recalled him only as the eldest of the Gray Hairs, the man who never seemed to leave the President's side, sitting quietly, patiently through most of the conference deliberations, as if he had heard it all before. Pyami's body was now mounted on a funeral pyre and he lay, smoldering, on the beach where he was cremated in a civil ceremony. It was Thanksgiving Day, not that it mattered.

Koyl said a few words in Kwitsa, a language that bore no resemblance to English and offered no inroad for the uninitiated. It was an odd feeling for Peter to listen to a eulogy, the final catalogue of a man's achievements, and feel no closer to understanding the person who was now being openly consumed by flames.

Peter had attended many funerals, but none of them had been as raw and confronting as this one. Most were somber, formal affairs where great pains were taken to shield those present from the ugliness of death. Western funerals were sterile events—the deceased wholly absent from the proceedings, like guests of honor who had failed to show. A fine casket might be on display, but it rarely seemed to contain someone so much as *belong* to someone. The coffin might as well have been empty, seeming to contain not a body so much as the idea of someone. Even open caskets contained little more than a crude impression of the departed, an effect the mortician painstakingly re-created from a photograph of happier times with the help of pancake makeup and formaldehyde—the show must go on. At the funerals Peter had attended, hymns were sung, readings were given, lunch was served, and as people munched on their sandwiches, caskets were discretely withdrawn and disposed of.

Things were different on the beach of L'Eden Sur Mer. Here, the old man's naked body had been carried out on a bamboo matt. It was then placed on a pile of logs and stones, covered in twigs and straw, then set alight. It was a simple ceremony. There were no special robes or ornaments. Pyami went out as he'd come in. It was all refreshingly plain. The congregation watched the fire burn, taking turns to poke the smoldering mound with sticks to agitate the embers. People talked. Some laughed. This went on for several hours, to the sound of crackling fire.

A man handed Peter a poking staff and made a gesture, inviting him to poke the fire. He refused but the man insisted, pushing the staff into his hands.

"*Maht, maht,*" said the man, smiling. He was missing several teeth.

At the funerals Peter had attended, invited guests usually offered clichéd platitudes to the bereaved: *"I'm sorry for your loss"; "He was a good man"; "She was a beautiful woman"; "A person lives on in our memories"*, and so forth. These were the modern conventions of grief.

Peter thought of his own father and what memories his death had promised would live on. There hadn't been much to recall, really. Roland Van Dooren had been a uniquely uninterested man. He had no hobbies. Peter had known fathers who belonged to exclusive clubs and social orders; fathers who had sheds where they built things with their hands; fathers who presided over vast collections of treasured objects that had taken them a lifetime to accumulate; fathers who loved sport or gardening or cars with an enthusiasm they passed on to their sons. Roland had no such interests. He liked football, but never hesitated to switch the game off when called to dinner. He mowed the lawn, but treated the chore as an imposition on his spare time. He even seemed to treat the delivery business as more of a social activity than a business enterprise. He was a passenger in life.

Roland hadn't been a bad father. There had been no rift, no central trauma between them. But there had been no real warmth either. Peter recalled no tender moments of being taught to swim, play catch, or ride a bike. They hadn't built sandcastles or flown kites. He had offered no inherited craft or sage advice. Roland had always just been there. He had always just been a man. He had no pretense of greatness, no ambition to succeed. Peter had come to think of his father as an example of what a man becomes when he merely accepts what he is given. *Go with the flow.* Isn't that what he always used to say? Roland had even approached his diagnosis with an air of resignation. He seemed to make no commitment to the modern medical treatments that were available to him. He had no fight in him. Peter could never forgive him for that.

"*Maht, Maht,*" said the toothless man, inviting Peter to copy his use of the fire staff—a sweeping motion to fan the flames and separate the burning embers that were gathering underneath the corpse.

Poking the fire, watching those coals grow hotter, Peter recalled a family trip. He hadn't thought of it in years. Mother had sat in the front seat, Roland was behind the wheel—he had always been a safe driver. They were holidaying in the Italian Alps, an extravagance that Roland had allowed the family only because he had recently been ill and the doctor had recommended rest for his wellbeing.

As Peter recalled it, most of the trip had been spent watching the world go by from the back seat of the family car. Europe had been a much larger place then, before cheap airfares, fast trains and the highway system, back when there were borders. Peter remembered watching the flat, green pastures give way to rolling hills, to steep peaks and valleys, and he remembered feeling ill as the car lurched around sharp corners on its steady climb up the mountain pass.

Roland had slowed unexpectedly, and steered the car to a rest stop at the side of the road. Peter noticed a row of white, wooden crosses, each with a bouquet of flowers withering in the noonday sun. His father rolled down the window and pointed at a peculiar-looking mountain in the near distance. It had been the site of a massive landslide less than a decade before. Half the mountain had shorn off, burying people in their cars as they made their way up the pass below. There had been no effort to search for survivors. In all, nine people had been buried under a torrent of pulverized rock, mud, and debris, ninety feet deep and two miles wide. Their death had been instant and it had been certain.

"Those poor people," his mother had said.

The road had eventually been rebuilt, re-routed to circle the devastation, and it now swung five miles further from the mountain than the path of the original road. But the original road was still under there. Peter imagined the bodies inside their cars, keys in the ignition, road maps in glove boxes, buried somewhere below that rubble. Trees had sprouted between the boulders, softening their hard edges. Shrubs and wildflowers drew nourishment from the mineral deposits layered in the sediment. To the untutored eye, this hallowed ground looked no different from the landscape that surrounded it, just another valley.

"It's tragic," said his father. "But still beautiful." Roland explained how pre-existing tectonic structures, faults and shear zones had caused the landslide. Locals said that the conditions that spring had favored a rupture of the mountain. The region had recently experienced a series of small earthquakes. It had also been unseasonably rainy. These natural forces had increased the shear pressure on the rock. It had finally become too much for the slab to hold. Roland had explained all of this matter of factly, as if listing the necessary ingredients for baking a cake.

"Why did all those people have to die?" Peter had asked his father.

He remembered Roland looking out towards the broken mountain. "When it's your time to go you have to accept it," his father had said. "There's nothing you can do about it." He seemed almost cheerful.

Peter could not forgive the wanton cruelty of that disaster. That mountain had stood on this spot for millions of years. It had been witness to a time when the earth was mostly fire, and had cast its long shadow over this valley before man had even gazed upon its glacial peak; the mountain had looked on as mankind took its furtive steps on the barren plain below. In all that time, the natural fissures of the rock had slowly widened. Atmospheric pressure and erosion, the snow and sleet and rain that poured down the mountain face, the searing heat of summer and the bitter cold of winter, had coaxed the slab to finally let go, and tumble towards the pleasant valley below. This could have happened at any moment in the millennia that had past. But it hadn't happened. Until one April morning in 1963 when the force of gravity finally won, and geological time collided with the Easter holidays, turning a natural spectacle into a human tragedy. Nature had no mercy.

Peter stood there, poking the fire, watching the embers glow red at the end of his stick. A deep reservoir of anger welled up within him. He felt an inexplicable hatred towards this man, this pile of ash, and was annoyed by the delay his death presented in the struggle to save this needy little island.

He had privately shared his vision for the floating island with Holden Nash, seeking to garner in-principle support for the idea before committing himself in front of the others.

"What happens to the old island?" said Nash.

It had seemed an odd question to Peter, who had rather expected Nash to take more of an initial interest in the finance of the project or its engineering.

"I'm not sure," said Peter. "It could be used as an anchor point, I suppose, and allow people to transition to the new island over time. Or the structure could be entirely separate. I really haven't worked out the details yet."

"Keep them together," said Nash, immediately. "The President's not going to want to just leave this place behind. Keep them together and I'm in."

Nash had responded more quickly than Peter had expected. Even with only a preliminary pitch, Peter had secured a $1 million initial investment from what Nash called his green syndicate. He also offered in-principle ongoing support to further develop the project. Nash had been resolute in his belief that you needed twenty-first century technologies to tackle twenty-first century problems.

Peter had spent his morning runs mentally developing the engineering of the floating island. He loved ships. For Peter, a boat was one of the purest forms of engineering, a symbol of man's ingenuity, his conquest over nature. The 'hull' of the island—it helped Peter to think of the structure as a ship—could be made of high-density plastic, boxed with molded concrete and insulating foam. A jagged, mineral-rich shell below the water line would encourage plant growth and coral. The fish would return, and, with them, the promise of a sustainable local economy. The platform would feel stable, even on top of a generous swell. The integrity of the outer material would last more than five hundred years, even in the unforgiving environment of seawater. The bottom of the vessel would plunge some eighty or a hundred feet below sea level and could be fitted with any number of useful devices: hydro-electric generators, desalination tubes, all of it enabled by the passing current. The whole thing could be tied to the seabed by cabling or telescopic moorings that moved up and down with the rising tide. The 'deck' could be filled with arable land, shaped and used like an industrial-sized planter box. Sur Merian farms could be relocated there, cemeteries could be re-established, ancestral land titles honored; every detail of the existing island could be transposed onto the new one. The island would be fixed to the existing continental shelf, on top of L'Eden Sur Mer's original geographic coordinates. Keeping to the original sovereign boundary would circumvent the United Nations Law of the Sea.

In his excitement, Peter had drawn up a number of preliminary sketches of a prototype for the floating island. It felt good to draw again. To create.

Figure 1: 'Floating' structure anchored to seabed on telescopic mooring

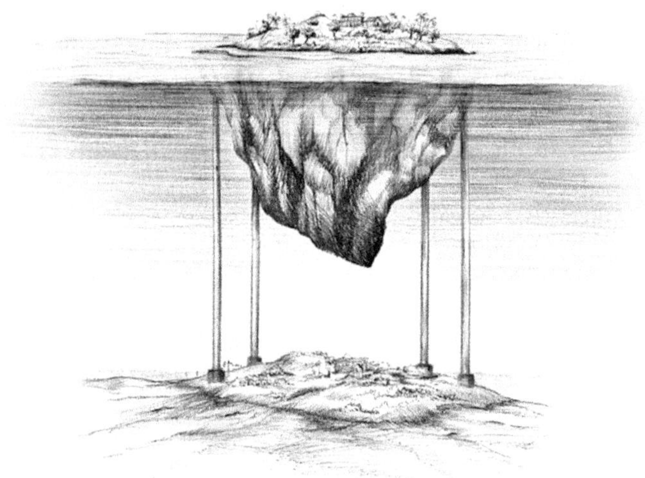

Figure 2: Internal structure showing possible hydroelectric and desalination network

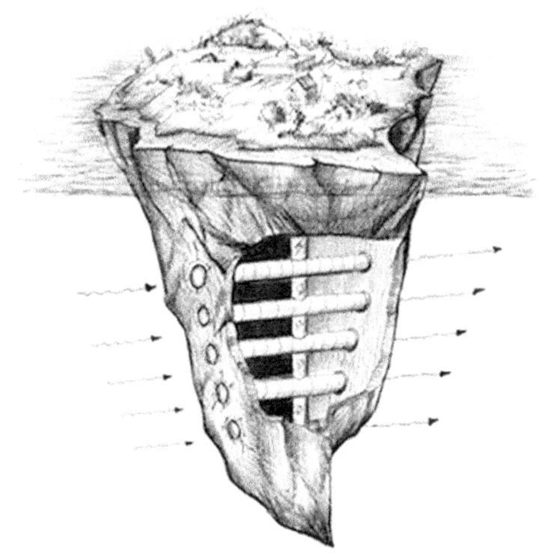

This was no life raft, wobbling around on the surface of the water. This was a triumph of engineering. This was a solid structure, at once independent from and dominant over the very environment that threatened the original land. If God had indeed created the Earth, it was up to us to improve his original and flawed design.

It would be expensive to build, yes. Initial costing put the finished project at about $900 million. But prototypes always cost more. Once completed, the island could be a self-contained landmass. This was pioneering, a way of establishing completely new lands—countries—and ecosystems even—in international waters. Groups or individuals could be free to set up their own societies and govern them by their own values. It was the next logical extension of the liberal democratic ideals of liberty, equality and self-determination. Governments might not like the challenge to their authority but that would be their problem. This idea could potentially resolve geopolitical divisions, cultural and religious conflicts; this was tribal sovereignty on an industrial scale. The potential applications were staggering: private armies, religious zealots, breakaway states, and the *uber* rich. Peter allowed himself to imagine self-contained communities living life by their own design. That was the apotheosis of freedom. The possibilities—and profits—were limitless. He just had to prove that it could be done. The problem was one of perception. The technology existed. It was just a matter of finding the will. And the money.

He had already started mapping out the details of a global public relations campaign. The idea had come to him, fully formed, like a vision, a prophecy. It had been an odd thing to see on a deserted stretch of beach, but there it was, an old television half-buried in the sand. It had probably washed ashore after being dumped from a passing vessel. Whatever its past, it now lay on the beach with seaweed and barnacles clinging to its weathered, plastic frame. It had reminded Peter of family trips to the beach at Zandvoort, Holland's middle-class resort town when he was a boy, strolling along the foreshore, imagining what it might be like to find a message in a bottle. It might contain a call for help or a treasure map that had been tossed overboard somewhere, for someone else to find. Peter had loved the idea that such a bottle could have floated for miles on the open ocean and that of all the places in the world, and of all its people, he would be the one to find it.

He called a friend he knew in Vancouver who operated a large prop-making studio for the film and television industry there. He employed the studio to make working models of architectural or shipping projects for Van Dooren International. This time Peter gave the studio a different kind of brief.

The box arrived that morning. Peter tore it open like a child at Christmas and pulled out a small, oblong, white and green plastic vessel, a roughly hewn model of L'Eden Sur Mer. His message in a bottle. It was time to convince President Koyl, and the rest of the world, that their savior had come.

Figure 3: Message in a 'Bottle'

Chapter Fifteen

Gracie had been in the café for much of the afternoon. It was exam time. She had a pile of reading to do but kept being distracted by the comings and goings of those around her. This time it was a tall hippie guy with dirty dreadlocks, wearing Thai fisherman's pants. He came out of the pizza place across the road and took a seat at a picnic table. Gracie watched him through the grimy window. A seagull watched the hippie as well, eyeing off his slice of pizza. The bird took only a few steps back from the hippie's waving hands. It was concentrating on the slice of pepperoni with a Zen-like focus. When the guy turned his head the seagull lifted the entire slice and flew off in the direction of the chemistry building.

It was almost time for Gracie to meet the girls. She left the café and headed towards the student union building. That was where Lucy and Joanne had asked to meet, despite Gracie's belief it was an odd and somewhat desperate place. The student union was essentially a mall. It had a food court, a pharmacy and a few haphazard shops: a place that sold stationery and branded clothing, one that sold last-minute gifts like brandy-filled chocolates and novelty bottle-opener key chains. People congregated there between classes. They ate, drank coffee and socialized. To Gracie it was really just a place to buy and sell things.

There were posters recruiting for groups with competing political interests: Marxism Today, the Anarchist Club, and the

Young Conservative Alliance.

The student union also housed shared office space for various social and political groups that operated from campus. It was home to the Earth Coalition, the Food Cooperative; there were Jews for Social Justice, Baha'i for Civil Liberties, and Hedonists for Organ Donation; offices were held by the Polish Club, the Iranian Students Association, the Japan Society, and the Buddhist Meditation Group. The Plexiglas partitions between rooms offered group members a semester's worth of tribal sovereignty, paid for by compulsory student union fees.

Gracie peeked inside the windows of a self-proclaimed Queer Space where half a dozen kids lazed around on beanbag chairs. She was growing impatient and a little annoyed that Lucy and Joanne were running late. *Look at them all in there, cuddling, hanging around. Didn't they have anything better to do?*

She browsed the community noticeboard that people used as free ad space. Some people designed rich and colorful advertisements; others just put a felt marker to any old scrap of paper and tacked it to the corkboard.

Selling:
2nd year biochemistry textbook - $180

> Large, brown bookshelf—$50.
> Bottom shelf missing.

> Repco guys mountain bike in excellent condition 30" 18 sp—$150

Buying:
Movie posters, all sorts. Call Jake.

> Old tapes and 8 tracks (for an art project). Contact Sherrie.

Looking for:
Kitchen/Wait staff, some experience required
A ride to Edithvale for the Xmas break (I can pay)

> Funky chick to share 3 bedroom house with socialist collective. Must be a non-smoker.

Gracie had always enjoyed reading the classified ads. The things that people wanted, and the things they wanted to get rid of, offered a fleeting yet intimate glimpse of their personal life. What circumstances had made Beth "desperate" to sell her Lasko Cyclonic Digital Ceramic Heater?

Nowhere was the blur between public spectacle and private confession more obvious than in the Personals section.

> Single, Caucasian male seeks lovely Oriental lady. Oriental women are hard to meet. Why do you work such long hours?

> I am 28 years, 5'7", brown hair, green eyes and have fit physique. I enjoy listening to house/electro/dubstep music and spend most of my free time watching tv/movies (esp post-apocalyptic sci-fi) or playing video games. Looking for someone who's cool with spending the night in watching television/ movies or playing video games. 18-25.

> No need to waste of my time any more. i am from one of asia country, high educated, 39, got a professional job. Must be motivated. No players!

Here, people summarized themselves and their ideal partner in fifty words or less. People invested hope in the idea that sharing common interests would ease their sense of isolation and social displacement.

A tap to her shoulder and Gracie jumped, turning around quickly.

"Hey," said Gracie, her heart slowing to a normal rhythm.

Lucy and Joanne both wore university-branded hoodies. Lucy was holding a fan of printed leaflets.

"Sorry we're late," said Lucy. "We were totally on the other side of the building."

"That's okay." Gracie chewed the inside of her lip. "What are you guys doing?"

"Oh, we're just handing out some flyers for this group we kind of got involved in," said Joanne.

Lucy handed Gracie one of the black and white photocopies put out by the Christian Fellowship. A line drawing of a cross and two embracing hands dominated the front page; the back offered a 'Did-you-know' section about Jesus that included a few biblical references:

Whoever wants to save their life will lose it, but whoever loses their life for me and for the gospel will save it. What good is it for someone to gain the whole world, yet forfeit their soul? (Mark 8:34-38).

The Son of Man came here not to be served but to serve others, and to give his life as a ransom for the many (Matthew 20:28).

Gracie didn't like the brochure. It looked amateurish and corny. She handed it back to Lucy.

"What's this?" said Gracie with a nervous smile.

"We met these guys last week and they seemed, you know, pretty okay," said Lucy with a shrug.

"Yeah." Joanne tucked a loose strand of hair behind her ear. "Anyway, so we started talking and found out we were into a lot of the same stuff."

"They invited us to come along with them to this, like … what would you call it?" said Lucy.

"It was like a discussion group where you just talk about Jesus and, you know, ways that you can keep him with you in modern society. It's really good, Gracie. I think you'd like it."

An announcement came through the speakers. A red jeep parked in a handicapped zone. The accusing voice momentarily joined their conversation. Gracie waited for the voice to disappear. Did they really have to repeat the license plate number twice?

"When did all this happen?" said Gracie. She passed her tongue over her bottom lip. She could taste the metallic sting of her blood through the dry cracks.

"Last week," said Lucy, leaning against a wall under some band posters.

"Thanksgiving," added Joanne. "You went home, remember, to your mom's place."

"Oh yeah." Gracie swallowed her bottom lip. Her tongue explored the blistery crack. *Was it bleeding?*

Lucy tapped the stack of flyers against her thigh. Joanne twirled the loose strand of hair around her index finger.

"Well, we've got to hand these flyers back to the office. You should totally come and meet Daniella," said Lucy.

"Yeah, come on Gracie! You have to meet Daniella," said Joanne, already turning towards the staircase.

The Christian Fellowship occupied one of the larger office spaces in the student union building. Inside, the place was a hive of activity: people talking on phones and clicking at computers with an intensity that gave the impression of urgency.

A few mismatched and empty chairs were arranged in a semi-circle around a whiteboard on which someone had written a jumble of words in friendly, bubbly letters:

```
relationship              technology              power
value          I/me   duty    be/have         Fear=Hope
meaning vs usefulness             You/it          Love
               noise   wealth/richness/value
"Brotherhood"                     Time            Home
```

Without the benefit of the discussion behind these words, they just dangled there on the board, emptied of meaning.

Daniella was busy talking into the microphone of a headset. She was as big as a sofa, and she gestured with chubby fingers for Lucy and Joanne to approach. As the three of them walked closer they could make out one side of Daniella's conversation:

"That's right ... no, it has to be twelve ... because that's what we've budgeted for ... "

Daniella raised her stubby index finger to indicate she was

almost finished with her conversation.

"All right ... I'm counting on you ... it'll be fabulous ... one hundred and ten per cent ... okay... look forward to seeing it. You'll give me a call next week then? ... I don't know, maybe ten o'clock?"

Daniella rolled her eyes at the three of them, and made circles with her hands as if to hurry the person on the other end of the line.

"Okay ... okay ... great ... Thank you Mike. Talk to you next week. Bye."

Daniella tapped the Off switch on her headset and sighed. "Hi girls, sorry about that. Just putting together a couple of fundraising events so it's been a bit crazy around here. Some people just need a little extra pushing, you know what I mean?"

Lucy and Joanne nodded meekly.

"And you must be Gracie," said Daniella, gathering herself from her office chair.

"Hi," said Gracie, uncomfortable at the thought that she had been discussed without her knowledge. She had only gone home for a couple of days over Thanksgiving, but it now felt like she had been gone for ages, that she was out of the loop.

"Lucy and Joanne were telling us last week about how the three of you came up through high school together. Sounds like it wasn't always so easy."

"I guess not." Gracie didn't want to commit any more details to flesh out Daniella's impression of her.

"Well you can see from everything going on that there's plenty of people like you here that want to make a difference, and there's lots of things you can help us out with. How'd it go with the flyers, girls?"

"Great," said Joanne.

"Yeah, we handed out about half of them," said Lucy, stuffing her hands in her back pockets.

"Well done. You guys coming to the open mic next weekend?"

Lucy and Joanne nodded.

"You're welcome to come too, Gracie, it's just an opportunity for some of us to get together and let our hair down a bit. We book out the café, put a microphone on stage and people are invited to just come up and do whatever."

Daniella, eyes magnified under the convex lenses of her glasses, searched Gracie's face. "You could do a reading of something that's important to you," Daniella continued. "Or you could sing." Daniella looked to Lucy and Joanne for encouragement. "It's a chance to share some hidden talent you might have. Basically a chance to show off a little."

Gracie leaned back on her heels. She swung her satchel around so the bulk of her bag now rested in front of her.

"This isn't one of those things where everyone hugs at the end, is it?" Gracie chuckled to lighten the mood.

"We might," said Daniella, laughing. Lucy and Joanne chuckled along. "Don't worry, Gracie. This isn't a cult or anything. We're not going to make you do anything you don't want to do."

"Thanks," said Gracie. "I'll think about it."

"That's all I'm asking," said Daniella. She held her hand to the headphone, still on her head. "Oh, there goes the phone again. Got to take it. Thanks again for the flyers, girls. See you tomorrow, okay."

Daniella pressed a button on the headset near her ear to answer the phone, "Daniella speaking ... Oh hi, Carl." She waved goodbye to the girls.

"So?" Joanne said, as the three of them descended the stairs to the food court.

"So ... what?" said Gracie.

"Well, what do you think?"

Gracie slowed her pace. She swung her bulky satchel to her back. "What do you mean? Like, what do I think about Daniella?"

"Well, yeah, about Daniella, and the group. You know, the whole thing?" said Lucy.

Gracie's eyes wandered down the staircase, to the food court below. "I don't know. I was there for all of five minutes."

"Yeah, but you get a feeling, right?" said Joanne.

"Yeah, didn't you think Daniella was pretty great?" said Lucy.

Gracie quickened down the stairs. "She was all right, I guess," she said, perusing the fast-food menu boards as they came into view.

"Sooo, you didn't like her?" Joanne stopped walking.

"I didn't say that," said Gracie.

"That's just it, though, you usually have a lot to say."

At the bottom of the stairs Gracie fidgeted with the clasp of her bag. She hoped her phone would ring to interrupt this conversation. "I don't know," she said. "I guess I just didn't really like the way she assumed I was, like, a member of her staff or whatever."

"I think she was just asking you if you wanted to help out," said Lucy.

"Yeah, I think you're reading a little too much into that one," said Joanne.

"Well I don't know," said Gracie, leaning against a pillar. "I guess it's a bit weird. It's not like I know any of those people so ..."

"Well, you should come to the open mic thing, then," said Lucy.

"I don't know; it sounds kind of lame." *What was all the intensity about? Who cares? Why had Lucy and Joanne so embraced this fat woman with the bad skin?* There was something not quite right about this whole thing.

"It'll be fun," said Joanne.

"Yeah, I don't know," said Gracie, ignoring a pack of guys walking by. "I'll have to see. I've been pretty tired lately."

Lucy rolled her eyes. "Okay, well, we can talk about it more tomorrow." Lucy got her phone out, fiddled with it.

"You going to class in the morning?" Joanne turned to Gracie.

Gracie sighed. "I think so, yeah."

The three of them stood there, Lucy half-read something on her phone. A pack of guys laughed in the distance, someone dropped a tray of something. Gracie shallow-breathed to avoid the assault of fried chicken on her senses. *Those poor chickens.*

"Okay, well ... let's just catch up tomorrow then," said Joanne.

"Well, what are you guys doing now?" asked Gracie.

"I've got class," said Lucy, without looking up from her phone.

Gracie looked at Joanne.

"I could hang out," she said. "I'm pretty beat, though. I'd just be into watching a movie or something."

Gracie looked at her watch. "You could come back to my place if you wanted. Crash there."

Joanne scrunched up her face. "I kinda want to just sleep in my own bed tonight. Sorry."

Gracie swallowed; her throat was dry. She wanted out of the student union building. Now. Its maze of corridors, the clutter of posters, flyers and sandwich boards … her throat tightened. The do-gooders in their little hives upstairs pressed down on her. The sight of the slack-jawed loafers in the food court chewing on their hormone-injected meat products churned her stomach. Complicit, all of them, in the degradation of the planet and the mistreatment of the animals now caught in their gnashing, gnawing teeth. She looked away.

"That's okay," said Gracie. "Think I'll just head off now, then. The bus only comes, like, every hour after 7:30." She turned to the sliding glass door, which opened with a mechanical hiss. A guy wearing a ball cap walked in, mercifully letting some fresh air in from outside.

"Okay … cool. So, we'll see you tomorrow then?" said Lucy.

"Yeah," said Gracie, forcing a smile.

"Okay. See you later," said Lucy smiling back. It was a short smile.

Joanne hugged Gracie. She was skinny, Joanne.

"Want us to wait with you at the bus stop?" said Joanne. "It's already dark."

"I'm good," said Gracie, pulling away. "Thanks."

Gracie forced herself not to run from the student union. The automatic glass doors wheezed open then closed behind her with a thud.

Chapter Sixteen

The paper bags rustled, breaking the silence inside the car. Stephen and Alma were parked outside a fast-food restaurant. Stephen dipped his fries in a blob of mayonnaise and folded each long, soggy strand of potato onto his tongue. Alma didn't eat her burger so much as pick it apart. She didn't bite into burgers, didn't like the way the layers slid around and shifted between the bun. Alma preferred to build each mouthful, tearing off pieces of bread and pulling individual bits of lettuce and onion out of the burger. Finger food. She had suffered her children's ridicule for this habit, but she just couldn't take to holding a burger with both hands and biting into it. That seemed too … American.

Gracie and Peter never ate fast food, calling it greasy and dirty. Stephen and Alma had grown tired of their moralizing whenever they brought home the tell-tale brown paper bags. So they had adapted. Sharing a meal like this in the comfort and privacy of the family car had become one of their guilty pleasures. Even now, with Peter away and Gracie out of the house, they continued to enjoy the ritual; their strawberry and vanilla milkshakes seemed to taste better when pulled from the cup holders of the SUV.

"It's good?" asked Alma.

Stephen nodded, folding two limp fries onto his tongue.

Alma's phone vibrated from the glove box. *That goddamned phone.* It was never convenient to have it ring. And even when it was, Alma always felt a rush of anxiety.

She knew it stemmed from the call she'd received from her father's palliative care nurse. She had agreed to the phone for calls just like that one, but regretted it the moment that call finally came. Every time it rang it took her back to that crowded intersection.

Alma's father had spent the last ten years of his life in France, and his health had deteriorated noticeably during his last two. The last time she had seen him, his suit swam on him; now three sizes too big, its bulky shoulder pads bunched around his ears. Mostly, they had talked about his daily routine, and Gracie had been too conscientious, too thoughtful to mention that she had sat down in a puddle of *Grandpere's* urine that slowly absorbed into her summer dress while Alma talked to her own father about the importance of showering every day.

The nurse told Alma her father had slipped into a coma overnight. It was time to say goodbye. Hours, the doctors expected. Hours before her father disappeared. That's how the nurse had put it, as if her father would just vanish the moment he stopped breathing. *He did.*

The nurse put the phone to the dying man's ear before Alma had a moment to gather her thoughts. *He might still be able to hear you,* the nurse whispered. It wasn't supposed to be this way. She lived too far away. It was the life she had chosen. She had dutifully visited her father every year, and always imagined that when the time came, she would have a chance to get to him before things turned grave. It was too fast. She had no hope of getting there in time. So there she was, hunkered under the awning of a Starbucks while somewhere across the Atlantic, in some hospital she had never been to and would never visit, a phone was put to her dying father's ear.

She heard him breathing. It was more of a deep snore, the sleep of someone already gone from this world. Alma thought about all the things she might say. Were people really expected to be articulate at moments like these? "I hope you're not in pain," was what she said and had felt stupid saying it, aware of the nurse—a complete stranger—listening in on her last words to her father. What else could she have said? What else was there to say?

And now the phone dared to interrupt her while she was sharing a moment with her son. No. It was just hamburgers and fries, but that didn't matter, the contents of those brown paper bags were sacred.

"You going to answer that?" said Stephen.

"Not now."

Stephen half swallowed his mouthful. "What if it's Dad?"

It probably *was* Peter. He usually called about this time. *A man of habit.*

"Well if it is, he'll call back later," said Alma smiling. *Too brightly?*

She pinched off a piece of hamburger bun and brushed it across the condiments now oozing out of her disassembled hamburger. The phone continued to ring, insistent, like a third person hijacking the space between them.

It stopped suddenly, restoring a sense of present-mindedness to the atmosphere inside the car.

"How's work?" asked Stephen.

Alma caught a glimpse of herself in the rear-view mirror, her mouth full of hamburger. The years had dulled the mischievous intensity she had once seen in her eyes, and a puffy layer of fat now rounded the once sharp features of her face. What a silly, dowdy old woman she had become. But she had her son. He was a good boy.

"Work's good," she said. "Work's good."

Alma finished her mouthful. She offered the burger's disemboweled remains to Stephen. He pulled the remaining meat from the bun and popped it in his mouth. Alma watched him and smiled. She crumpled up the cardboard boxes and paper bags and clicked in her seatbelt, about to start the car.

Maybe they were both tired, maybe it was the shared mischief of eating forbidden food, but whatever it was, Stephen sensed a fragile atmosphere of trust and shared understanding. Perhaps Alma was predisposed to sympathy, to a generosity of spirit that would evaporate the moment his mother turned that car key and started the engine. Now was the time to tell her his plans.

"Hey Mom?"

Alma's hand stayed poised on the clump of keys in the ignition.

"Do you think it would be okay if I got a job?"

Alma released the keys, lowered her hands and turned to face her son, who was chewing the end of his straw. He had always done that.

"What kind of job could you get?" The question sounded more patronizing than she had meant. But it was true that Stephen had no work experience. He didn't even have any particular skills or interests.

"I found this sales job that could be pretty good," he said.

Alma searched Stephen's face. He was an earnest boy, a good boy. She had sometimes worried about him not finding his way in life. He had always been more fragile than Gracie, more sensitive, and she resisted the familiar urge to protect him.

"You know that no one is asking you to be like your father, right?"

Stephen furrowed his brow. "I know. I'm not."

Alma glanced at the dashboard; it was dusty. "I mean you can do whatever you like," she said. She wanted to make sure that Stephen felt supported, that he should feel free to be himself.

"I know," he said.

It *had* been silly, hadn't it, this principled objection to the kids working. For the first time, Alma considered what role her own acquiescence had played in her acceptance of that prohibition. It was really Peter's position. *Why hadn't I stood up to him?* Of course it was good for the kids to work; she remembered her insatiable appetite for experience when she'd been Stephen's age. It had been wrong to prevent the kids from exploring those opportunities. Besides, Peter wasn't here. As far as Alma was concerned, he had forfeited his right to decide. "You like this job?"

"Well I don't have it yet."

Alma's hands dropped from the steering wheel and she turned to her son. "What is it doing?" she asked. "I don't like the idea of you working with big machines and stuff. You can be injured very easily, you know." Her mind wandered to a factory or a fast-food restaurant with its hot grills and vats of bubbling grease. She was already imagining burns and scars and cut fingers.

"It's just, like, online sales. I just do it from home on the computer."

This sounded fine. Harmless. "Just don't let the job get in the way of your school work, okay?" She gripped the steering wheel once more.

Stephen smiled. He felt at once closer and more independent from his mother, as if the prospect of a job sharpened the edges of his individuality. Self-assured, the feelings inside him were indeed his own.

Turning on the engine seemed to turn off something inside them, as if the trembling of the car reawakened them both to the world outside. They had been safely harbored in the parking lot. Veering back onto the road, towards the city, they were pulled into the flow of traffic, into the pulse of life.

Chapter Seventeen

Peter hit 'Send' on his text message: *Wish you all well. Have a good day.* The same message went out simultaneously to his whole family.

He leaned his head back and watched President Koyl, who sat with his hands folded in front of him, staring at some invisible spot on the floor a short distance beyond his feet. The President had not quite been the same since Pyami's funeral. He seemed quieter, almost resigned. Half the conference delegates had left, called back to other responsibilities. Peter would stay until the President considered his idea.

At dinner, Koyl sat at the head table, where he had always been, but he felt more removed from the remaining group than ever. Organizing the conference had been expensive—Koyl had only just managed to convince his government that the summit was a good idea. The President's dissenters had questioned his motives from the outset. His more conservative, but nonetheless loyal, supporters had voiced their concerns about the cost of the undertaking.

Even though it wasn't much to look at, construction of the resort had exacted a considerable toll on the federal budget. While much of the basic construction had depended on recycled local materials—village women had built the thatched palm roofs of the huts—but many of the extras had been imported at enormous cost. Wooden posts as foundation stumps for the resort were purchased from Fiji. When they arrived, the Canadian-made composting toilets intended for the guest suites didn't fit the dimensions of the space as designed, forcing their relocation to communal lavatories that had to be erected as an amendment to the original plans. All of this had cost money, which was progressively siphoned from the remittances, the international aid payments and other revenue streams that L'Eden Sur Mer relied on.

Koyl's decision to temporarily allow the open consumption of alcohol was widely unpopular. Adherents of tribal law believed drinking alcohol was an inexcusable sin and roundly condemned the President for enabling such egregious foreign excess on their sacred lands. But these voices belonged to the cultural fringe, whose real political influence was marginal. It had been harder for Koyl to dismiss appeals from the women whose husbands worked on merchant ships and had seen their families torn apart by drink. It would send the wrong message to the youth of L'Eden Sur Mer to allow these foreign visitors to consume liquor, they said.

The President had approached the whole business of the conference as other governments might have made a case for hosting the Olympic Games. For Koyl, his plan was a short-term investment to momentarily hold the world's attention. It was an opportunity to build lasting networks that had the potential to access new technologies, new ways of thinking, and yield untold dividends.

"We stand to gain more than we risk losing," had been his catch cry throughout the parliamentary debates that followed. In the end, it had been Pyami who had cast the deciding vote in Koyl's favor.

Pyami had been the eldest in a line of ageing chiefs. His death would be the first in a coming wave of successions. Soon the others would follow—the men who Koyl had not always agreed with but had nevertheless known from the beginning. They too would pass and, one by one, their youthful, energetic rivals, men whose visions extended beyond the horizon, would replace the Gray Hairs. Koyl, too, had been young once. It was the way of things.

Thani Malhoun had taken Pyami's seat and would now tip the balance of power. Thani was part of a different generation, one that had never experienced the oppression of colonialism. They had never been a subjugated people, and would never understand the passionate yearning for freedom that had driven Koyl to carve out his nation's independence.

Sur Merians believed in *Vaktanoa*, the interconnectedness of all things, and had long used this belief as a basis for tribal dialogue, to help resolve conflicts and to facilitate their adaptation to external factors. An early account of Sur Merian dealings with missionaries told of a people who "seem to take up the cross with no real commitment to the principles of Christianity it represents".

This ambiguity was changing, and more and more Sur Merians sought refuge in the Christian church. Despite nearly two centuries of a marginal presence on L'Eden Sur Mer, the church was gaining influence, ironically because it was seen as something new. Attendance at church was a proclamation of modernity. Youth were among the largest converts to the Baptist Church. Many of the island's youth saw membership in the church and adherence to its rules as a de facto challenge to official authority. Their faith was a kind of rebellion, allowing them to observe God's authority as superior to the one claimed by their President or their elders. Whatever their outward sense of social stagnation or political oppression, religion offered these young people a sense of inward strength, of personal expression, a liberty of conscience.

Malhoun was a new and emerging leader, and he was part of this youthful tide. He knew how to use scripture to galvanize his followers. He invoked the biblical flood as historical fact, a parallel storyline to the island's predicament, and used Noah's resourcefulness as an incentive for the islanders to move forward.

President Koyl tolerated these youths as an opportunity cost of progress. Many of them were the sons of parliamentarians. Pyami had cautioned him about the pace of change. "It comes suddenly, without warning," he had said. But Koyl remained unconcerned. They were only boys, who understood little about the deep culture of island life and even less about the ways of the world. Kinship, based on bloodlines or marriage, had always defined traditional social ties on the island. It was a concept this new tide of youth didn't quite understand. Their insolence was rooted more in naivety than in rebellion. Their dissatisfaction was a phase, not a cause for concern.

But government support for the conference had waned. It would have to produce some compelling results.

The event had been unremarkable. The pair of academics who had given the opening presentation now seemed content to get drunk most evenings, ogling and pestering resort staff until politely asked to retire to their bunks. Their behavior left Koyl reconsidering the wisdom of allowing alcohol at the event.

Although not all had been a loss. Satoshi Utitsu had made a number of useful suggestions about using genetically modified algae to reduce the salinity of the soil and encourage crop growth.

Francois La Larc, who had been so enthusiastic about the potential of harnessing tidal energy, now conceded the idea was impractical without some way of storing the energy. According to La Larc, that technology was no more than a decade away.

For Koyl, these ideas offered only short-term solutions. They failed to acknowledge that the sea was rising faster than the recommendations accounted for. As useful as it might be to grow organic crops or generate clean, exportable power, these ideas bought L'Eden Sur Mer no more than fifteen or twenty years with its head above water.

The question of who would fund these projects was also evaded. Koyl felt like the headmaster of a class that would not quiet down. His cabinet was slipping from him and he had invested what little political capital he had left in the outcome of this conference. People were already leaving and he had nothing to show for it.

It was time, said his colleagues, to align with the Russians or the Chinese. Their checkbook diplomacy in the region was the most likely source of additional funding for any initiative they could agree on. They could not afford to choose political independence over commercial viability.

Koyl knew in his heart what was right. Sovereignty mattered. Independence was a worthy cause. He wanted his people to know their country as he had known it, pulling cat fish out of the freshwater ponds, sipping mango juice in the shade of the coconut groves, looking out to sea wondering what pleasures the future might bring. They deserved more. They deserved a future that would endure. Koyl was determined to wake the Sur Merian dreamers, those young, urban elites; arrogant sons of his own parliamentarians, kids who had never known or understood village life, who talked about leaving as if the idea offered real promise.

Koyl winced when he heard the younger generation speak flippantly about moving the population offshore. They had romanticized notions of emigration and little sense of what they stood to lose. They were like children who understood nothing of freedom and failed to comprehend the personal responsibilities, the self-discipline it required. Abroad, their fates would be no different to those of the wretched souls locked up in that detention center. Those people were condemned to live an unsettled life, no matter what happened to them in the future.

Theirs would be a living purgatory, only ever half-knowing where they came from and only ever half-belonging wherever they ended up. They were doomed with an insatiable nostalgia, and would never forget the pain of longing to return.

The conference failed to grab the international headlines Koyl had allowed himself to imagine. The *New York Times* had run a piece on the conference but had put it in the Travel section. The *Globe and Mail* published a more significant piece, though Koyl bristled at the article's suggestion that the President was, himself, delaying the inevitable decision that would have to be made on behalf of his people to get them off the island. *Damn them all.*

Sunlight faded outside Koyl's parliamentary office as Peter handed the President one of the models he had made. Nash leaned against the bookcase, hands in his pockets.

"What's this?" said Koyl, looking at them both. The President took the bundle wrapped in cloth.

"It's the future," said Peter.

Koyl unwrapped the package, revealing the little island with its transparent bottom. The President held it in his lap and narrowed his eyes. He turned it over in his hands, caressing the edges of the plastic mold with his long, smooth fingers.

"You can do this," said Peter. "This idea, it came to me all at once. Now I know it's going to sound crazy at first, but just hear me out." Peter stood, moved towards the President, towards the little island. "Mr President, you said The Peak was a failure. I don't think that's quite right. I think it was a good idea. But it wasn't done right." Peter searched Koyl's face for disapproval. The President looked back blankly, authorizing him to continue. "You see, the problem with The Peak," said Peter, tensing his shoulders, "is you had to move people from where they lived to somewhere new. What I'm suggesting is the same thing done differently." Peter looked at Koyl, at Nash. "I'm suggesting we start over. Make everything new."

Peter explained about the piles and the concrete and the telescopic moorings anchored to the seabed; he spoke about polymer foam and steel reinforcement and solar capture, of prototypes, patents and development grants. He talked about the long transition between moving from the old island to the new. Through it all Koyl listened patiently, never wincing, never smirking, his gaze locked to Peter's, his concentration broken only by the occasional glance at Nash and the object still turning in his hands. Nash stood almost motionless throughout Peter's technical explanation.

"You can do this," said Peter. "You're the father of the nation, Mr President. Respectfully, this could mean something even bigger. The whole world will marvel at what you've done here. At what you've accomplished. It can be done. I just need you to believe it, Sir."

Koyl swallowed hard and nodded, absorbing Peter's speech. "What do you think of this?" He looked at Nash.

Nash cleared his throat. "I think there are some interesting possibilities here, Mr President."

Koyl rubbed his chin, glanced out the window. "This is … ah. You don't see this as a risk? I mean … I can only imagine what this idea must cost."

Peter moved to answer Koyl, but Nash put a hand on his shoulder and cut him off.

"It'll take money," said Nash quickly. "Thirty million to start with. More later. A lot more. We'll need investors."

Koyl kept turning the little island over in his hands, flipping it over and back to front.

"The development of this project will be a long road, Mr President," said Nash. "But I see no short-term risk in pursuing it. As Peter says, the long-term possibilities could be worthwhile."

Koyl rose from his seat and walked around his office, still holding the model of his island with both hands. He stopped at the window, searched the pink clouds on the horizon. "Is this crazy?" he finally said, turning back to them. "This is crazy, no?"

Peter dared not look at Nash, lest his expression be misinterpreted as hesitation or doubt. "A little," said Peter, "but a crazy idea is better than no idea."

Koyl looked to Nash, gestured for him to speak.

"We can do this, Mr President," Nash said. He took a step forward. "I think we have to."

The three of them looked at one another. Koyl smiled. The President laughed. They all laughed, a bond as good as any written contract.

Chapter Eighteen

Stephen shuffled through the revolving door of St Martins Tower and emerged in the lobby. It was warm inside. The interview wasn't scheduled for another fifteen minutes but already he regretted the sweater vest. It was too hot. It was also too late to remove it; dark sweat pools had already formed under his arms. This was no way to make a first impression.

He read down the directory of organizations in the tower:

Sagitec Consulting—3301

Zable and Associates—3302

Gaia Enterprises—3303

He was almost surprised to find the company's name on the list. Given its wholesome-sounding motto, *Inherit the Earth*, he hadn't expected Gaia's corporate headquarters to look so … corporate. It had been easy to get this far in his search for work. He had wanted to avoid working in kitchens and dish pits, so he had set up an automated job search using the key words: computer + part-time + sales + marketing NOT kitchen + service. A list of new vacancies appeared in his inbox daily: *looking for telemarketers; wanted: sales assistant for busy sports emporium; we need funky, alternative people who like to sleep in and work late.*

Gaia's ad had looked the most promising: *Want to save the planet? Be part of the solution! Low hours, high $$$$.* Gaia was a carbon broker. It offered businesses and individuals a variety of carbon-offset packages through which to reduce their carbon footprint. Individuals could buy annual offset credits worth 28 tons of Co_2 for $260. A family of four could purchase a yearly offset worth 98 tons for $960, and $17,340 bought you a lifetime offset of 1,643 tons of Co_2. The offset credits were tied to various 'industry-leading projects in reforestation, research in increasing efficiency and the development of renewable energies'. Gaia's business model was all part of 'the future of our global economy'. Stephen was eager to see how it all worked.

The lift shot up to the thirty-third floor so quickly Stephen could feel the atmospheric pressure change in his ears. When he exited the elevator, a young man sat behind the desk at the front office. That was odd; you didn't usually see a man doing that job.

"Gaia Enterprises, can you hold please? Thank you."

The man behind the desk looked up at Stephen. "Hi. You here for the orientation?" he said impatiently.

"I have an interview," said Stephen.

The man behind the desk looked unmoved. "Okay, so you replied to the ad?"

"Uh, yeah."

"Okay, everyone's in the conference room, just down the hall there to the right. Thanks."

The man didn't wait for Stephen to respond but looked back down at his desk and stabbed a blinking light on the phone console with his bony finger. "Hi, welcome to Gaia, thanks for holding."

Stephen wandered down the corridor. What had the receptionist meant by everybody? Stephen thought he had been invited to a one-on-one interview, but started to feel foolish as he approached an open set of frosted glass doors at the end of the hallway. He could hear a male voice from inside the room.

"That's right," he overheard, "which is exactly why now is the right time to get involved."

The volume, the pitch of the voice convinced Stephen that whoever was beyond the doors was addressing a crowd.

Stephen always felt uncomfortable entering a room full of

people who had already begun a collective experience. He hated being late, dreaded the idea of wandering into a class after it had already started or entering a movie theater after the lights had been dimmed. He disliked the way the spotlight would soon turn on him, the way people would look up from the comfort of their establishment in the room. *He* was interrupting *them*. They would watch him adjust to the group, and make the dozens of tiny decisions that would begin to influence a shared opinion of him: where he chose to sit, where he put his things down, it was inescapable. He put his hand on the wall beside the door.

It was clear that Gaia was orchestrating some kind of group interview session, a bulk process for screening potential candidates. He had heard about these kinds of interviews and didn't much like the thought of participating. There was still time to walk away. All he had to do was turn around and head back towards the elevator. No one would ever have known he had been there. It's not like he really *needed* the money.

"Hello?"

The question had come from inside the room. Stephen froze.

"He-looo? Is there somebody there?"

If Stephen left now, he would have to pretend he hadn't heard the question. What if the presenter came out of the room to get him? He might even have to run. It would be a scene. It would be ridiculous. Stephen took a deep breath and edged into the conference room.

Inside, the chairs had been arranged in a semi-circle around a man he assumed was Jack Schroeder, the person Stephen thought would be interviewing him personally.

"Hi there, what's your name?" said the man.

"Uh, Steve."

"Well hi there, Steve. My name is Jack Schroeder. I'm one of the executives here at Gaia. Come on in; we've only just started, so pull up a chair. Anywhere's fine." Shroeder gestured to the empty chairs with open palms.

The interruption had not fazed Jack Schroeder, who swaggered back to the center of the room. Stephen sat. There were about twelve other people and Stephen was the youngest. Most of the others looked to be university students. There was an Arab-looking guy wearing sandals and one of those white robes with the mysterious wraps and folds that kept it all together. Stephen wondered if those things were comfortable. Would there be a lot of fussing around to get it off when you had to go to the toilet?

There was another guy with a turban, probably Indian, earnestly taking notes. Then there was an older woman, maybe his mom's age. Stephen gave them all a back-story; it always took the edge off of meeting new people … like it offered him some influence over another's opinion of him.

The Arab-looking guy was probably a doctor in his homeland—no, an engineer—and he was pissed off about having to consider a sales job he felt was beneath him. That's why he was frowning and had his arms crossed.

This was probably a second or third job for the Indian guy, who probably drove a cab or ran a small cleaning company or a vending-machine business on the side. Whatever he was writing in that notebook of his, he was probably scheming something.

The woman was sad; a single mother who had to pay for her son's operation—no, wedding—no, legal fees. Her son was experiencing an ugly divorce and she had plenty of advice to share with him on the subject.

As he worked and embellished these fantasies, Stephen started to feel more part of the group.

"So … like I was saying, guys, if you're not part of the solution you're part of the problem, right?"

Schroeder looked around the room with raised eyebrows. He had given this presentation before. The Indian guy scribbled in his notebook.

"Right? I mean who can argue with that? And that's what I like to talk about, guys. Facts. I like to deal in truths, okay, and here are the truths we're facing. We shouldn't be dependent on foreign oil; the environment is not a threat, okay, it's our greatest resource; and the country must create a workforce for the twenty-first century. True or false?"

Jack searched the room again; it wasn't clear if he was expecting an answer or not. The older woman nodded furiously.

"Okay, right, so if we know all that, your next question ought to be, what are we doing about it? And by showing up here today, you guys all demonstrate that you've already asked yourself that most important question, okay. You're here. So, like I said, there're three things: foreign oil, valuing the environment, building a twenty-first-century workforce for a twenty-first-century economy."

Jack listed these using his fingers, starting with the pinkie. Struggling through the confining cut of his jacket; he silently held up those three fingers, and dramatically panned himself around the room, emphasizing the significance of those three points and fingers.

"That's all. That's all there is. These three things." He held those fingers up as high as he could. "At Gaia, we don't see any reason why those three things can't be achieved, okay. That's our business. But it gets better than that. Not only are we going to do those three things. We are going to do them simultaneously, and we're going to do them with the help of the people right here in this room, starting today."

Schroeder paused slightly, allowing the idea to settle in on the group. Perhaps a previous audience had broken out in applause at this point of the presentation. This group sat motionless. Schroeder cleared his throat.

"The federal government has been nudging industry towards 'green' or 'clean' energy, or whatever you want to call it." Schroeder delighted in over-gesturing the mimed quotation marks around these terms.

"We've all heard those words before, right. Yes?" Schroeder scanned the room. "Well, the big players have been slow on the uptake. You know the companies I'm talking about, right?"

"Cars," said someone from the back.

"Yes," said Schroeder, snapping his fingers. "It's the big guys. You know the kinds of businesses I'm talking about. I'm talking your power companies, your airlines, your car manufacturers. These are the big guns, right, the command and control centers of the national—hell, the global economy. But guys, guess what? They're going to have to change." Schroeder was panting lightly. A rose flush brought out the burst capillaries on his face. "They may not like it," he continued. "They might go kicking and screaming, but they're going to have to go there." Schroeder paused. He ambled up to the first row, and looked down at the mother, the one paying for her son's legal fees. An easy target. "You fill up your gas tank lately?" The woman nodded slightly. "Yes?" Schroeder nodded as well, emphatically, encouragingly. "Well don't think these guys haven't noticed their prices going up too. You see, this isn't me talking horoscopes or telling you what I've seen in my crystal ball, okay." Schroeder waved his arms around mockingly. He sighed. "These companies, they already know the path they're on. They know," he repeated with a touch of melancholy. "Ever heard of an oil company?" Schroeder searched the room. Nobody answered. "Of course not! No one calls them oil companies anymore. We used to call them oil companies, but you know what we call them now? We call them energy companies." Schroeder clapped his hands together with a loud snap. "You know why? Do you know why? Because they know. They know there's only so much oil out there and they know they've already found most of it. Better call themselves something else then, right? So hey, overnight, we're not oil companies anymore, we're energy companies now, okay. We've rebranded."

Shroeder laughed at his own joke.

"You see, they don't care where the power comes from, guys. Their job is to turn the lights on. End. Of. Story."

Schroeder looked down at the little group. His congregation. "You see they already know all of this," he whispered. "They know we're living in a different world to the one they started," he pointed at no one in particular. "They already know they're going to have to run their businesses differently, more effectively, more efficiently, with different revenue streams, and the public against them every step of the way." Beads of sweat threatened to trickle down Schroeder's brow. He struggled to control his breathing. "Now all of that is hard. And it's going to take more than a few solar panels and convincing people to turn the lights off in the office after dark to make a real difference. Change is an economic reality, okay. And that's where we come in. We offer that change."

Schroeder put his hands deep in his pockets and cocked his head to the side. He looked out the window. He cleared his throat. "Now I told you at the start that I was a salesman, remember?" Schroeder turned back, his gaze lingering on all those seated.

A lot of nodding.

"Right, so I was honest about that. And I told you I was going to give you one sales pitch today, right?"

More nodding.

'Well here it is."

Jack Schroeder was a master. Even though there were only a dozen people assembled in the room, he held his ground as if he had captivated a stadium full of the party faithful. It worked. Stephen was swept up in the moment, as if a great wind was blowing and he had but to step into it to be lifted off and carried away. It didn't really matter where. It was enough to feel that he was moving.

"Want to know a secret?" Schroeder leaned in close. "One of the only ways these big companies are going to be able to afford to stay in business in the twenty-first century is for them to invest in carbon offsets. Okay? That's it. That's my pitch. It's as simple as that. Unless someone invents a magic potion that turns water into gasoline, or it turns out that carbon pollution is good for the environment, these companies are going to have to learn to operate in a world where they're going to have to pay for someone else's green to offset their gray, if you know what I mean. It's like oil and water, okay, or yin and yang, the two things cancel each other out. Make sense?"

The Indian guy shot up his hand.

"Yeah, question," said Schroeder, briefly closing his eyes.

The Indian guy stood while Schroeder took a long drink from his crinkled, crumpled, plastic water bottle.

"Yes, Sir, can you please tell us about some of the offset programs that you are offering?" said the man.

The Indian guy was blushing, darkening his brown skin. That color reminded Stephen of the only black girl in his collection of videos on his hard drive; she also blushed like that, the little slut.

"What's your name, Friend?" asked Schroeder.

The Indian guy smiled, as if he had been singled out, as if forgetting that he had willingly chosen to enter the spotlight with his question. "Jasbir, Sir."

"Well Jasbir, I want to thank you for asking that question. It's a hell of a good one. First off, I want to say that we're not the only ones doing this, okay, this isn't some hocus pocus, and if you don't feel right about any of what I'm saying, then please … you go off and do your own research, or whatever it is you've got to do to get your head around it all and I will always welcome you back when you're ready."

Schroeder leaned down slightly, hands on his knees. "Look, guys, there are plenty of clean-tech companies out there, okay, and we're in business with a lot of them. The thing we've got going for us at Gaia, though, is that we're doing what they're doing, it's just that we're doing it on a global scale. You know that company ByWay, right? The one that recycles all the old tires?"

People nodded a lot more slowly this time.

"Well we do that too. But we don't stop at recycling tires just here at home. Any of you ever been to Mexico? Sure you have. Cancun. Playa Cozumel. Pretty ain't it? Well away from the "tourist spots, away from all of those nice beaches and palm trees, you know what you find? Well you find a lot of junk. And among that junk you find tires. And I'm not talking a couple of tires along the side of the road. I'm talking a lot of tires. I'm talking like a mountain of tires, okay. And there're whole mountain ranges of these tires in places like Mexico and Guatemala and Belize. And guess what? Gaia's there too. Gaia's there helping to get those tires off trash heaps, off the side of the road and into places where we can make useful stuff out of them, like sidewalks and that spongy playground matting. How many of you have heard of that US company, Acorn?"

The room filled with raised hands. Or was the Arab guy just stretching?

"Right. Good. So everybody knows they plant trees. Great. Nothing wrong with that. I like trees," Schroeder grinned. "And they plant a lot of them. But they're only doing it in the United States. What about the other places in the world? Places like the Trafina Gorge in Venezuela? Or a place like the Taimyr Peninsula in northern Russia, where the permafrost is thawing and, even though not a living thing could grow out there for thousands of years, you can now grow trees?" Schroeder put his hands on his hips and looked down at the floor. "I mean that's amazing. So this isn't reforestation I'm talking about guys, it's forestation. We're actually building a forest where there wasn't anything there before." Schroeder lifted one eyebrow as he looked around the room. "Pretty cool, huh? I mean, think about it, guys. You know what success is? You know what it is? I mean, if you go out there and ask any successful person what it is they do differently than people who've failed, and they'll all tell you the same thing. And I'm going to boil it down for you, okay. You ready?"

Schroeder cupped his hands around his mouth, as if he were about to shout. "Success is about seeing opportunities where everyone else sees problems. That's it. You read any billionaire's story and that's the ending, okay, I've saved you a lot of time." Schroeder leaned back slightly. "This isn't just about protecting the environment, guys. That's what hippies do. God bless 'em. This is about more than that. This is about valuing the environment, investing in it, using market forces to protect an appreciating asset. I'm not a hippie. I'm an investor and I don't mind telling you I'm pretty good at it. But I'm just the local boy in this operation. Gaia's got contacts all over the world. For example, South-East Asia."

Schroeder motioned to Jasbir as he said this, as if mentioning India somehow implicated Jasbir as already having a personal stake in Gaia's business model.

"We've got a bunch of interesting projects in India that'll be ready to come on line in a couple of years. Another really interesting project we've got going is a forest conservation project in Bolivia. Rather than paying cattle ranchers to cut down trees to make pasture, we're working with a company that's paying them not to cut down trees. Those trees represent carbon offsets that we can then sell on the open market to a company that, you guessed it, is looking to reduce its carbon footprint. Like I said, guys, twenty-first-century solutions for twenty-first-century problems. So it's real exciting times over here. Good time to get in on the ground floor. For you, this is an easy decision. I'm not asking you to put up any money. You got that? No money. Not a dime. All you've got to do is hop online, social networks and stuff, and just promote this thing, get the word out. You're the experts there, okay, I'm just an old fart. About the only thing I know about the Internet is the Google, right." Schroeder invited others to join his gentle self-deprecation. "My knowledge of technology pretty much stops there."

"So, it's like door–to–door sales?" asked the Arab guy. It was more of a statement than a question.

Stephen was surprised that the Arab guy didn't have an accent. He would have to adjust the Arab guy's back-story. Jack Schroeder didn't blink. He had clearly fielded this question before.

"Sure, if it helps you to think of it like that. But it's not like you're selling encyclopedias. You're selling action. You're selling solutions. You're selling hope. Plus you're doing it all online. That's the beauty of it. We're not asking people to sink big bucks into this, guys; it's a personal investment of twenty, thirty, fifty bucks in carbon offsets; it's crowd investing. This is stuff your grandparents can get involved in. Again it's about using twenty-first-century technologies to tackle twenty-first-century problems. That's what Gaia's all about."

This was all sounding good to Stephen. He mentally purchased a number of items in recognition of his new-found status as an employee with an income. The daydream was satisfying. He imagined himself taking Sara out for dinner somewhere. He imagined buying her jewelry and boots and bags. She looked so happy. So good.

His English teacher had asked the class to keep dream journals. The teacher had promised the students would one day come to think of them as windows to their soul. They took the first fifteen minutes of every class to write in their journals. They were encouraged to write about their hopes and experiences, and whatever dreams they might have remembered from the night before.

Sara figured prominently in Stephen's journal. She sat two rows in front of him in class. Sara Anthemusa. The teacher always flubbed the pronunciation of her last name.

When they were supposed to be writing in their journals, Stephen would often watch Sara nibble the end of her pen, as if she were trying very hard to gather her thoughts. He could see the top of her underwear peeking out from under her jeans. It was all lacy. Stephen didn't think she would be the kind of girl who would wear underwear that was all lacy like that. He wondered if they had been a gift. But then who would buy her underwear like that as a gift? She didn't have a boyfriend, the whole school knew that, and it would be creepy to get something like that from your parents. She must have bought the underwear herself. He took pleasure in allowing his eyes to follow the delicate spirals of cream lace. He registered the pattern, archived it as a detail that he could later recall, incorporating the design, the color and the imagined texture of the fabric into a subsequent fantasy.

Sara intoxicated Stephen. He could recognize her bouncy walk in the crowded hallways between classes. She was confident and intelligent. She asked questions in class, but not in a dumb way. She had big teeth, or at least a broad smile that curled her lips back all the way to her gum line. Even her gums looked fresh and healthy. Her skin was so smooth, and her smell lingered in rooms long after she'd left. Strawberry lip balm and some musky, earthy perfume that would have smelled a bit fungal on an older woman, like a hint of decay, but on Sara, that smell flouted the inevitability of ageing, as if she imagined herself exempt from the world's natural cycle, as if she believed that her body was too young, too vibrant, too filled with life to consider anything so human and sad as death. Sara would never get old. What would it be like to touch her? What did she look like naked? What might that musky perfume taste like when it filled his mouth?

Stephen sometimes sat in Sara's desk, just for a minute before class started, when the room was empty. He wanted to sit where she sat, where she would sit. Stephen reveled in the molecular proximity of his connection to her. He imagined his body, touching hers, as if superimposed, the two of them sitting there as layers of being, of pure potentiality, separated only by the relativity of time and space. He collapsed these distances in his mind, and dwelled in a place where he and Sara were joined in a quantum realm where anything was possible.

Sara had arrived from somewhere at the start of the semester. Not much was known about her. In the absence of facts, the student body had generated a rapid succession of competing rumors about her: she was local; she was foreign; she was nice; she was a bitch; she had been expelled from her last school for using drugs; for selling drugs; she was a nark; she was a stealth marketer, placed in the school by some corporation to gather market intelligence on teenage consumer trends; her father beat her; her family had moved here as part of the federal witness relocation program.

There must have been people close enough to Sara to know these details for certain, but most students accepted that all this gossip probably contained some half-truths about Sara, which nonetheless reinforced her mystique.

Stephen decided he would give Gaia a chance. If it didn't work out he could just pull the plug. He just wanted to work, not for the money, but to feel more self-possessed than he did living in his father's house, under his father's rules.

He walked up to Schroeder, who was hunched over a woman filling out some paperwork. She was joined by Jasbir and the Arab guy.

"Hey, sport," said Schroeder, standing up. "You interested?"

"I think so," said Stephen, blushing.

Schroeder's hand shot out. "Stephen wasn't it?" he said. Stephen nodded and shook hands. Schroeder's hand was hot and soft. It felt … right.

Dizzied by the prospects of self-employment, Stephen headed to the mall—the cosmetics section. He had never shopped in that area of the department store, had only ever walked through on his way to somewhere else. He nervously browsed a shelf of women's perfume, turning the oddly shaped bottles in his hands and sniffing at nozzles, aware that a counter woman closely watched his every move.

No one asked him if he needed any help. They probably thought he was there to shoplift. They had no idea. No idea that he would one day have more money than all of them combined. Then they would line up to help him, these cougars, in their starchy, white lab coats. Who did they think they were? Doctors?

"Can I help you, young man?" asked one of the shop attendants.

Stephen hated being called that. It sounded so patronizing. "I'm just looking for some perfume," he said.

"For … a girlfriend?"

Stephen could almost hear the sneer in the woman's voice. Was that her lip curling up? "For my mother," he said.

The woman's eyes widened and her hard face seemed to soften. "Oh, aren't you a thoughtful boy. I wish my boys would buy me some nice perfume. But they're all grown up now. Did you have something in mind?"

"I've smelled the stuff before that I like, but it doesn't smell anything like these ones." He gestured to the shelf of colored bottles.

"Okay, did you know what brand you were looking for?"

"No, I just know what it smells like."

"Okay, well why don't we just try testing a few of these."

Stephen began to relax. He had felt conspicuous, lumbering around the shop with its little stands of creams and colored liquids; it was all so feminine, and he was overwhelmed by the selection. He felt fat and clumsy among these dainty things.

The woman wore a broad and friendly nametag.

'Hello, my name is: MARTINE'

Martine was here now, and she would help him find the perfume. She reached under the counter and produced a jar of coffee beans and unscrewed the lid with a look of private amusement.

"We use these to help you reboot your sense of smell," she said. "Just stick your nose into there and it'll help you smell the different aromas better, otherwise it can all get to be a bit too much."

Stephen breathed in the beans. He didn't like coffee, but he didn't mind the smell of these raw beans. Martine turned away from Stephen and sprayed some perfume on a small card. She fanned it dramatically. The movement reminded Stephen of when he was sick, and Alma would whip the thermometer to re-set the mercury before taking his temperature.

"Have a smell of this." Martine handed Stephen the little paper card. "It's called *Détente*. It's a beautiful scent."

Stephen smelled the card and crinkled his nose. "No, it's not this stuff. That smells like ... oranges or something. The stuff I'm looking for is ... I don't know... different."

Martine smiled. Stephen could tell she had been quite pretty once. She still had a pretty good body, even though it was probably all wrinkly.

"You're right, there's some orange blossom in that one."

Martine shelved *Détente* and turned back to face Stephen. "Would you describe the scent you're looking for as fresh or earthy?"

"Earthy, I guess."

"Okay, well we can forget about this range, then. They only do fresh," said Martine, dismissing the row of little glass jars on the display case. She rummaged around under the glass counter and produced another bottle. This one was blue, and in the shape of a pyramid.

"This one's called *Isis*. It's one of our most popular products this season."

Stephen sniffed the coffee beans while Martine prepared the next sample card. He liked Isis, but it only smelled like an approximation of what he was looking for.

"This is close," he said. "The one I'm looking for is more ... fuzzy. I don't know if that makes any sense."

"It does, actually," said Martine encouragingly. "I'm pretty sure I know what you want now. Hang on."

Martine came out from behind her counter and removed a small, plain glass bottle from its lighted perch. "This one's called *Autumn*."

Stephen held the card to his nose. The aroma filled him like a warm breath. It flowed through his nose and swelled inside his mouth, coating his tongue. He could taste it. The perfume spread inside him, carried through his bloodstream, seeped into a stream, carried by the current on its silent journey to the sea. It entered his heart and from there it radiated to his fingertips, dancing on the end of every hair on his body. The perfume filled his every sense and directed his eyes, his nose, his mouth, to indulge every encounter he had ever had with Sara, real or imagined, delivering them into one concentrated experience. He was at the cosmetics counter of a mini mall, but he was also holding Sara and kissing her neck where her perfume, this perfume, came from. He was kissing her neck but he was also in class, staring at the gentle, spiraled pattern of her underwear, and as he did so, he also wrote and read and reread every passage that he had ever written about Sara in his dream journal.

Time to go home.

The computer screen glowed in the darkened room.

Overturned tanker forces evacuations, click to view raw

video—Doping allegations claim Olympic hopeful, read more—Senator Grows Cold on Carbon Pricing—Coaches say the 17-year old was devastated to hear of his suspension and—Rate cut forecast to stimulate retail gloom—90 presumed dead in ferry tragedy—For full playoff coverage click here

How could he get Sara to notice him?

Chapter Nineteen

Dusk crept over the beach, gradually extinguishing the last shimmering reflections of the setting sun as night closed in around L'Eden Sur Mer. From out there, beyond the shore, the island's coral atoll would now be dimly visible, a slight undulation on the black, open ocean. Unless you were looking closely, you might miss the island completely.

The beach hummed with people, their shadowy forms wandering up and down the foreshore in the flickering of firelight. People sat in clumps on the sand, eating, drinking and singing songs; their voices carried out to sea by the passing breeze.

A pod of canoes bobbed in the shallows, glowing in the torch-light, their hulls cut in half by the black water below. Little children, oblivious to bedtime, darted in and out of the shadows, swung on tire swings and ran between legs in the crowd.

Peter, Koyl and Nash looked on from a small jetty that stretched out into the water; the steady thump of lazy waves lapping against the wooden boards below their feet.

Peter turned his attention to the beach, to his islands. There, on the shore, 50,000 model replicas of L'Eden Sur Mer, cast in watertight silicone, were ready to be launched. It had everything you could want from a media campaign: drama, hope, and global appeal. Sur Merians would float the tiny islands out to sea like messages in a bottle. A screw cap on the bottom could be removed. Inside was a message:

Congratulations! You have found our message in a bottle. What you are holding is a vessel that represents the island where our people have lived for 3000 years. Our land is now sinking and we need your help. Please visit www.SurMer.com to find out how. Our home is in your hands.

The web page was linked to the country's national website and described the whole project of the floating island, complete with technical specs and Peter's preliminary sketches. It contained an interactive world map where people could pin the location where they had found their message in a bottle. The idea was to track the vessels, feeding a global interest and growing dialogue about L'Eden Sur Mer. The website also contained short video clips, introducing visitors to the island, with footage of the sodden mangrove fields, the inundated coffee plantation and vegetable patches choked out by the salt water rising up through the ground.

The website was Nash's idea.

"You don't need heavy hitters," he said. "Even small donations, we're talking a couple of dollars, maybe a few hundred, can really add up. Even if it doesn't, look at this thing," said Nash, holding up one of the little island boats. "It's freakin' cool. It's going to start a global conversation about this project that'll attract bigger investors. No one likes being the first one out of the gate."

Nash seemed confident about this public-relations model, and confident that people would respond generously if given a sense of personal involvement in the outcome of the island's fate.

"We have to draw people in," he said. "Make them feel connected and invested in the stakes. Then they'll care about the outcome of the project. It's just easier to engage people on a relative scale," he said. "A hundred bucks here, a few hours of volunteering there. No one person can save the world, not even you, Van Dooren. It takes a bunch of us, swimming upstream, to change the direction of the current."

On the jetty, warm water washed over the three men's bare feet. Koyl crouched down near the blackened sea. He placed his little island on a passing wave.

"No turning back now," said Nash. Koyl did not look back. The President watched his island bob on the swell.

The three of them watched as those little islands drifted out to sea. Children took two at a time, ran into the water as far as they could go, pushed the vessels out to sea and came back for more. It wasn't clear if Sur Merians launched these boats with any sense of intent, any stake in the outcome. It seemed more like a game. It was fun, whatever the objective.

Some thought the floating island was a good idea. Others thought it was folly. But most probably didn't think about it at all. There was little sense in worrying too much about the future. Tomorrow would take care of itself. People enjoyed launching a little island; the game was to watch it as it touched the water and try to remember which island was theirs, to try and keep sight of it as they all floated out to sea together.

People huddled along the shoreline, silhouettes against the firelight. They pointed and giggled and called out to their friends, their children hustling in and out of the water.

Peter put his hand on Koyl's shoulder, surprised by a gesture he seldom committed. It had felt like a natural expression of their like-mindedness, a symbol of their partnership. It was *they* who had created this scene. It was *they* who refused to be deterred by something simply because it was difficult. Peter felt an affinity with Koyl—they were giants among men. It was men like them who had once dared to make fire and build spears. Were it not for men like them, human kind would still be shuddering in caves, defenseless against the hostile world outside.

Koyl turned his head slowly and stopped to look at that hand, just the hand, until Peter felt compelled to take it away. He retracted his hand slowly, sliding it down Koyl's shoulder like a serpent unfurling itself from a branch. Peter put his hands in his pockets and turned to look out towards the sea.

Koyl turned to look at the horizon. "Thank you," he said.

Chapter Twenty

Gracie pinched the little pills of wool that hung off her favorite sweater. The cuffs were frayed, but the sweater was warm and baggy, and Gracie felt safe inside its embrace.

She usually avoided crowds, but the lecture hall was buzzing. Whenever she entered a large group of people, she felt her individuality subsumed by the collective throng, as if her joining a group robbed her, turning *her* into an *it*, a *them* over which she no longer had control; people begat people, which contributed to Gracie's anxiety.

She was forever consumed by the thought of seven billion people. She could not shake the image of that writhing mass of humanity swarming the Earth all at once, and had begun to imagine them all as a squirming, wriggling ball of maggots heaped on a decomposing carcass. They crowded her mind, these people, and her own thoughts competed against the volume of their imagined conversations. These people. All of these people lived and loved, and lost, and cried and did so just outside the fragile prism of her own reality. How many people were dying—or had died—the minute she finished that very thought? Hundreds? Thousands? They were people that she would never meet and never know, and yet she felt the weight of their presence was never far removed from her own experience. She imagined them all in rapid succession, gasping their last breaths, just as somewhere, someone else would be drawing their very first. How many people were sleeping right now? How many were eating? How many people were defecating this very moment? Vomiting? Coming? And what would it look like to assemble the total mass of that effluent? What was the scale of the excrement produced in that moment, and what would it look like all heaped together?

This colossal mound would be enough to fill stadiums, lakes and rivers, and all of that damage excreted, inflicted in the time it took her to imagine the activities of a few nameless, faceless people half a world away. The thought of them all would have driven her mad, were it not for the calming reassurance that above it all, looking down, was the peacefulness of God. He was not some old man living on a cloud. She thought that image ridiculous; felt that image of the bearded patriarch had done a great disservice to the church. It was bad branding. God was so much more than that. It was people's attempt to understand Him that caused them to invent such petty and earthbound approximations of His true grandeur.

The lecture theater fell silent as the professor handed out the astronomy midterm exam. "Keep the booklets face down until I say you can begin."

The exam had been a source of worry for Gracie. There would be calculations to make and formulas to employ. The whole class, really, was more math than stars, and Gracie had never been very good with numbers.

She had studied for the exam, but each practice question had only intensified her anxiety. The questions demanded a discipline and order of thought that felt wholly unnatural to her.

Gracie had always hated math, ever since grade school. Times tables, algebra, trigonometry, the formulas and equations had piled up in her mind, an untidy heap of numbers and symbols. An exam expected her to dive into that clutter and retrieve a single item. It was too much. Solving a math problem felt like tracking a single minnow in a writhing school of fish, and soon overwhelmed her sense of the individual. Any fish seemed like *the* fish.

Why had she taken this course anyway? It was supposed to be the easy way to a science credit. She could have taken geography, or earth and ocean sciences. Joanne had taken biology. But all of those subjects were too hard. Joanne could have her biology.

From her seat in the back row at the top of the lecture theatre, Gracie looked down at the other students with their pens, pencils, calculators and scrap paper at the ready. She tried to pick out the people whom she imagined would ace this exam and envied the discretion of their minds, longed for the mysterious thing that enabled them to block out everything they knew except the 'right' answer. *Why were Asians always so good at math?*

The whole of university was a bit of a joke, really. It was all just a lot of talking.

"You may begin."

A fluttering and flapping of paper ensued as students turned over their exam booklets.

"You have just under ninety minutes to complete the exam," said the professor. "If you finish early, I strongly recommend you take the extra time to double-check your answers."

Some people had already begun scribbling on their pieces of scrap paper. Others quietly flipped through the booklet, getting a sense of what lay ahead.

- What is the difference between an inertial reference frame and a non-inertial reference frame?
- Light travels at 3×10^5 km/sec. There are 3×10^7 seconds in one year. How many kilometers are there in the approximate distance to the Andromeda Galaxy (2×10^6)?
- A right triangle, shown in the above diagram, as it would look at rest, moves with respect to you at a speed of 198,294 km/sec in the x direction. In an instant, you measure the length of the side that lies along the x direction, and you get?

A familiar disquiet settled over Gracie as she approached each problem set. She read the questions carefully, determined to unpick the hidden clues and apply the desired equation for the correct answer. Did this question call for Kepler's law? Wien's law? What was the difference again? Wien's law was about temperature, wasn't it? Was it (lE/ lV) = (TV/ TE)? Or was that the Minkowski formula?

- Travelling in the family car at 60 mph, how many years would it take you to reach the outer edge of the solar system (10^5 AU)?

Gracie looked at her scrap of paper. She drew a quick sketch of a car. It was a frivolous thing to do, she knew that, but it had felt good to make long, fluid lines with her pencil, before attempting the short, brisk strokes of a calculation. She began to work out her answer.

v1 = v2 + V

1+v

~~3 x 105 km/sec~~   ~~30,000 x 10, 0000 – 60sec~~

3 x 105 km/sec   2 x 106 light years AU

149 597 871kms

3 x 105 km/sec x 3 3 x 107 seconds =   ~~2.2 miles per Km~~

2.2km per mile

Gracie's breathing was shallow; she took a deep breath and looked up at the clock. *Taking too long.* At her current pace, she would run out of time. Maybe she could buy some time if she skipped the calculations for now and moved on to some of the multiple-choice questions. She could always come back to the calculations later. She flipped through her booklet.

- A planet whose semi-major axis from the Sun is 3 AU would have an orbital period of how many Earth-years?
    - a. 3
    - b. 27
    - c. 12
    - d. 9
    - e. 81

    Flip.
- This reference frame is $\Delta x2 = 0$. Calculate the—

    Flip.
- A wave's velocity is equal to the product of:
    - a. The frequency of the wave times the period of the wave.
    - b. The period of the wave times the energy of the wave.

c. The amplitude of the wave times the frequency of the wave.
d. The frequency of the wave times the wavelength of the wave.
e. The amplitude of the wave times the wavelength of the wave.

This was a waste of time. The green light marking the exit door glowed invitingly. There was nothing keeping her here.

Gracie looked down at the Asian girl who sat in front of her and could clearly see the girl's exam paper.

- A wave's velocity is equal to the product of:
  a. The frequency of the wave times the period of the wave.
  b. The period of the wave times the energy of the wave.
  ©. The frequency of the wave times the wavelength of the wave.
  d. The amplitude of the wave times the frequency of the wave.
  e. The amplitude of the wave times the wavelength of the wave.

The answer *was* c. Now that she saw it, Gracie *knew* that it was the right answer. She had known the answer all along. Her professor was pacing at the front of the lecture theater, way down below. Gracie had a narrow window of opportunity. The Asian girl would soon be finished with this page of the exam.

This was wrong. She knew it was wrong. But she *had* studied. She had studied long and hard, and she had known the answer was c. The Asian girl had just confirmed it. Gracie knew the answers but needed more time. Perhaps at her own pace she might have been able to answer these questions, but here, in this artificial environment, with constant time pressure, she could not come up with the solutions.

Maybe this opportunity was God's way of helping her? Surely He recognized that she had worked hard, that the answers floated around inside her somewhere but that she needed help to pluck them out. Surely He knew that her intentions were pure. Gracie knew that she could do well on this exam, she just needed more time. If *she* knew it, then God must know it too.

Gracie circled 'c' and waited for the Asian girl in front of her to work out the solution to the next problem. It became easier for Gracie to transfer the answers as the Asian girl worked her way through the exam.

When the Asian girl finished, she flipped back to the beginning of the booklet to double-check her answers. Gracie watched her make a few indecipherable scribbles on her scrap paper, some baffling calculations on her serious-looking calculator, paused, closed the exam booklet and handed it in. Gracie sat there. The seat in front of her was now empty. She scanned the room. About half the class was still scribbling away. She could hear the flipping of pages, the clicking of calculator buttons, the intense quiet punctuated by the occasional cough. How long should she wait before she should leave? Would it look suspicious to leave so soon after the Asian girl?

Gracie sat there for a few more minutes—or were they seconds?—thumbing the pages of the exam booklet. She stood and made her way down the aisle to hand in her exam. The professor was sitting on his desk and fidgeting with the cap of a whiteboard marker. He nodded kindly as Gracie placed her midterm on the growing pile. Was he still watching her as she made her way back up the stairs and out of the auditorium?

The light outside seemed harsh and bright after having been inside the lecture theater for so long. The world seemed louder. She was aware of people talking and traffic noise and passing airplanes. Gracie noticed a girl wearing heavy white makeup and all black clothes leaning against a tree outside the exam room. The girl was smoking a hand-rolled cigarette and tapping it constantly with her index finger.

"That was a hard exam, hey?" said the young woman to Gracie.

Gracie realized she had probably paused for longer than she was aware. She had essentially courted this unwanted conversation. "Yeah," she said, and turned to walk towards the bus stop in the distance.

She couldn't see the young woman's face anymore, but Gracie could feel her looking to make contact, like a missile locked on a target. Gracie would not make eye contact.

"Okay then, see you later," said the girl as Gracie passed.

On the bus ride home, Gracie had doubts about what she had done. What if the lecture hall had been under surveillance? They did that kind of thing nowadays, didn't they? What if the Asian girl had given the wrong answers? It would just be a matter of watching the footage, or matching two identical exam papers to reveal that Gracie had cheated. *How could I have been so stupid?* She would be thrown out of university. Humiliated. Gracie was sure of it. Why hadn't she just left the exam room when she had the chance? Why wasn't she stronger? Worse, this experience had been a test from God and Gracie had failed. Evil had tempted her and she had succumbed to it. She was weak and had chosen the path of cheats and liars. Gracie could see that now. She wept for guilt and shame, and fear. God was angry. There was no telling what He might do. But mostly she felt bitter regret at having so disappointed Him. Even if she could fool the lecturer, she knew she couldn't fool God. She would have to set things right.

Gracie rode the bus back towards the city, back to her apartment. It was a twenty-minute trip. She had made it often. But it seemed different tonight. Longer. It was already dark outside and the bus that carried her through the cold, wet night seemed to pass through unfamiliar surroundings, along eerie patches of vacant land and menacing, bare trees. It felt like she was on a much longer journey. She felt like a stranger entering an unknown city in a hostile land.

Her apartment complex stood tall in the distance, its floodlit exterior twinkling with perennial Christmas cheer. She stepped off the bus. It was cold outside. She could see her breath. She pulled the steel handle and opened the heavy glass lobby door. The concierge waved to her from inside his little glass box. It was more of a slow salute, and Gracie never really understood what he meant by it. The concierge had a clear view of her as she waited for the elevator in the lobby. He watched. That's what he did. He was like one of those isolated Siamese fighting fish that stared, motionless, at the world outside of its miniature aquarium. Gracie shifted the strap of her schoolbag so the bulk of the satchel rested behind her. She waited for the elevator doors to close before she turned around, and breathed deeply as the lift drew her up towards the clouds. Finally she was alone.

It was dark in the apartment. Even though she knew the glass windows were mirrored on the outside, Gracie didn't like to turn on too many lights. She preferred to look out at the view. She liked to look down at the streets and buildings, the cars and the people she had been among only a moment before. It all looked so different from the forty-fourth floor. The maze of streets that had overwhelmed her just minutes ago now appeared as neat, straight lines—part of a distinct and orderly grid. The traffic that had sped past her, the motorcycles that went too fast, it now all seemed like a disciplined convoy moving slowly downstream. It was possible to imagine all of those headlights and taillights were headed to the same place. In some way, they were. The world made more sense from up here.

Chapter Twenty-One

Malhoun held up one of Peter's little vessels, his message in an island. He hoisted it up over his head. His congregation looked back, waiting for Malhoun to speak.

"What is this?" said Malhoun to his congregation. No one answered. Malhoun searched the room. Fat ladies fanned themselves with paper brochures. Someone coughed.

"They want you to see this as a sign of hope." He held the model in front of him.

"This," he said again, panning it around the room for all to see. "Does this look hopeful to you?" Malhoun shook his head slowly. "No? Me neither. I don't see hope. Do you know what I see?" Malhoun raised his eyebrows. "I see desperation. I see pride. I see fear. We should not build this. This is our tower of Babel. If God chooses to reclaim this land, then who are we to stand in His way?"

Cheers from the congregation.

"No. I will not fight God. Do you want to fight God?"

A chorus of disagreement.

"Are you going to fight God?" Malhoun pointed at members of his congregation. "Will you fight God?"

Shaking heads.

"You?"

Another head shake.

"I will not fight God. You cannot fight God. If God is every-thing and we are part of it, then fighting God is to fight ourselves. Is it not better that we seek to learn lessons from our worries?"

Shouts of approval.

"We should not wait for these boats to return. We should follow them. We too should ride the currents beyond the horizon. It is there, not here, and not in this, that our salvation lies." Malhoun threw the model out the window.

The congregation stood, clapping and cheering.

Thani Malhoun was a young upstart in the island politics of L'Eden Sur Mer. The twenty-eight–year-old had resolved a number of minor local disputes about fishing rights, earning him a reputation as a gifted and sensitive problem solver. A member of L'Eden Sur Mer's Christian minority, Malhoun had also managed to synergize his personal beliefs with traditional Sur Merian spiritual culture. He associated his moderate Christian, pantheist notions of God with an essentialized version of Sur Merian spiritual beliefs, which held that all living things were endowed with an original, life-giving force. That he called that force God and that other Sur Merians might call it *Keolikahe* was, he explained, just semantics. His spiritual sensitivities had helped to make him popular in these uncertain times, particularly among the Gray Hairs who saw in Malhoun a reliable custodian of Sur Merian spiritual traditions. That his talents came wrapped in Christian idolatry was a small price to pay.

Peter sat on the landing outside of his little hut and watched Thani Malhoun walk towards him, head bobbing around on top of his skinny frame.

Koyl had warned Peter this would happen, that Malhoun would seek him out. Now here he was, holding out his hand in salutation long before he reached the top of the landing.

"Mr Van Dooren," said Malhoun, finally shaking Peter's hand. Peter gripped it with extra force and watched his face for any change of expression. Malhoun stared back, still smiling. The kid had confidence. Peter could respect that.

"Do you mind if I take a few moments of your time?" said

Malhoun. He had big, kind eyes.

Peter invited Malhoun to sit on one of the two folding chairs; the creaking of the plastic and cheap aluminum beneath them was loud on the air.

"I see you running sometimes," said Malhoun, leaning back in his chair. "You are very fast."

Peter didn't respond. If Malhoun wanted to talk, he would have to start the conversation.

"Me, I can't run," said Malhoun. He waved a long index finger. "Never. It makes me sick. But I understand. Healthy body. Healthy mind." Malhoun nodded sympathetically.

"Something like that," said Peter.

A cloud passed in front of the sun, softening shadows and chilling the breeze.

"Mr Van Dooren. Can I ask you something about these boats you have sent away?" Malhoun waited, as if genuinely awaiting approval. Peter shrugged.

"The thing is," Malhoun continued, "what if the messages don't come back?"

"They will," said Peter automatically.

"I wish I could share your certainty." Malhoun's chair creaked beneath him.

"What do you mean?" Peter crossed his arms.

"I mean that you and, respectfully, our dear President, have placed a great deal of hope, may I even say faith, in the help of others through this enterprise."

Peter didn't respond.

Malhoun continued to smile. "You see, I know you are not a religious man, but I believe that God helps those who help themselves." He seemed pleased with what he'd just said and looked at Peter expectantly.

"Well, Mr Malhoun," said Peter, "on that we can agree. Except maybe the part about God." Peter welcomed the opportunity to lighten the mood.

Malhoun's face tightened. He laced his hands tightly and placed them in his lap. "That is no offence to me, Mr Van Dooren.

God makes Himself known when you need Him most. I pray that you will open your heart to Him." Malhoun tilted his head as he spoke. He leaned in towards Peter. "Can I show you something?"

Malhoun reached into his pocket and pulled out a piece of paper. He unfolded it carefully, eyes sparkling. The sun emerged from behind the cloud. It glared off the paper.

"If I cannot appeal to your faith, then allow me to petition your sense of reason," said Malhoun, handing Peter the sheet of paper.

Reading it over, Peter discovered that the Fiji Real Estate Agents Licensing Board was selling a 6,000-acre property on Viti Levu, one of Fiji's main islands, for $9.6 million. The Fijian Methodist Church group that owned the land was looking to diversify its investment portfolio.

"For me this is a sign from God," said Malhoun, his eyes widening. "God wants us to relocate here." Malhoun tapped the paper. It flapped a little in the breeze. "But to you, I make a business proposition."

Peter handed the paper back. Malhoun folded it carefully and returned it to his pocket. "We can buy this estate as agricultural land," he said. "Look here," said Malhoun, rising to grab a fistful of dry dirt from outside the landing. He held it out in his palm for Peter to see. The sandy soil glinted in the sun. "The soil here is dead," said Malhoun. "But this," he said patting his pocket, "this is good land. It is alive. We buy this acreage and we can ensure food security for L'Eden Sur Mer. We would begin by sending our farmers there, maybe fifty or sixty to start. They will plant vegetables, grow fruit and keep livestock." Malhoun mimed things growing from the ground. "Sur Merian farmers will export the harvest back to L'Eden Sur Mer, at first." Malhoun paused, cleared his throat. "But if it is successful, the crop can become a business for export. You see?" Malhoun's bright smile returned. Such big teeth.

Malhoun never went so far as to call the Fijian acreage holy land, but he might as well have. The proposed solution was part of a broad migration strategy that he envisioned. If the island became uninhabitable, as was now clearly the case, its citizens would become global citizens, whether they were prepared or not. Rather than condemn the Sur Merian diaspora to a messy, uncoordinated exodus, Malhoun spoke of developing an Education for Migration program, aimed at up-skilling the local population to make them more attractive as migrants to international destinations like Australia, Fiji and New Zealand.

The idea was gaining traction. Fiji had already offered significant concessions for young Sur Merians interested in pursuing degrees at the University of the South Pacific, particularly in the fields of engineering and mathematics. Computer and English literacy classes were also offered on generous terms.

Sur Merian youth broadly supported Malhoun's ideas and had even started a quasi-political organization to publicly demonstrate their backing of Malhoun and his initiatives, particularly the young, urban elites who had cell phones and dreamed of bigger, better lives somewhere beyond the horizon.

"What do you think, Mr Van Dooren? Surely you can see the merits of this proposal." Malhoun leaned forward, expectantly. He rubbed his hands. Such long fingers.

Malhoun was angling for some kind of understanding between himself and Van Dooren International. That was clear. He needed money to help narrow the 1,500 mile distance between his Fijian holy land and L'Eden Sur Mer. Malhoun had spoken excitedly, idealistically, about his plans and Peter had let him speak, feeling that it was not up to him to put the young man in his place. President Koyl would do that.

"I don't know," said Peter. "I'm not convinced."

Malhoun shot back in his chair suddenly, as if he'd been wounded. "That is a very surprising answer. For a business man." He looked over his shoulder. A large wave broke against the coral reef in the distance. Malhoun swallowed hard. He hesitated then whipped back towards Peter. "I think I understand."

Peter shrugged. "What do you understand?"

Malhoun searched Peter's face and broke into a nervous smile.

"Very good, yes," said Malhoun, clapping his hands. "You say you are not a man of faith. "But …" he pointed an accusing finger at Peter. "Your investment in this … idea of yours. Well it suggests otherwise."

"Well," said Peter, "we'll see."

Malhoun leaned forward aggressively. "That's it, though, Mr Van Dooren. We will see. It's a shame." He rose to his feet. "Still," he said, "I would like you to think about it."

"I have," said Peter, remaining seated.

Malhoun rubbed his forehead, his face, his chin. "Be careful, Mr Van Dooren." He looked towards the horizon. "You do not have the control you imagine."

Peter sat back in his chair, half-smiled, half-frowned. "Is that a threat?"

"Not from me." Malhoun turned to leave. "Goodbye," he said from over his shoulder.

Peter watched him walk off until his skinny frame disappeared behind the sand dunes.

Koyl's face softened as he laughed. "Don't worry about Malhoun," he said. "He is just a boy. People understand the Sur Merian culture will not survive if they leave this land."

Koyl kept smiling when Peter told him about Malhoun's crumpled bit of paper, his Fijian holy land.

"He is no prophet. Leave it to me." The President suddenly took an interest in his own hands.

"Mr President," said Peter.

Koyl looked up without speaking. "There's something I have to ask," said Peter. Koyl blinked, authorizing the question. "The thing is, Sir," Peter hesitated, "why not evacuate? On some level—"

"Because if you move one person, you might as well move them all," said Koyl. "A phased evacuation is the first step to giving up on everything I have spent a lifetime to achieve. There is no coming back from that decision. It would divide this nation, and start a cold civil war that will never end."

Peter's respect for President Koyl deepened. Here was a man who shaped his own destiny. Peter could see the forces lining up against the President and yet he refused to yield. Pacific leaders distrusted him, the international community had abandoned him, the sea engulfed him and religious zealots threatened his plan—their plan, the *only* plan—to save the island, to save the Sur Merians from themselves.

Koyl understood Peter's proposal. Peter had felt self-conscious at first, showing the President his crude diagrams. He had prepared to be laughed out of Koyl's office, but the man had shown enthusiasm for the idea right from the outset.

"I understand." Peter stood and walked towards the door.

"Peter," said Koyl softly. Peter turned around. Koyl sat behind his desk, hands folded in front of him. "We're doing the right thing."

Peter nodded. He smiled, turned and left, his footsteps echoing in the empty corridor.

Koyl sat at his desk. He put on his glasses, opened a portfolio and began to read. The rustling of paper sounded loud in the quiet room. The phone pulsed with a soft, digital ring, quieter than the shuffling paper. Koyl peered over his spectacles into the hallway. No one answered the phone. It rang again. Koyl leaned across his desk to look down the hallway where his secretary was supposed to be. The phone rang again. Koyl picked it up, stabbed a flashing red light on the console.

"Yes?" he said. Silence from the other end. Then, a breath.

"Everything under control?"

It was Holden Nash.

Koyl's elbows dug into the desk. "Our friend received a visitor," said Koyl.

Nash paused, "Anything I've got to worry about?"

"No," said Koyl, his elbows heavy on the desk.

"You sure?"

"No one will do anything without my approving it," said Koyl.

Nash breathed heavily on the other end of the phone. "You've got to be sure, Mr President. Because we're not going to change our minds halfway through. I mean, once we start this—"

"Stop," barked Koyl. He breathed in deeply, composing himself. "Everything continues just as we discussed. I will deal with the young prophet in my own way. You just … continue to be useful. Everything will be fine."

"Okay," said Nash. "Thank you, Sir."

Koyl leaned back in his chair. He tapped the edge of the desk with his fingertips. "Nash," he said.

"Yes Mr President?" His voice was cheerful.

"Don't ring me here again." Koyl hung up the phone.

Chapter Twenty-Two

Tal and Stephen were in the pool house. The two-room bungalow sat some distance from the main building of the family home, which made it an attractive place to be. With Gracie now out of the picture, Stephen had swiftly commandeered the pool house for himself. Alma and Peter hadn't been comfortable with the idea of Stephen moving out there permanently—the pool house was reserved for guests, they said, so Stephen had moved in slowly: a poster here, a few clothes there, a sleeping bag for those nights when he decided to crash in front of a movie rather than make his way back to the main house. To keep his parents happy, he made a conscious effort to sleep in his dedicated bedroom upstairs at least three nights a week. The arrangement seemed to have struck a balance between Stephen's desire for private space and honoring his parents' sense of dominion over the family home.

Tal paced around the bungalow, air-drumming to the music. He browsed the contents of the room as if taking it all in for the first time, stopping to look over some family portraits that hung near the kitchenette, a leftover from when Gracie had occupied the place: a graduation photo, dinners at restaurants, mini golf. Tal looked at the photos, lingering on the pictures of Gracie, watching her as she grew up in them over the years.

"Your sister's hot. You know that, right?"

Stephen was slumped on the love seat, playing a video game. He was fighting his way out of a dark corner, angry that his online sidekick had suddenly decided to shoot him instead of the enemy they were both sworn to destroy.

"Super hot, man," Tal continued. "A smoking-hot hottie with hot sauce and peppers ... deep-fried hot." Tal looked over at Stephen, who appeared to take no notice of him. "You like it when I talk about your sister like that?"

Stephen shrugged and angled his controller. This fucker, whoever he was, obviously didn't realize he had picked a fight with the wrong guy. Stephen threw a smoke bomb and then peppered the traitor with a barrage of hollow-point bullets. It was overkill, but Stephen wanted the guy to know he had crossed a line and had pissed him off.

"You don't see how hot she is?"

"I don't know. She's my sister," Stephen muttered. Tal's badgering was preventing him from savoring the thorough and scientific beating that he was meting out to his opponent.

"Well brother, you really are the ugly sheep of the family, you know that, right. Say, does Gracie have, like, a bunch of hot friends who hang out at the house and stuff, because they do that, you know, chicks, they always hang out in groups of like three or more girls and there's always one ugly one. You ever notice that? There's always, like, one pig, right, who's just along for the ride. What is that about? She is seriously hot though, man. I'd be happy just fucking a couch she sat on. Damn."

"Shut up." Stephen applied a flamethrower to his former ally's broken corpse. That would teach him. Maybe next time he wouldn't be so cocky. You didn't turn on your own like that.

"Come on, man," said Tal. "This is boring watching you fuck around on that thing."

Stephen looked up from the TV. He had proven his point. Somewhere in the world, that guy was licking his wounds. He would think twice next time before turning a gun on his partner.

"Okay, what do *you* want to do?" he asked Tal, who continued to absently browse the contents of the room, twisting the knob on the dishwasher back and forth for no reason.

"Is your mom around?" asked Tal.

"I don't know. I think she's out. Pretty sure she works on Thursday nights."

Tal slowly drummed the countertop with the tips of his fingers. "I don't think she likes me very much," he said.

Stephen shut down the game console and tossed the controller onto a beanbag chair. "Don't take it personally. I don't think she likes anyone that much." He looked out the sliding glass patio door. The pool was full of leaves. It was usually empty by now because it was too cold to swim in at this time of year. That was usually his dad's job, but he hadn't been home in weeks. *Months?* Clearly no one had bothered to call the pool guy.

"I don't know," said Stephen. "I don't think she's very happy."

Tal leaned his arm against the wall and looked at the Van Dooren family portraits that hung there, at the smiling faces that looked back from inside the painted wooden frames.

"Who is, man?" said Tal. "Who the fuck is."

Alma had wanted to like Tal, had listened to Peter go on about their kids being influenced by the 'wrong' kinds of people and found herself determined to refute her husband's prejudices by giving Tal a wide margin for error. But the way he offered to help do things, set the table, put away the dishes, his obsequiousness reminded her of her father's friends and acquaintances, and the strategic niceties they had shown her growing up. She was aware of how absurd it would be to hold that comparison against Tal. But there was something else about the boy, too, a confidence, a bravado, some kind of intensity coiled up inside that lanky teenage body that made Alma feel uncomfortable.

Coming up the stairs one evening, she caught Tal coming out of Gracie's room. He said he had taken a wrong turn on his way to the bathroom, but there had been a blush on his face that made it difficult for Alma to fully believe him. She had seen more convincing liars get their cells tossed because of looks like that, and the exchange had put Alma on guard around him.

Gracie hadn't been home at the time, so there had been nothing to worry about, really, but it seemed odd, and the encounter had hardened Alma against Tal's charms.

"You know, I'm actually kind of beat," said Stephen. "I think I'm just going to crash."

Tal frowned. "Dude. It's like … eight-thirty."

"I know, I'm lame," said Stephen moving towards the door.

"Oh, you're serious," said Tal.

"What?"

"Look at you all showing me to the door. Bit of an assaholic move, dude, but very suave. Subtle. I give credit where it's due." Tal grabbed his coat.

Stephen laughed. "Whatever." He slid open the patio door.

Tal stepped outside. "Oh, fucking freezing out here." He turned to Stephen. "So you bunk here tonight, and I'm in the big house, yeah?"

Stephen smirked. "See you at school tomorrow," said Stephen, sliding the door closed.

Tal did a blowfish on the glass. "Don't jerk off too much. Kills brain cells."

Stephen gave Tal the finger and closed the blinds on his friend.

"See you tomorrow," said Tal, unseen and muffled from outside.

Stephen heard the gate latch jingle and the wooden door squeak open. Tal didn't close the gate behind him. It would bang all night in the wind if Stephen didn't close it. *I'll do it later.*

Stephen wasn't tired. He wanted to log some time on the Gaia website. He hadn't logged in for days and wanted to put in a few decent hours before going to bed. He hadn't told Tal about his new job. Tal had been offering to get him work at Motel 6 for more than a year and Stephen hadn't wanted to snub the offer. He worried that Tal would think him superior for passing up the kitchen job for something better.

Stephen agitated the mouse, waking the computer from its state of suspended animation. It never really slept, though, did it? The computer performed untold calculations and calibrations, even when dormant.

Gaia's website welcomed the casual visitor with a rolling banner of images. Urban clutter, mostly, juxtaposed against picturesque open landscapes. A highway clogged with cars dissolved to an open meadow fringed with cheerful clouds—dissolved to smoking factory chimneys—dissolved to a lush rainforest canopy.

Stephen felt a rush of pride logging in as an employee. On the Gaia site, Stephen understood the computer was no longer his own. Logging in allowed the company to passively commandeer his machine. His every movement on the Internet would now be tracked and recorded.

The company's business model was twofold. Stephen was free to access any legally permissible site he chose to visit (paid by the hour). Stephen's visited sites would be pooled together with data collected from other Gaia *messengers*, as they were called, operating throughout the world. This *shadowing*, Jack Schroeder had explained, enabled Gaia to get a sense of web-user traffic patterns and get a clear picture of where and how to target the company's advertising.

The second tier of engagement involved stealth marketing. Gaia *messengers* were encouraged to tastefully spruik the company's products through personal communications, emails, postings on social media, and by creating viral photo and video campaigns that captured the essence of Gaia's business ethos: twenty-first-century solutions to twenty-first-century problems. Remuneration was calculated on the relative *cut through* of any given message. How many times were a *messenger's* communications forwarded? Liked? Uploaded? And so forth.

Gaia reported that a few celebrated *messengers* were making thousands of dollars on a single well-placed posting. But Stephen had found no success in the direct-marketing angle of the job. He had tried once to spark some discussion in a chat room by planting a feeble question about the state of the Bolivian rainforest, but there had been little uptake on his posting. Someone who called themselves *Audmarspony* responded by calling him a fascist. Someone else named *Fiersomelover27* responded by uploading a poem about butterflies.

Those results were hardly the exposure that Gaia was looking for and Stephen had all but abandoned the marketing side of his role as a Gaia *messenger*. The truth was that he felt a bit strange about the whole thing. It's not that he didn't care about the issue, it just felt awkward duping his friends and even strangers into considering a thought or a question that he might have kept to himself, were it not for his getting paid to voice it. And so it was that he left others to spearhead Gaia's message. Letting the company track his usage and behavior would have to be enough. Stephen also bought some carbon-offset credits for himself. At least he was doing his part, more than most.

He sat there with a bag of chocolate chips, the kind you used to bake cookies and muffins with. He liked how the chocolate didn't melt in his mouth, how the little dollops of chocolate stayed hard, even if he took handfuls of them at a time, storing them in the warmth of his cheeks like a squirrel. Life was good.

Chapter Twenty-Three

The Sur Merian parliament was filled to capacity. Peter sat in the back gallery, looking down on the proceedings. People shuffled papers in front of them and turned in their swivel chairs to whisper asides as Thani Malhoun took the floor.

Malhoun put down the stack of papers he was holding. He cleared his throat.

"My parliamentary colleagues," he started, looking around at his fellow Sur Merians assembled in the hexagonal room. "There is no debating our predicament. We are past that. I rise because I believe the President fails to accept that ours is not a matter of choice. It is a matter of survival." Malhoun held his hand to his chest. He gestured towards Koyl. "I ask His Excellency to tell us, in this chamber, why he will not endorse a phased evacuation of this island? And why he, instead, pursues this foolish plan which offers us no assurances."

Mild applause accompanied Malhoun's speech. He sat down, keeping his wide eyes fixed on President Koyl.

Koyl rose. The crowd hushed. The President smoothed the fabric at the front of his shirt.

"We pursue this plan because we still have time to build our community," said Koyl. "We still have time to build our resilience and to avoid disaster." He pointed at Malhoun. "What you are proposing is the abandonment of our culture, our way of life."

Murmurings of agreement.

"You are suggesting that we rob our children and their children of their sovereign right to live as their ancestors lived."

Louder agreement.

"You bargain with our heritage, you wager our right to plough the same lands and fish the same waters as our parents did. And their parents before them. Beware." Koyl barked the word. He paused to look upon the faces gathered in the chamber. "I ask the members of this parliament to beware. Future generations will hold you responsible for the desecration of everything we have ever known. And they will never forgive you. I assembled an international coalition here on this island. We agreed that it should be done. That coalition has succeeded. We, as a people, launched small replicas of our land as a symbol of our hope." Koyl was no longer looking at Malhoun. He had turned to address his colleagues and the people assembled in the gallery at the back of the room. "This island can be saved. Success or failure in this cause depends entirely on our perception of what is possible. It can be done. It will be done. And I demand full parliamentary approval to dedicate our national resources to support this cause."

Koyl's words drew steady applause. The old man had fight in him yet.

Malhoun smoothed out his hair. He rose slowly. "With due respect," he began, "the President does not accept that we have already stepped over a threshold from which we cannot return. Saltwater has ruined our crops."

Murmured agreement.

"It has poisoned our drinking water."

Murmured agreement.

"Storms and cyclones are part of our everyday life. We face the inundation of our land, the disappearance of our homes and livelihood. We are damaged. We are lost. We are alone." Malhoun, too, searched the gallery and spoke generally, beyond the walls, above the ceiling. "Our hope lies elsewhere," he said. "Somewhere we can begin again, taking with us our cherished memories, the wisdom of our elders, the best of ourselves. From this rich history we can begin anew. We can build better lives for ourselves, a better future for our people. But we must leave. We have no choice."

Malhoun's words drew rousing applause. Koyl looked around the chamber. He rose quickly. "I ask the newly and temporarily appointed member who is entitled to make the decision about whether we stay or go? Are Sur Merians less entitled to self-determination because we are so few in number? Because we are isolated? Who says so? You? We are a distinct race of people who have been on this island for more than three thousand years." Koyl was clenching his fists. He looked rigid, even from the back of the chamber. "We have a unique language and a unique culture," he continued. "If you, Sir, or any institution, arrogates to itself the power to decide that L'Eden Sur Mer, or any other state, is unviable, then it and you assume colonial power. This is *our* island. It is where *our* ancestors are buried. *We* are entitled to be here. And one way or another, so will it remain."

The chamber divided, applause on the one side, grumbling on the other. Malhoun rose.

"Respectfully, Mr President, I can see your passion and I admire it. We all do." He made an all-encompassing gesture with his hands. "But I cannot share your sentiment. We must think of the future. Many people die here from conditions that could easily be treated elsewhere, or from a lack of safety standards, or from a poor diet. Emigration offers our people the promise of an education, reliable healthcare and employment. It would be grossly irresponsible of us to withhold those opportunities from our people. Not for sentiment's sake."

Koyl's eyes narrowed. It was not so simple, and he resented Malhoun's insinuation that it was. It was time to let him know who was in charge in this house. "Young man, you will stop at nothing until we are a nation of refugees."

Malhoun smiled. "No, Mr President. It is you, who by doing nothing, condemn us to that fate."

Koyl stormed into his office, Peter and Nash trailing behind.

The President turned to Peter, puffing and out of breath. He held a trembling index finger under Peter's chin. "Make it work," he said. "You make it work."

Chapter Twenty-Four

Lucy and Joanne were seated at a trestle table outside the university's Pendulum Café. Its rustic-chic interior and free wi-fi usually attracted campus hipsters, but tonight the place was booked out for the Christian Fellowship's Open Mic Night.

Gracie was going to skip the event but felt compelled to show up. The astronomy exam results had been posted that morning and she had got one of the highest marks in the class. She had to set things right with God.

Lucy and Joanne exchanged a surprised look as Gracie approached. The three of them fell into an awkward hug over the top of the trestle table.

"Hey, so good to see you," said Joanne. The brief neglect of their duty checking ticket stubs at the door left a clump of students backing up at the café entrance. They waited patiently, anxious to flash their tickets and get inside.

The venue was too large to be intimate. Most people assembled by chance at awkwardly spaced tables in the overly bright room. Too much food had been provided and people distracted themselves by taking handfuls of cookies and cupcakes served in their original packaging from the supermarket bakery section.

Gracie vaguely recognized a few faces from some of her classes, but depended almost entirely on Lucy and Joanne to facilitate formal introductions. Ruth was one of nine children. Her parents were forty and fifty years her senior and her worldview gave the impression of someone brought up by grandparents, with the wardrobe to match. Her physical appearance was deliberately *unfocused*—her own phrasing—because God loves what is on the inside.

Phil struck Gracie as weedy but sincere. He couldn't grow facial hair, not really, but his patience and determination had yielded a stringy patchwork of reddish brown that seemed to only temporarily cling to his face. He wore runners with jeans and wasted no time in telling Gracie that he was deeply into volunteering at church activities. The rest of the time, Phil studied sound engineering.

Chelsea hinted at a troubled past, if only to emphasize the timeliness of her salvation. She had found Jesus at the same time that she had met Aaron, who had helped Chelsea to develop a deeper understanding of her faith. She and Aaron were trying to date without kissing. It would somehow deepen their faith and their relationship.

Glen was a confident and exuberant young man. His fashion sense depended on his sluggish ability to gauge the national zeitgeist. Tonight it had instructed him to wear a designer tracksuit and a leather jacket. No shoes.

Glen removed the microphone from its perch and paced the stage with an exaggerated swagger. "Welcome," he said, and paused long enough for two people to clear their throats. "Wel-come," he repeated for no reason.

He leaned against the stand with rehearsed confidence. "Now most of you know that I have some issues with the way the modern church expresses itself," he said.

The group responded knowingly. Someone near the front made a complicated hand gesture, presumably drawing attention to some private joke that he and Glen had shared elsewhere.

He had some speaking ability, Glen, but lacked social polish, no doubt a hangover from an insular church upbringing. It was clear that Glen was a man driven towards extremes when placed in familiar confines; the common ground on which they all stood as Christians emboldened him to assume an air of familiarity with the group. He adopted a tone of reassurance that led others to praise him as a natural leader.

Aaron told those at the table that he found Glen a little offensive. Glen's cockiness came across as irreverent, bordering on disrespectful. Gracie didn't understand what Aaron meant. The whole table, really, seemed to hold a different concept of the Creator than the one she understood. They spoke of *Him* and *The Father* and of *God*, like He was an actual person, or at least something imbued with decidedly human—male—characteristics.

Gracie had come to think of God as something greater than the concept offered by the church, which seemed to present God as something closer to a human being. She understood the significance and utility of religious imagery, and that figures of Jesus and God—the bearded father—the symbolism had diminished God's grandeur and risked undermining the profound omniscience of the God she understood and loved, the God of a supreme reality for which crosses, churches and bearded men would only ever be superficial approximations. Aaron, especially, spoke of God as if *He* were no more than a powerful man. *That* image was more irreverent, more offensive than anything Glen had to say. She *felt* God, felt *its* unseen presence like heat or wind stirring within her, from the inside out.

This divine reality was, for Gracie, at once deeply personal and vaster, more disconnected from anything so trivial as the structure and rules of the modern church, with its rituals, its symbols, and hierarchies. And yet, she yearned to share this feeling, this faith that burned inside her with those who seemed to understand these feelings, whatever else they might think.

Glen went on to play acoustic guitar, saying his set would *redeem* the veiled biblical concepts that he interpreted in the secular songs he selected for his performance. He sang well, but the rapturous applause that rewarded each song seemed overly generous. Maybe the Christian Fellowship was sympathetic towards Glen for reasons of which Gracie was unaware, reasons that might have nothing to do with his musical ability at all.

As an audience, the Fellowship's disproportionate show of appreciation might be in support of Glen himself, rather than as a show of gratitude for his songs. They were tight, this group, they were a real community, and Gracie felt like an imposter, a spy with no orders except to avoid detection. Everyone seemed bound by a genuine respect and affection for one another. It was all nice on the surface but tinged with a fanaticism that made it creepy. You had to belong to be loved.

From the banter at her table between acts, Gracie learned that many of these people had known each other for years. Chelsea knew Ruth; Phil knew Aaron; and Glen knew everybody. There was talk of jogging and shoes, evidently Phil and Aaron cycled together competitively, and the mention of someone or something named *Patch* drew hearty laughter from everyone. Gracie felt alone. For all their niceness, she wasn't now, wasn't ever, going to be part of this group. They were a closed circle.

Lucy and Joanne were working behind the scenes, filling cups of water and ushering performers to the foot of the stage. There was a juggling act, a stand-up comedian, someone read poetry, and there was an awkward skit involving people carrying cardboard boxes as if they were the heavy weights of sin.

Gracie belabored clearing her throat a few times between performances to establish a credible excuse for leaving early. Her stomach rumbled but she refused to eat the cakes and sticky buns the others seemed to consume with such abandon. *Junk food*. Sugar and flour from who knows where, combined with mistreated-animal products. *Just get up, pretend to go to the bathroom then slip out the side door.* She was getting ready to excuse herself when a hush fell over the crowd.

Daniella took the stage, the microphone held gently in front of her with both hands. Her ascent of the stage had left her breathless. She took a moment to compose herself. The silence, the tension, added gravitas to her stage presence, as if the physical investment of her labored breathing increased the value of whatever it was that she was about to say.

"God-given talents," she began, still breathing heavily. "You ever hear people use that phrase?"

Daniella looked out encouragingly at the nodding silhouettes.

"Yes?" she nodded vigorously. "Sure we have. We hear people say it all the time. Heck, we saw some God-given talents on display here tonight."

Grins and searching looks rippled through the audience.

"But what does it mean?" Her gaze traveled the crowd. "What. Does. It. Mean?" the microphone sputtered with static.

Daniella caught her breath. "Well, guys, the things you can do, the things you can feel." She cleared her throat softly. "These things are all gifts. They're gifts from God. That's what God does. He gives. He provides."

People were nodding so much now some moved their whole bodies in agreement.

"Your talents. The food we eat. The water we drink. The air we breathe. It's all there for us, whether we want it or not." Daniella was bending forward, leaning towards her audience, as if reducing the height, the pedestal of the stage. "We don't have to ask for it," she said. "It's just there." She nodded, slowly.

Gracie nodded slightly.

"Pretty good deal, right?" Daniella looked around the room. A few voices called out in agreement. "All these gifts," said Daniella, throwing up one of her hands, "and they're just for you." Daniella walked to the side of the stage, to Gracie's side of the audience. "All we have to do is show up," Daniella continued. "Pretty easy, right?" She said rhetorically. A few people nodded; a few more shook their heads. Daniella furrowed her brow. "What you do with it though, guys, well … that's the part that's up to you."

Gracie leaned forward in her chair. She put her arms on the table.

"You know why God has done all of those things?" Daniella was smiling now. "Because God likes you," she said. "He really likes you," she added softly, personally. "You see, He made you. And He thinks you're pretty great." Her face softened. There was near silence in the room now. "That's why God provides for you. Because He loves you. And He will love you and support you, and help you, no matter how bad you've been or how many times you screw up. Because He believes in you. He will always be there when you need Him."

Glen's guitar played softly. Gracie didn't know the song. It seemed sad. But also hopeful. He played beautifully. A hand reached for Gracie's. It was Ruth, sitting beside her. Chelsea took the other. Gracie let them. Singing started somewhere from behind her. It soon filled the room.

Gracie cried. And she didn't care who saw.

Chapter Twenty-Five

Palm leaves swayed in the breeze as the last helicopter took to the sky.

The storm was on its way. It had been building for days and was now 125 miles north-east of Fiji, and carrying sustained winds of 65 mph—not quite enough to officially classify as a hurricane, but that didn't stop the colorful headlines appearing in the regional press about a deadly hurricane alternately 'blowing', 'howling' and 'heaving' its way across the South Pacific.

Peter had followed the red and blue blobs of data on the Doppler radar. He watched them creep over the open sea, the same dots that would make landfall on L'Eden Sur Mer by six o'clock that evening.

Talk of the coming storm had even made the evening news back home, and he'd called Alma.

"Don't worry," he told her. "The media always exaggerates these things."

"I will worry," she said. "Just promise me you will not do something stupid."

"Like what?"

"I don't know. I cannot imagine. But if there is an opportunity, just please, do the right thing."

"Okay," said Peter, unsure of what he was agreeing to. Alma needed reassurance; she was easy to reassure.

It didn't look like a storm was coming as Peter pounded the sand on his daily run. The skies over L'Eden Sur Mer were patchy but otherwise bright, and the Pacific gently lapped the island's bleached pebble shores.

He had run every day since arriving on the island, at least ten miles. It was a regimen he hadn't followed since university, and the exercise had left him feeling lithe and nimble. It had been heavy work trudging through the sand dunes on those first few mornings, but he now sprang over them with effortless grace. Some days he felt like he wasn't even running, but floating over the landscape, his bare feet hardly touching the ground.

The coming storm had already claimed its first casualties—those who had stayed on after the official conference proceedings had left the island, called away by the embassies and insurance companies unwilling to shoulder the risk of their people riding out a tropical storm in a developing country.

Nash had left suddenly, a scrawled message stuffed under Peter's door: Sorry. *All that glitters is not gold.* A change of heart? Nash's involvement in the project was vital, and his sudden departure threatened to sink the whole thing. Nash's reluctance to support him had seemed to Peter an example of what he hated most—a man who had lost his hunger, his taste for ingenuity. Nash was, after all, a man whose confidence was built only on what he had achieved, not what he might still accomplish. In the end, Nash was just like Peter's father: conservative not by choice but from a lack of imagination.

Peter took another's cowardice personally, as if it somehow weakened him, diminished the whole of his species. Who was it said that idleness always favored the oppressor? Nash's inaction was an example of mankind's fundamental reluctance to get involved. He would have to change Nash's mind, but he would have to worry about that later.

The thought of Nash spurred Peter on. He quickened his pace through the shallow water along the coastline, leaping over the occasional wave that broke higher than his knees. He was in the best shape of his life. He was breathing easily, despite the exertion, imagining the steady, rhythmic pump of his heart, dutifully feeding the rest of his body as he ploughed through the still morning air. He was a machine, an engine designed to move forward and never stop.

With the sun just risen, there weren't too many people around. A few clumps of women were doing the family washing, beating the clothes against the smooth rocks of the lagoon; a handful of men hauled buckets of water out of a well and farmers sprinkled fertilizer on their crops from hand-held plastic bags. *Didn't they know the storm was coming?* People had started waving to Peter as he passed; he wasn't sure when it had started, but he now looked forward to this morning ritual. He depended on it to complete his experience of the day.

Kids thought it funny, the way he ran. They sometimes mimicked him, flailing their arms in the air, puffing and snorting. Peter supposed they weren't used to seeing adults run for no reason. He motioned for them to join him. They were reluctant at first, but a few of them eventually did, half playing tag with each other, laughing, but following him all the same. They were good runners, some of these boys, and Peter wondered what some of them might do, what they might become, had they been born in a different place, under different circumstances. He liked these moments, when two or three village boys joined him for a jog along the shore. They might stay alongside him awhile, a mile or two, but they would soon peel away and return home.

Peter had always wanted to run with his own son. He had tried to encourage Stephen, but the boy had shown no interest in sports. *Perhaps I spoiled the children.* Maybe he should have been stricter with Stephen and Gracie? Or maybe less strict? His own father had been such a reluctant parent, a generational characteristic he supposed, but Peter had sought to correct the shortcomings of his own father's approach to parenting by being a strong role model in Stephen and Gracie's lives. Peter hadn't always been there for them. He knew that. It had caused problems. But he had wanted to lead by example; he wanted to demonstrate that life must be taken; it must be shaped; it must be controlled.

Otherwise it just slipped through your fingers like a handful of sand. The island would be his legacy.

A chainsaw interrupted his thoughts, cutting through the thick quiet of the morning. A man was carving a hull out of a single tree, gradually shaping a canoe.

Peter kept to the shoreline, his bare feet cooled by the long reach of the incoming waves. On the horizon the soft glow of the rising sun made that ball of fire seem friendlier somehow, more personal. It would rise into the sky, growing hotter as the day wore on. By noon it would beat down on the shadowless landscape. But the sun had not yet chased the cool from the morning; it had not yet sent life retreating to the shade and under the ground. For now it cast long, pleasant shadows across the landscape and drew people out to greet it. For now it was their star. Peter spotted a sand fly swooping and diving just a few feet ahead of him, whizzing away from his legs as they spun through the sand. He sped up, chasing the fly for no reason but to enjoy watching it dart his coming footsteps. The fly got tired of zigzagging so low to the ground and lifted up and away, over a cluster of palm trees that were beginning to sway.

Peter drew to a stop. A light breeze stirred the morning's humidity. He heard the slow tearing of the surf breaking against a distant reef, where the raw waves of the open ocean, having travelled untold distances, finally broke ashore. He knelt at the edge of the water where the waves arrived in gentle, frothy mounds and picked up a handful of sand; let it sift through his fingers. It was a mixture of bleached pebbles, bits of clamshell and shards of coral reef, all of it ground down by years of pounding surf. How long had they been out here, these bits of detritus? Was he the first person to touch them, these pulverized fragments of the Earth? It seemed possible. Out there was the ocean. Different parts were called by different names but they were all connected, weren't they, swirled and mixed by the currents. The water didn't care about maritime borders.

He looked out to sea and wondered where in the world his little boats might be. To what far-flung reaches of the globe would those little islands travel? He imagined them bobbing along the ocean currents, crossing shipping lanes—maybe even his own ships—twirling in the wake of the freighters as they circled the globe. Some of his little islands would be out there already battling against the coming storm. Others might have reached the safety of land. He thought of them scattered on distant shorelines, the little green and white pods, landing on resort towns in Bali and Fiji, where children would be distracted from building their sandcastles by something floating in the water. They might pick up his island and bring it to their parents. He thought about his islands running aground in Australia and Europe and North America. He thought about all the beaches he had visited and imagined the settings with his models drifting ashore. His conquest. He thought of couples strolling along the beaches of Sydney and Miami and Vancouver and Hong Kong and coming across one. He liked the idea of those little islands creating a moment of wonder and connection for those who might find them, his messages in bottles. That was the way it was supposed to work.

Nash's website recorded a few vessels that had already made landfall in Fiji and Indonesia. The rest would come. This flotilla would start a global conversation about his plan. It would become his greatest achievement. He would win this war with the sea. The sea could be beaten. Nature could be tamed. The Dutch already had their triumph. This one would be his. Peter washed his hands in the shallows of the water and continued on his way.

Chapter Twenty-Six

Mall decorations were in transition. It was a holiday vacuum, the space between Halloween, Thanksgiving and Christmas. Gone were the jack-o-lanterns, the plastic spiders and the cotton cobwebs. The turkeys and autumnal baskets of yams, too, had been stashed in boxes for another year. Gracie and Alma strolled along the mezzanine, looking down into the food court, a panopticon of world cuisine.

Gracie had been busy, throwing herself into work at the Christian Fellowship. She had stuffed envelopes and answered phones, ordered stationery and paraded around the student union building handing out flyers to people she knew would just turn around and throw them in the trash. Some didn't even bother to wait until they were out of her sightline before dumping the leaflets she had given them. Why did they take them in the first place? People were so wasteful. Gracie had fundraised, she had sold raffle tickets and magazine subscriptions; she had spent a whole weekend putting up posters for a Christian rock/pop band that was apparently well known and well respected in the university music scene. It was not glamorous work. It was far from tending to wounded soldiers or walking among grateful lepers in some remote colonial outpost, but she hadn't expected that. The Christian Fellowship wasn't perfect, but it was something. She knew what she was getting into. Gracie had expected to feel better, though. She had expected to feel something like relief, a fulfillment at answering God's call.

She had agreed to buy a few items to put into a silent auction at an upcoming fundraiser and had asked Alma to help her shop. So here they were, browsing the shops at Westgate Mall. They had been there an hour and had only spent half of the $500 allocated for the purchases. Gracie had wanted to buy a few gift certificates and be done with it, but her mother had insisted the two of them be a little more creative in their approach to the silent auction.

Alma was excited, and buzzed from shop to shop. This task offered her a rare opportunity where her interests merged with Gracie's. She was not about to let the experience slip through her fingers.

"What about these?" Alma held up one of a pair of carved, mahogany bookends in the shape of Atlas, but instead of holding up the world, Atlas was holding up a stack of books.

Gracie looked at her mother, blankly.

"Not cool?" said Alma.

"Mom, the stuff's got to be for students," she said. "Think twenty-something. Not … retired."

"Well I don't know," said Alma, sliding the bookend back onto the shelf.

They visited a florist, a chocolatier, a jeweler and an electronics superstore. The two of them browsed through a novelty gift shop that promised 'all things weird and wonderful'. Neither Gracie nor Alma felt comfortable looking at each other among the tee-shirts with fake boobs on them, penis-shaped drink bottles and decks of playing cards decorated with pornographic images. Alma thought these things tacky, Gracie found them confronting, and they both agreed to leave the store after only a few minutes spent absently browsing the contents of its shelves.

They strolled the wide, heated boulevards of Westgate Mall and ate frozen yoghurt even though it was freezing outside.

"Hey Mom," said Gracie. "How did you know when you were

grown up?"

The question came from nowhere. Alma wasn't sure she understood it. Did Gracie mean physically grown up? Emotionally? Alma was hesitant; she didn't want to spoil the intimacy of the moment by having to clarify what Gracie had meant. She feared Gracie might catch herself and withdraw if she felt her mother wasn't following her meaning. Alma so wanted to understand— her own life had been so different from her children's. Alma had already learned to be self-sufficient by Stephen's age; had learned to speak three languages, and had seen first-hand what real poverty looks like, all the while surrounded by diplomats and Saudi royalty. When she and Peter had started their life together it held the intoxicating promise and enthusiasm of youth. Now it seemed distant, muddied by years of disappointments and compromise. What could she say to Gracie? How could she answer truthfully without pouring water on the flames of passion and intensity that still flickered inside her daughter?

"It's when you're no longer sure," said Alma.

Gracie crinkled her nose. "Sure about what?"

"About anything," said Alma, already regretting her words. She should have said something else. But what? It didn't really matter what, but something more … uplifting. She tried to recover the ground, the trust she felt her answer had lost. "You know things change in life. Things don't stay the same. Sometimes change happens fast. Sometimes slow. But it happens. Do you know what I mean?" She felt sure there was something helpful, something constructive in what she had to say. She had mentally translated what she might have said in French, but her meaning was no clearer in either language. There was a thought in her mind, but it danced around in the air, like a mosquito on the breeze, unable to stay still for long enough to bear down on it with both hands. Maybe if her English was better. Maybe if her French was better. Even now, after all of these years, she would sometimes struggle to remember a word and wonder if it was a word she had ever known.

"Is everything okay?" said Alma, trying to change tack. It was a more motherly thing to say.

Gracie wanted to talk to her mother—to someone—about the world and about God. But she felt certain her mother would not understand. Gracie felt sorry for her. She was so fragile and skittish. She could be closer to her mother if she weren't so desperate. So needy for the attention. It was pretty obvious. Look at her, at the mall with her golden shawl and her fire-red shoes, wanting so desperately to stand out and fit in.

Alma studied her daughter; she wanted to reach out and touch her, hold her. While she didn't feel comfortable expressing physical affection, it didn't mean that she had no desire to be close. She wanted to have a different relationship with her children than the one she'd had with her parents. She wanted it to be open and honest, and real. She wanted to understand and support them, but she hadn't wanted to spoil them either. Perhaps she should have taught them her native language. Maybe then things might have been different. They might have understood her better. They might have known where she had come from, what values she had grown up with. But things were never that simple.

Moving from country to country, Alma had decided that she would speak English to them from the moment they were babies. She had wanted her family to be normal, for her children to fit in. She didn't want them to be the weird kids with the foreign parents and the exotic past. Alma had resented that all her life. She wanted normalcy. The decision to speak English at home had been part of that goal. It had been strange for her at first, whispering a foreign language into the crib at night. It felt unnatural. But it had been for the good of the children.

"Yeah," said Gracie. "I don't know. I think I'm just really tired."

"You okay?" said Alma.

Gracie nodded.

The moment, if it had been there, had passed.

The mall exit was streaked with slushy footprints. It had snowed while they had been inside. The grey asphalt of the parking lot was transformed into a fluffy and glistening white.

"It's so beautiful, don't you think?" said Alma. "I always like this, you know, when winter starts."

Alma breathed in the crisp air. People pushed past them on their way into the mall. The stairs were icy and Gracie lost her footing but Alma caught her before she fell. Gracie hung on to her mother's arm, dangled there a moment. They stayed there, the two of them, levered against each other, a clumsy circus act, swinging oversized paper shopping bags to regain their balance. They laughed as people walked by.

"Be careful, it's icy," said Alma, smiling, and to no one in particular. "That could have been really bad."

"Oh look," said Alma, making her way down the stairs. She reached the bottom and held her hand up, offering to help Gracie down the rest of the stairs. Gracie took it. Alma tilted her face to the sky. "Look at the size of the flocks."

"Flakes," said Gracie.

"Oh, it's so beautiful," said Alma. "They are really floating. You see?"

The flakes drifted down, thick and brittle. Alma stuck out her tongue and closed her eyes. "They are so soft," she said, snowflakes collecting on her eyelashes.

Gracie watched her mother, standing at the entrance to the mall with her arms outstretched and her tongue out.

"It's a bit gross if you think about it," said Gracie.

"No, come on, don't spoil this for me now. You try."

Gracie looked around. People streamed in and out of the mall, loaded up cars, not appearing to give them much notice. She rolled her eyes and stuck out her tongue. The flakes tickled her nose and melted on her tongue. The snow thawed as it fell, warmed by the glow of life in her body. Gracie peeked at her mother, whose eyes were still closed, her tongue out. Gracie smiled.

Chapter Twenty-Seven

A man's silhouette slipped inside the door and pushed hard against it, fighting to keep it from being pushed open again by the screaming wind outside. The door shut, muffling the noise from outside. The silhouette walked up the corridor of the Sur Merian parliament building and reached President Koyl, whispering in his ear, "Communications are down."

Koyl nodded and dismissed the messenger. The President rubbed his palms together, massaging his own hands as he glanced around the room.

A few members of parliament and their families had opted to ride out the squall from inside parliament's thick grey walls. The rest of the government were bracing against the weather from inside their concrete shacks.

The parliament building was built in 1981, paid for by a combination of low-interest loans from the International Bank for Reconstruction and Development, and the International Monetary Fund. A symbol of the country's nascent independence, L'Eden Sur Mer's Parliament House was really no more than a low, sprawling bunker, but it had narrow, double-glazed windows and was made of reinforced concrete. It was a good place to wait out a tropical storm.

The stout frame muted the sound of the howling wind, yet the storm was picking up speed. About a hundred people had gathered inside the chamber of the Legislative Assembly, a plain, oblong room at the center of the building that comfortably sat fifty people when parliament was in session. With a hundred bodies trapped for an indeterminate period of time, the place was decidedly less comfortable.

The coughing and spluttering of old men echoed in the chamber. People had hastily bundled their belongings into tarps, sheets and plastic bags, which were piled up around the room. They sat on cushions on the floor, or sprawled out on blankets, or busied themselves stringing bed sheets on clotheslines to carve out some privacy in the large, damp room. Mothers shushed their crying babies, bounced them on their knees, rocked them over their shoulders. There was no consoling them as the wind and rain beat down.

President Koyl had invited Pyami's widow, Mareta. It was the least he could do for the wife of one of his most loyal supporters. Even at her advanced age, Mareta had agreed to take charge of her daughter's three young children, who now played with the microphones on the desks in the chamber and spun around on the wide, black leather chairs.

"*Maht, Maht.*" Mareta called the children down from the furniture.

Peter had heard those words many times since he had arrived. It seemed to him like a catchall phrase for getting someone's attention. Peter watched Koyl touch the old woman's shoulder. He seemed supported by it, leaning ever so slightly. From a distance, it wasn't entirely clear who was doing the consoling.

Mareta had once been a beautiful woman, Koyl thought. Her looks had faded, or rather, had sunken just below the surface of her weathered face. It was not easy for women once their husbands were gone. Mareta reminded Koyl of how much time had passed, of the history they had shared, and how much he missed his old friend. Mohala Koyl felt the weight of the years gone by, how they folded in on top of one another, each one less distinguishable from the previous, like the waves upon waves upon waves of crashing foam now shattering the open ocean as far as the eye could see. Koyl held Mareta's hand. It felt small.

"You'll be safe here," said Koyl. He wanted to get out of the Legislative Assembly chamber. It made him feel listless. He walked aimlessly, his footsteps echoing in the empty corridors. In his office he passed his fingertips across the spines of the books on his shelf; it had been a long time since he had entered that room without any real reason for being there.

All of these books, what use were they, really? He stood there, in the room, his room, taking it in. The picture of himself with French President Pompidou, taken on the eve of L'Eden Sur Mer's independence, hung crookedly on the wall by his desk. Koyl straightened the frame, stood back and cocked his head to peer through the narrow window. The wind blew a low and constant hum, broken by the occasional thump of debris hitting the building: a fence post, a piece of sheet metal.

The storm was here.

Communications were down across the island. Emergency shelters had been set up inside the school and the town hall at the other end of the island. Sur Merians would now have to rely on themselves and wait out the worst of the weather. Houses would blow over and be rebuilt. This is what they had always done.

The waves weren't big, but broke with such precision and came one after another, each crest slamming on top of the one before and leaping its way up the shore, lifting everything in its path.

Thani Malhoun held a prayer vigil inside the small brick building that housed L'Eden Sur Mer's Methodist church. A number of new faces had walked in, people who didn't normally attend, but they were all welcome in this house that trembled and bowed beneath nature's onslaught.

"Our Father who art in heaven, hallowed be Thy name
Thy kingdom come, Thy will be done, on earth as in heaven.
Give us this day our daily bread.

And forgive us our trespasses,
As we forgive those who trespass against us.
And lead us not into temptation,
But deliver us from evil.
For Thine is the kingdom,
and the power, and the glory,
for ever and ever."

The storm wailed and a great wind tore the roof off the church. Malhoun and his congregation held hands, praying as the rain poured down around them and the lightning lit up their faces.

Peter stood before one of the bottom-floor windows of the parliament building. The thatched-palm roofs of the spa resort had already been carried off by the wind. He stared out to where, for weeks, he had looked upon a gentle gradient of colors: the white of the coral, the blue of the ocean, the thin line in the distance where the turquoise of the sea met the azure of the sky, all of these separated into neat, geometric bands of color that stretched all the way to the horizon.

There was none of that now.

Across the beach, swollen with rain, the sky raged in gray and black, and the sea boiled. Waves smashed anything that got in their way. A wire-link fence that had once marked some boundary was now half underwater, seaweed clinging to its metal skeleton. The churning sea whipped up a murky, frothy mixture that blew inland, the dirty foam clinging to shrubs and palm leaves like blobs of canned Christmas snow. Whole trees were torn from the ground and palm fronds, shaken loose by the wind, were cast adrift in the water, where they swirled like empty life rafts.

The breakers slammed against fences and sea walls, sending salt spray into the air like geysers. The tidal surge dislodged the mounds of garbage that collected behind houses and on the side of the road. The flotsam of tin cans and plastic bottles fanned out across the island, torn plastic bags snagged on shrubs and caught in the branches of low-hanging trees. Cardboard boxes rolled down the street, tumbling end over end until they grew heavy and sodden with water then collapsed under their own weight. Palm trees with their leaves blown back to one side swayed like giant, menacing heads with their long green hair blowing out behind them. *How could they withstand such a battering?* The wind hissed through the steel rigging of the giant flagpole. No one had thought to lower the flag, which the wind tore off its moorings and carried into the darkened sky.

What of those little wood and straw shacks he had passed on his morning runs? Those villages set back from the beach? Of Tebano, Mote and Rui, the three village boys who sometimes joined him for a few miles on his run along the beach. He had introduced himself as Peter, pointing at himself as they ran alongside him. *Pidah, Pidah* they had repeated, laughing. They hadn't said much more than that. Where were they now? In what trembling hut were they now taking shelter? They were tough, those boys, tougher than most of the men Peter knew. They would be all right. They had to be.

The lights flickered then died. There was a bustling of bodies, a rustling of bags in the dark room. One by one, candles were lit, warm pools of light hovering in the darkness. A silhouette handed Peter a candle.

"*Maht,*" said Peter.

He saw Mareta, sitting in a cave of sheets and blankets. She was stroking the hair of a little girl curled up on her lap. Peter sat next to Mareta and showed the children his candle. The children smiled and looked deep into its light.

Mareta smiled.

Peter smiled back.

He took her hand.

Chapter Twenty-Eight

Alma walked on the polished tiles of the new kitchen. The under-floor heating warmed her bare feet. She caressed the cold granite counter top; ran her fingers over the smooth, brushed steel of the drawer handles. It was all clean and new and perfect. The kitchen renovation had been completed just in time. The caterers would be arriving in a few hours, and it was a pleasure to be able to offer them a space to work in that was a cathedral to the gastronomic arts.

A kind of ceremony attended Peter's return from trips abroad. Alma always made sure the cleaners came the day before so that the place gleamed. It wasn't that Peter was particularly fastidious about cleanliness. He was partial to order, but Alma wanted to blank the canvas for his homecoming, as if disinfected tiles and a freshly vacuumed carpet helped support a literal clean start to resuming their lives together.

The Van Dooren family traditionally ate together on the evening of Peter's homecomings. Tonight would be no different.

Peter appeared thin when Alma saw him stride through the arrivals gate. His weight loss and deep tan underlined the duration of his absence. They embraced, and the body Alma felt against hers was different; sharper, more angular bits where she hadn't noticed them before.

"You didn't have to pick me up," said Peter. "I could've ordered a car." Peter hadn't meant to sound ungrateful and knew that he should modify his response. "But I'm glad you did."

Alma smiled automatically. She knew not to expect things to be different. They would be for a time. Peter would hold and kiss her, look and listen to her, even if he wasn't really interested in what she was saying, and Alma would be all the more grateful for his patience at hearing her out. They would talk about what they had done while apart; about the children, the house, but that closeness wouldn't last. She knew that. Maybe a week, maybe ten days at the most, but eventually Peter's deep kiss would become a peck on the forehead.

She understood Peter needed his trips away to generate longing for his family, to create a novelty out of his home life. She knew his affection would wear off with the jet lag. He would eventually become distracted again, preoccupied and grouchy, but for now, Alma enjoyed the temporary pleasure of his full attention.

"What was the highlight of the trip?" It was the same question she always asked when he returned.

"Coming home, of course." It was the same answer he always gave, and they chuckled together at the familiar routine of it. "It was a confusing place." Peter let the words hang there, unsure even what he had meant. "Really strange."

The two of them walked the short distance through the airport lounge to the waiting car. There were no gift shops or crowded gates to walk through, one of the benefits of flying privately. Peter noticed that he was walking slower than Alma, and that she was adjusting her natural gait to keep pace with him.

"You want me to drive?" said Alma.

"Sure."

Alma was surprised. Peter usually preferred to drive.

Once they were in the car, Peter reclined the seat. God it was comfortable. He shut his eyes. For weeks the world had seemed … flat. And then, rising in that helicopter seemed to add a new dimension. Peter saw more than he understood. He looked down at the wreckage of that land, at the twisted, molten landscape. The force of the propeller blades had sent a giant blue tarp flapping and twisting in the wind, and, as the helicopter rose, the tarp settled back, blanketing a row of stacked cadavers.

As Peter ascended, he perceived the scale of the disaster all at once, the flattened matchstick houses, the way the water had carved out the landscape, hacking channels through the brush. He saw bodies partially buried under the mud. The sea was calm now, bright and gentle; a gesture of peace. The sharp, white coral outline of L'Eden Sur Mer appeared against the deep blue of the Pacific. From this height the islands' narrow reef systems spread out like the bleached skeletons of giant cattle.

That was, what? A day ago. He didn't feel much like talking, but knew that he must. Alma was pulling the hair at the base of her neck, a sure sign of anxiety. Was she even aware of it?

"You ever hear of a guy by the name of Holden Nash?" he said.

"No," said Alma, concentrating on the road. "Should I?"

"No," said Peter, his eyes still shut. "I'm just replaying a few conversations over in my head. Sorry."

"It's okay," said Alma. "You've been through a lot. I'm glad you're okay. You don't have to talk if you don't want to."

Peter opened his eyes. He smiled at Alma, put a hand on her knee then turned to look out the window.

Alma did care about Peter's interests, and she was interested in that ill-fated island, she just felt that Peter launched into these kinds of details too quickly. He always did that. Didn't warm up to a subject; he hit it head on. Alma felt more comfortable talking around something first, feeling the subject out. Doing so allowed her to come to grips with the implications of what she was saying. It took Alma a discussion to discover what she thought about something. Peter didn't work that way. He said nothing until he was certain about it. Peter committed an opinion only once he had weighed and considered and debated the thing inside his mind.

She was frustrated. Jealous. She had not been part of his experience, had been fed only the tiniest morsels about his adventure on those cursed discussions via cell phone. Now she was expected to sit through this … this silence? No. It was her turn. It was her turn to be considered, her turn to be asked questions, her turn to be heard.

There was a limit to human sympathy. She had seen the news. She knew the storm had been bad. There were bodies, little bodies. She'd seen them on the news, wrapped in blue plastic sheets. She'd had enough. Enough of droughts and fires, and dustbowls bankrupting farmers, enough of stories about wars and earthquakes, and tsunamis, and poor little Afghani children with their limbs blown off. It was all too much. Too much to be shown pictures, day after day, of babies with distended bellies and their eyes covered with flies. It was all too much. The stories of pedophiles and serial killers, and shallow graves dug in suburban backyards, of child prostitutes smuggled across the world in shipping containers, of women imprisoned and beaten in their own homes. No one person could expect to take all that in and make sense of it, much less respond in any meaningful way. The world was not her community; it was not her family.

She was not a saint, and she had never claimed to be. Alma had done her best. She had raised two children, had taught them to respect others and to stand up for what they believed. Surely that counted for something. Surely that made a contribution. What more could the world ask of her. The more she thought about other people's problems, the more pressing and significant her own family's needs became.

The car was hot. Peter had cranked up the heat. He always did that.

"Do you mind if I turn down the heat?" she asked.

Peter studied the console. "It's a dual system," he said. "Each seat has its own climate control. Here, I'll adjust your side of the car."

Without waiting for Alma's response, Peter started to fiddle with a knob on the dash. "Here, what temperature do you want?"

It was so like Peter to oppose her opinion on mechanical grounds. She was hot, dual system or not. And yet, it was just like Peter to see the utility of these devices because they *should* work, even when they didn't, as if, above all else, his duty was in defending the engineering of the thing.

"There," he said. Peter sat back in his seat and watched the landscape whiz by outside. The distant trees and houses seemed to cruise past his window as if the whole view were being carried on a conveyer belt. It had been weeks since he had been in a car, and he became aware of just how fast they were travelling. This freeway bypass had been a godsend. Its completion had meant one could avoid the maze of suburban streets and traffic lights below. But Peter felt there was something unsettling about the speed at which they hurtled down the freeway. Alma drove too fast. That was it. She didn't have a great sense of the road, of what other cars might be doing around her. She followed them too closely. There would be no time to react if something went wrong.

"That better now?" said Peter, hearing the fan stop on Alma's side of the car.

Alma adjusted herself into her seat. "It's fine."

Tires crunched gravel as the sedan wound its way up the driveway. Moments later, Peter stood at the foot of the staircase in the entrance hall of his own home. It was bright in here.

"Where are the kids?" he said.

"Stephen is here somewhere; I know he wants to see you. Stephen!" Alma called up the stairs. No response. "Stephen?" Alma's eyes wandered up the long, gentle curve of the staircase. "Maybe he is out," she said without looking back.

Peter stood in the hallway, a hand in his pocket.

"You must be tired?" said Alma.

"Not really." He rubbed the back of his head. "Think I'll have a shower, though."

"Oh wait. I want to show you something first." Alma smiled. She took Peter gently by the hand and led him through the long sun-lit hallway. "Come on."

Peter followed, his other hand still in his pocket. He could smell paint. Alma flicked on the lights in the kitchen.

"Ta da," she said. "What do you think? Do you like it? It's beautiful, don't you think?"

"Wow," said Peter. He squinted in the glare of the track lighting overhead. "It's a real difference." The smell of fresh paint was sharp in his nostrils.

"You like it?"

"It's really, ah, modern." He panned the expanse of the new kitchen's gleaming glass and metallic surfaces.

"I wanted it to be a surprise for when you came home," said Alma at his side. She was looking up at him expectantly.

"No, yeah, it's a great idea." He nodded enthusiastically. Too much? "I like it," he said.

He put his arm around Alma and drew her near. She leaned into his body, head on his chest. Peter rubbed her shoulder with one hand, the other still in his pocket.

"I really like it," he said. "Thank you."

The dining room had been off limits to Gracie and Stephen until a few years ago. Its thick white carpet and heavy antique table—wood salvaged from some important ship—were reserved for the most special occasions. Stephen had once spilled glue on the table while assembling a model airplane, and the panic that his accident caused had left him wary of the room. It was not so much a space for living as an area set aside, shielded from the family's collected inadequacies that threatened to undermine the order of the place. The way the room was tucked away from the rest of the house, shut up behind lockable glass doors, also made it uninviting, a hermetically sealed, life-sized diorama of upper-class respectability. And so it was in this room—the room in which Peter and Alma had once hosted the French ambassador who had, by all accounts, made a complete fool of himself; the room where champagne corks popped and turkey was carved; the room better known to caterers than to the Van Doorens them-selves—that Peter, Alma, Gracie and Stephen now ate together in celebration of Peter's return.

The four of them were grouped together near the center of the table to avoid making a mockery of its grand proportions. The caterer knew what he was doing; he had prepared a simple, three-course dinner of goat's cheese salad, poached salmon and a citrus-fruit sorbet. With winter setting in and the nights growing colder, he had originally proposed a more seasonally appropriate menu: pork loins, maybe, or even a duck curry, but Alma had wanted the dishes to attune with Peter's sojourn in a more temperate climate.

"It's wonderful. Just wonderful," said Alma as the caterer poured the segue dessert wine into a pair of long-stemmed glasses Alma had never seen.

Good idea. That had been Peter's reaction to the new kitchen. Maybe Alma had expected too much from him, but his reaction left her wondering how much less of a reaction there could have been. He could have ignored her, she supposed. Maybe it had been a dumb idea to redo the kitchen. The old one had been perfectly functional. But that wasn't the point. Alma had invested herself in the project, had thrown herself into looking at color swatches and tile samples, and shades of grout. She had made the thousands of tiny decisions that collectively accomplished the seamless, coordinated look of the place. He could have said more. She downed the wine.

Stephen slouched forward in his chair. He could feel the dense ring of fat gathered around his belly, like a half-deflated buoy around his waist, preventing him from moving too far forward. He had long felt shame about his body. He often moped in front of full-length mirrors in his underwear, grabbing handfuls of flab and kneading it between his fingers, imagining what he might look like—how he might feel—if he could gather up all the fat that he could hold with both hands and make it disappear. Better yet, he could donate it to skinny people, a bit here, a bit there; they wouldn't even notice. That would be a cool superpower to have.

But he didn't feel that way tonight. He didn't feel lopsided or clumsy, or awkward. He didn't feel soft or slow. He felt heavy. He felt solid. He felt strong. Stephen felt protected by his weight. It was a shield as his father watched him eat. His father seemed small to him—shrunken—his diminished authority no less arbitrary than the absurd prohibitions surrounding this very room. Stephen took a third, exploratory helping of sorbet, if only to goad Peter into responding with one of his trademark quips:

The sorbet's nice, isn't it?

Or …

I think fruit is the best dessert.

Or …

Did you have gym class today?

But Peter said nothing. He just sat there, eating precise spoonfuls of sorbet he scraped out of his bowl like a surgeon with a scalpel. Stephen's thoughts drifted to Gaia; he had logged ninety online hours for the company. He felt smug about that, about not having told his father what he was doing. Secrets were empowering. An image of Sara's round, perky behind rose in his mind. He imagined sliding himself between those thighs. He wouldn't even thrust. He would be happy to just stay there, knowing he was inside her.

"Your father's taking me to New York," said Alma. What would she wear? A dress? That Chanel suit was still in the basement. *See, I knew it would come in handy.*

Gracie, who had barely said a word all evening, looked up from her untouched plate with raised eyebrows.

"President Koyl is going to address the United Nations and we're going to be his guests," said Peter, a frown forming as both Stephen and Gracie neglected to acknowledge the grandeur of the occasion.

"I hear he's a crook," said Gracie.

Peter briefly felt about Gracie the way he imagined Koyl must have felt about Malhoun. For all its charm, there was nothing so grating as the naïve exuberance of youth.

"You shouldn't talk about things of which you have no idea," said Peter.

Gracie stared at her father. Was his spoon trembling at the end of his bony fingers? *Geez, relax.*" She took in a spoonful of sorbet. "Sorry. I didn't mean to insult your dictator friend."

"Gracie!" said Alma sharply, frowning.

"Okay. Sorry," said Gracie.

"So when are you guys taking off?" said Stephen.

"When did you say we'd go? Thursday, was it?" Alma looked to Peter.

Peter stared at Gracie then took a deep breath. "Thursday," he confirmed and lowered his eyes.

Stephen slowly slid a large spoonful of sorbet into his mouth.

"And Gracie," said Alma, "We were hoping you could come and stay at the house while we're away."

Stephen's attention snapped back to the conversation. "What? Why? I don't need a babysitter?"

This was so typical of his parents. To talk about the importance of maturity, of independence and self-belief and then do something that completely undermined all of those things. They must really think of him as a child. Carol often went away for the weekend and left Tal alone. Stephen never told his parents that, of course, fearing they might not agree to his going over there on those occasions. He could feel his pride deflating. He felt tight in his clothes again, could feel the pressure of his stomach against the button of his trousers.

"It's not that we don't trust you," said Alma. "We would just feel better knowing that the two of you were together, that's all."

She did that, Alma. She said things like that, things that somehow turned what she had said into something else.

"Whatever," said Stephen.

The caterer reappeared in the room, which had grown quiet, save for the tinkling of silver spoons on fine crystal bowls.

"How was everything, Ma'am?" he said.

"Very nice," said Peter without looking up.

"Thank you, Tom," said Alma smiling broadly.

Chapter Twenty-Nine

The Van Dooren house was quiet, its large, bright rooms slowly filled with the morning sun. Alma and Peter had left for New York two days ago, leaving Gracie and Stephen together at the house. It had only been a few months since Gracie had moved out, but it still felt odd to Stephen to see her around all the time. His sister had always been a little intense, but there was a new, brooding quality about her that made her seem permanently unapproachable. What was with the haircut? It was completely shaved at the back, leaving only a few of her curls around the crown of her forehead. It looked to Stephen like a bit of a hack job.

In an unexpected act of generosity, though, Gracie had let Stephen retain control of the pool house. She said it smelled like boys in there now, and pretty much left Stephen to himself. Gracie stayed in her old room upstairs, where she kept to herself, locked away for hours at a time doing God knew what. His sister had never been into the kind of stuff that normal kids were; she didn't really like music. She did, but it was always something weird, some world music with kooky instruments that no one had ever heard of—not the kind of thing you really enjoyed.

Stephen thought Gracie tried too hard to be different and he believed she would be a lot happier if she just lightened up and let herself have fun every once in a while. He didn't dare invite her over to the pool house to watch a movie or play video games, expecting that she would probably offer some kind of fundamental rebuke of those activities. She was a downer and Stephen didn't want to have to deal with Gracie's high-handed condemnation of the things he liked to do, so he mostly left her alone.

Gracie woke up and rubbed the back of her head. It felt strange and bristly. She had taken to waking up late. She had dropped the astronomy class that had forced her to go in early on Mondays and Wednesdays. It seemed the right thing to do. But she felt no better for it. How much penitence was enough? If she woke before 10am these days, she rarely got out of bed before noon. She would doze fitfully, waking occasionally, and glance around the various items she had collected over the years.

She now regarded many of these artifacts with a kind of distant curiosity. The stuffed animals, the throw cushions, and the movie posters now seemed like set pieces in a re-creation of her own life. Whatever had motivated her to buy, much less string up, a pink and blue Chinese parasol was now lost on her. Gracie might wander downstairs to prepare a plate of something if she was hungry—mostly just chunks of iceberg lettuce—but she would always bring it back upstairs and eat it in bed. The world just seemed more manageable if it was limited to the small slice of it that was visible outside of her bedroom window. It was enough to watch the shadows creep across her carpet and wait for the few remaining birds, the ones that had not yet travelled south for the winter, to hop along the bare branches of the maple tree outside. She could see part of that tree from her bed, its leaves in full autumn retreat. It was enough to wake in the morning and see which leaves remained and which ones had blown away in the night. She fell asleep without expecting dreams.

In the pool house, Stephen ate a microwaved burrito. He had stopped at the grocery store on his way home from school to pick up a few supplies. It was fast food, mostly, stuff that he could either just cook in the microwave or eat out of a box, but it had felt like a grown-up thing to do: browse the aisles and think about what he might need for later. He even bought some toilet paper, having noticed he would probably run out soon.

The pool house was now *his* house, *his* domain, a personal enclave on the Van Dooren estate where he was afforded a kind of limited sovereignty.

It was 9pm. *Still early.* Maybe he would watch a movie later, but first he would log an hour or so with Gaia. He clicked on the homepage and frowned. The Gaia website was recognizable in the background, but it had been ghosted out, its links deactivated. A full-page banner had been posted over the homepage.

The domain name associated with Gaia Enterprises has been seized by IPCAA (Intellectual Property and Consumer Affairs Authority), Fraud Investigations, Department of Justice. The contents of this page have been appropriated in accordance with a seizure warrant obtained by the Department of Justice and issued pursuant to 18 C.F.C.C. Sections 981 and 2421 of the Supreme Court.

A Federal grand jury has indicted several individuals and entities allegedly involved in the operation of Gaia Enterprises, its related websites and holdings, charging them with the following federal crimes:

Fraud by False Representation [18 C.S.C & 612 (f)]; Conspiracy to Commit Racketeering [18 C.S.C & 1962 (d)]; Criminal Copyright Infringement [18 C.S.C & 1956 (h)]; and Conspiracy to Commit Money Laundering (18 C.S.C 505, 302, 221 & 303).

Stephen stared at the panel plastered over the familiar Gaia website. He clicked around the screen a few times, but the site was completely frozen. He hadn't done anything wrong. Had he? At this thought, he half braced himself for … what? For someone lurking in a darkened corner to say: "Freeze! Gotcha!"? For a swat team to come bursting through the window? Absurd.

Stephen got up from his desk and drew the blinds on the patio door to look outside. What was he even looking for? *Something, anything out of the ordinary.* Outside everything looked as it had the night before and the night before that. It was raining. The lights of the main house were all out, only the garden lights glowed around the sodden, uncut lawn.

Mohala Koyl arrived in New York City for the second time in his life. He absently leafed through the tourist brochures in his hotel room. He had no intention of visiting any of the destinations they suggested. Staring out the window at the clutter of buildings, he yearned to see the horizon.

The President of L'Eden Sur Mer was scheduled to address the United Nations General Assembly that afternoon. Koyl's own parliament had openly criticized the President's decision to go abroad so soon after the storm. He was needed at home to rally support and marshal aid, to bind the community as he once had. For some, the President's willingness to go abroad at this time was further evidence of his essentially foreign nature.

Koyl paid no heed to these criticisms. He understood the world had a short attention span. There was no better moment than the aftermath of the storm to remind the international community of their moral responsibility to assist him. His people were in need. The storm had irreparably damaged churches, had torn up schools and flooded roads. Koyl would make the international community see that without their help, this was the beginning of the end for his country. The storm would make them understand the Sur Merians were doomed without help. Soon, there would be nothing to show the island had ever been there. It would be a shipwreck, lost under the vastness of the open ocean, forever eyeing the surface.

There was a knock at the door. Koyl continued to stand and leaf through some notes he had made for his speech. There was a second knock and Koyl remembered there was no one but him to answer it. It had been a long time since he had answered a door.

A black man dressed in a baggy gray suit stood before Koyl,

staring at him and saying nothing.

"Mr President, Mohala Koyl," he finally said, reading off a small index card.

"Yes."

The little man looked withered and rumpled in his suit, but wore his ensemble with a kind of reserved dignity. "Sir, I have your car downstairs. I'm to take you to the Assembly."

He was deferent, this little black man. Professional. "Give me a few moments," said Koyl, disappearing into the bathroom. He splashed water on his face; it felt fresh, his skin cooled by the filtered air that circulated, unseen and unheard, through the hotel complex.

This would have to be the performance of his life.

Gracie, Joanne and Lucy were packing boxes of imperishable food to send out to the local homeless shelter. The food had been piling up in the donation box the Christian Fellowship had been granted permission to set up at the entrance of the student union building. It was student food, mostly—noodle soups and canned pasta—but Lucy and Joanne prepared each cardboard box with care, smoothing out the little wrinkles and air bubbles that formed under the packing tape they used to close each box. They taped the perpendicular line over each box slightly off center to form a vague cross.

The rattling and squeaking and tearing of the packing-tape roller annoyed Gracie. She felt stale and cagey under the fluorescent lights. She wanted the Christian Fellowship to do something truly meaningful and had tried to convince Daniella they should try to raise money to sue people for international war crimes or the like instead of just raising money for local homeless people.

"We fight battles, not wars, Gracie," Daniella had said.

The answer was entirely unsatisfactory. This was all too little, the stuff they were doing; it was all just Band-Aid solution stuff, and it bothered Gracie to see Lucy and Joanne so gleefully taping boxes of crappy food to send to homeless people like they were saving the world.

She sighed audibly. Lucy and Joanne must have heard her but refused to take the bait. Gracie packed her own box of goods: white one-minute rice, a sachet of Gatorade crystals, two cans of stewed tomatoes. She stopped to read the ingredients listed on a pack of soup-in-a-mug. She scanned the paragraph list of numbers and additives: skim milk powder, corn meal, preservative 270, food additives 621 and 635. It made her angry to collect this poison, give it to people, and pass it off as a good deed.

"This sucks," said Gracie.

Lucy and Joanne kept packing, squeaking and rattling and tearing the packing tape.

"What?" said Joanne dragging her tape roller across the length of a box.

"All this is just … I don't know." Gracie tossed the box of soup sachets onto the table.

"Are you going to start again on how homeless people don't matter?" said Lucy.

Gracie furrowed her brow. Is that what they thought she had said? "Of course they matter. That's not what I'm saying. Why would you think that's what I said?" Lucy and Joanne wouldn't make eye contact.

"Well, what are you saying?" said Lucy.

"I'm saying there's an element of choice there, that's all." Gracie leaned on the table. "Some people choose not to get help, you know, and I sometimes wonder if we're really doing people any favors by giving them stuff." She picked up the pack of soup again with two fingers as if it were a dirty sock.

Lucy and Joanne stared at Gracie, and she sensed they had taken personal offence to what she had said. Did they think she'd meant to belittle their commitment to this cause, maybe even to their faith? She hadn't. She'd meant to galvanize them, to embolden them. She wanted to show them there was no end to what they might accomplish if they pursued their cause with passion, knowing that God was on their side.

"I just think we might want to do something for people who really don't have anything, you know," said Gracie.

"Like what?" said Joanne defensively.

"I don't know. Take your pick." Gracie threw up her arms. "Like women in Somalia who can't even leave the house without getting raped. When they're not getting raped in it, that is. Or, like, prosecute warlords who steal all the food that's sent to people by international aid groups. I don't know." Gracie sat back in her chair. She crossed her arms. "I'm just saying this all just feels a little … safe, you know? Like it's all a bit easy. I mean, missionaries used to be willing to die for Jesus. Now we, like, write blogs for Him."

Lucy raised her eyebrows and looked at Gracie for the first time. "I think you're being a little unfair," said Lucy. "We're doing good stuff here."

"Yeah, Gracie, you're being a little … intense." Joanne kept looking at the contents of her cardboard box.

"So I'm intense. Big deal. I think we could all be a little more intense." Gracie gesticulated. "What's so wrong, so uncool about taking stuff seriously? I mean, it's like people think you're stupid just because you're not being ironic all the time. I'm sick of it."

"We *are* involved," said Joanne. "You're the one on your high horse about everything."

"It's never good enough for you," said Lucy. "You think just because you shave your head we're supposed to be all impressed."

Gracie half expected these outbursts from Lucy, but not from Joanne. She was the gentle one.

"What's my hair got to do with it?" Gracie rubbed the back of her head.

"You look like a freak," said Joanne.

Anger churned Gracie's stomach, burned up her throat. "Fuck you, Joanne."

"Seriously?" said Joanne.

Gracie felt a flush rise to her cheeks as Lucy and Joanne shared a silent look, confirming some earlier pact. The two girls then turned back to Gracie.

Lucy spoke first. "Look, you can sit there and say whatever you like, okay. Thing is, though, you go to church and everything, but you're not really part of things. You always have negative stuff to say about the people there, like they're never good enough or something."

Gracie nibbled at the inside of her lip and felt herself blinking uncontrollably.

"It's always been like that." Joanne was gentle yet firm. "It's like you're the only one who's allowed to set the rules."

"What rules?" said Gracie.

"And now," Lucy continued, ignoring the question, "you live in that apartment and then pretend like you're all uncomfortable with it and stuff … but really, I think you're pretty happy up there away from regular people. I don't see you moving out of there or into a dorm room or anything. So you can talk about suffering and dying for Jesus and everything, but really … it all ends up kind of sounding like you're just a bit spoiled, you know? Sorry, okay, but it does."

The three of them sat there at the cream-colored trestle table under the blinking fluorescent lights. Lucy stacked cans inside her cardboard box. Gracie leaned over the table, trying to get her attention. *At least look at me.* Joanne pretended to pick at a roll of tape.

"So, what? You guys are saying … that we shouldn't be friends anymore? Is that it? How after-school special is that?" said Gracie, shoulders bunched up around her ears.

Lucy and Joanne glanced toward each other before dropping their gaze to the ground.

"I'm saying I'm not sure that we ever were." Joanne didn't look up.

"Look," said Lucy, eyes blazing. "I know you love Jesus, okay. I believe that. I just don't think you really get him." She resumed packing.

The squeaking, croaking sound of the tape unfurling across the box tore through the silence of the room. Joanne slowly returned her attention to filling up her own half-filled box of food.

Gracie stood, still holding the packet of soup. "I'm going

to go."

Joanne turned cans around in her box of supplies. Lucy ironed out the wrinkles on a fresh band of tape.

"Okay," said Lucy, retying her ponytail.

Gracie zipped up her bag and walked past the girls without saying a word.

"See ya," added Lucy chirpily.

Lucy and Joanne obviously had no idea of the depth of Gracie's faith. What did they know about suffering?

Alma stared around the massive hall of the United Nations General Assembly. She felt unsettled by the stern and serious faces that filled the theater. They were men, mostly, fidgeting and rifling papers. They were smirking and laughing, shaking hands and turning to one another to whisper before the official proceedings began. Alma looked up at the rows and rows of twinkling lights, following them along the entire length of the hall. Up there were the booths and the galleries; up there the interpreters were readying themselves to feed the substance of the proceedings to their mute delegates waiting on the floor below. She was actually here.

Peter had meant well by inviting her to join him; he had meant it as a kind gesture, a gift. She was excited to be here but also missed the children and imagined the simple joy of an evening spent in their company back home.

The lights dimmed.

After a lengthy preamble from a number of delegates, the President of L'Eden Sur Mer took the stage. Peter looked around for Nash. He was nowhere to be seen. That was a battle for another time. For now Peter felt proud of Koyl and puffed up by his own association with the man.

As the President got to the top of the stairs, Alma clapped too, this was like being at the center of the world.

Mohala Koyl now stood firm at the podium, grasped its sides with both hands and leaned forward with broad shoulders. Even so, he looked small on that massive stage.

Mr President, distinguished guests, ladies and gentlemen.
My message today is simple and genuine.
Climate change is a world problem. Perhaps the first such problem that we, as a species, have faced.
For some countries, there is room for debate. There is time for discussion. For us, there can be no discussion. Our time has run out.
Strong winds, long droughts and high tides are all too real in my tiny country. I have come here as my nation still languishes in the devastation caused by one of the largest storms I have witnessed in my lifetime. One half of my people are now without a home. The storm has taken everything.
Our time is up.
Ladies and gentlemen, I say without exaggeration that our very existence is at stake.
Our existence is in your hands. We need your help. Being a small, isolated country with few people and few resources is no excuse for us not to do our part to resolve this problem.
We are in dire need of development assistance. With your help, we can fortify our land against the future comings of such a destructive force. A force of nature that is not natural, but unnatural. A creation for which we all share a measure of responsibility.
Tiny island countries like mine will feel the consequences of the decisions you make. Just as we now feel the consequences of past decisions made in rooms like this one.
L'Eden Sur Mer is sinking. My people are in danger. Our sovereignty, our language, our culture will be lost forever. If you will not assist us, I fear that we have no choice but to drown alone. Our home, and everything we have known, will be swallowed by the ocean. And we will never get it back.
In my country, we believe in vaktanoa. It is the interconnectedness of all things. More than any other event in the history of our humanity does climate change represent this belief. Our hope is that these United Nations can truly join together for the good of our collective fate.
Thank you.

As Koyl spoke, the honorable delegate from Malia thought how tragic these circumstances were, but his country too was small and poor, and he knew that his own President believed that Malia and Malians deserved to develop their country's economy on the same principles and with reliance on the same resources that the great western powers had used to propel their political and economic ascendency. Through the interpreter, the delegate from Malia heard a revolutionary tone in what Koyl was saying and, while he sympathized with the plight of the Sur Merians, it would not be his country that would pay the ransom to save them. Besides, it was increasingly clear that countries like L'Eden Sur Mer were simply unviable. Politically, economically, geographically, many of these Pacific microstates should not exist. They were nations in name only, their sovereignty inherited in a brief pang of post-colonial guilt. Sovereignty was not sacrosanct; nationhood was not an inherent right. Independence was an outcome of particular political and economic conditions. It was not a given. Failed states were no more deserving of aid than failed companies; they designed their own extinction.

The honorable delegate from Kyrgyzstan thought much the same, as did representatives from Angola, Kirwan, and Bangladesh. Mongolians, already enjoying the spoils of their recent economic development, quietly echoed those sentiments. Their country's vast natural resources of gold, copper, zinc, uranium, coal, molybdenum and oil had only just started to attract huge international attention. Mongolia was the darling of the international commodities market. It was this lonely country's turn to help fuel the insatiable appetite of the global economy and Mongolians were ready to reap the rewards. No Mongolian would entertain the thought of entering a coalition that might weaken the prospect of an increasingly brighter future for themselves and their country. If L'Eden Sur Mer needed assistance, it would have to come from the traditional centers of power and wealth. Mongolians had lived out in the cold for long enough.

The General Assembly's reception of Koyl's address was cordial. Delegates clapped politely. It was no uproar.

It was hot in here. Alma was baking inside her pantsuit. She wriggled. Trickles of perspiration slid down her rib cage. The air was stuffy; she had to remove her jacket. She stood and made her way down the row of chairs where black-suited knees thwarted her exit. She waded past them. The least they could do was stand up for her—it would have been the polite thing to do. But they didn't. They just sat there, those gray men in their black suits. They peered around her, through her as she tried to make her way past. They didn't even see her. They never had.

It was cooler in the bathroom, but not cool enough. She peeled off her jacket and put it on the counter then turned on the tap. It was good to hear the sound of running water, and she splashed some on her face before looking at herself in the mirror. She was pale. Shriveled. Her heart began to beat faster. Or was it beating slower? Or was it skipping beats? She heard it pulsing in her ears.

Alma's legs were shaking. She braced herself against the wall, setting off the automatic hand dryer. Startled by the noise, her breathing was shallow, she couldn't draw enough air into her lungs. It wouldn't go in deeply enough, leaving her hungry for the next breath. Her palms were tingling, and she scratched at them, knowing it would be of no use. The itch was inside her body. The feeling would pass. It usually did. She just needed some time. Some space. What was she doing here anyway? It was stupid. She didn't belong here. She belonged elsewhere. She belonged back home. Everything was all right there. She had made a life, a place, a home. She wanted to sit on her chair by the fire and drink a glass of wine. She turned around, back against the tiles, and slid down to sit on the floor.

She smiled to herself. She felt a bit nauseous, a bit short of breath. But she felt great. Alma had made it. She had finally been to the United Nations, and had a whole life to go home to. She was blessed.

Alma and Peter returned to their hotel room after a late dinner. She had meant to tell him about the feelings that had overcome her earlier, and had waited for the right moment to tell him that she was fine. She had meant to tell him that she was proud of him and of what he had achieved, but she hadn't. The right moment never materialized. Or rather, it seemed an even better moment would soon present itself. Even after dinner, when the warmth of the wine and the soft candlelight seemed to dim the rest of the world around them, Alma said only that she was glad she had come. It would have been too easy for him. Peter had disappointed her; he had neglected her and taken her for granted. She could not allow herself to say anything that could make him feel he had been absolved. Not yet.

It was late, but Alma wanted the evening to continue. Back in the hotel room, she poured herself a drink from the minibar. She didn't offer Peter one. He never understood why she liked a drink after dinner. Peter was in the bathroom—his evening preening routine. He spent more time in there than she did. She could just see the side of him, lit up by the glow of the bathroom lights.

Even though the hotel suite was large, Alma's movements felt constricted. Her agitation began to grow as she thought about the parade of nameless, faceless people who had temporarily stayed between these very walls. They all seemed to crowd together behind her, invisible but there nonetheless. Ghosts in white terry cloth robes.

"Stephen's got a job," she announced.

Peter had his back to her, but she watched him pause momentarily. It wasn't even a pause, it was more of a hesitation in his body language. It would have been invisible to anyone but her.

"Oh," he said.

It was more of a question left dangling in the air. Alma let it float there a moment longer, teasing Peter, testing his interest in pursuing the matter.

"What's he doing?" he asked finally, portioning out a length of dental floss.

"I'm not really sure. Some kind of sales. On the Internet."

Peter still had his back turned and peeked over the reflection of his shoulder in the mirror. "Well, good." He started to floss. "He needs to start taking on more responsibility," he added, examining the string between his fingers.

The answer surprised Alma. She peered out the window to the street below where an advancing row of cabs circulated people throughout the city. It was a ceaseless flow of activity—

The ring of her phone interrupted her thoughts.

In his hotel room that evening Koyl stared out across the city. How awed his people would be with the view before him. A skyscraper must once have seemed no more a defiance of nature than his own plans were today. Koyl wanted to feel the wind on his face, but the window was hermetically sealed. He pressed his face against the glass and stared down at the passing traffic. He was startled by a knock at the door. Three hard thumps.

Koyl opened it to find two men standing outside. One man was white and the other black.

It was the black man who spoke. "Are you Mr Mohala Koyl?"

Koyl noticed the white man stood a few steps behind the black one, as if to seal the corridor with his wide frame.

"I am President Koyl."

Koyl had assumed these men had been dispatched from the offices of the United Nations, like the chauffeur from that afternoon, but there was a gruffness about them, an absence of courtesy that didn't fit Koyl's expectation.

"Mr Koyl, I'm Special Agent Lassiter and this is Agent Hicks with the Department of Homeland Security, we'd like to ask you a few of questions."

The two men flashed badges automatically and entered the hotel room without invitation, looking the place over as they walked in.

"Sir, is there anyone else here in the hotel room with you at the present time?"

Koyl shook his head. What was the meaning of this intrusion? These men obviously had no idea who they were dealing with. Didn't they realize they were creating an international incident? It would be embarrassing for them and for their government. Fools. He mentally relished the thought of crushing these men, destroying their careers, and wondered how much of their smugness would remain after they hadn't eaten for a few days. He had broken tougher men than them.

"I am Mohala Koyl, President of the Democratic Republic of L'Eden Sur Mer. You have no right to ask me anything. You have neither the jurisdiction nor the authority."

"I'm afraid we do, Sir," said Agent Hicks. "Mr Koyl, we want to ask you a few questions about your relationship with Holden Nash and your involvement with Gaia Enterprises."

It had happened.

Koyl knew it was over.

Malhoun had been courting China for months. Koyl's principled avoidance of strategic international relationships within the region had gone on long enough. If Taiwan and China wanted to vie for influence in the region, Malhoun saw no reason why his country should not also benefit from their check-book diplomacy.

Malhoun was not alone. A growing number of parliamentarians agreed that L'Eden Sur Mer should assert itself on the international stage. President Koyl was too insular and too rigid in his opposition to these strategic alliances. There were other incentives too. Pacific microstates that recognized China were given grassroots development funds, cash payments ostensibly designed to enable members to help their local communities undertake small-scale development projects without having to jump through the bureaucratic hurdles or reporting requirements of international aid programs. Of course these funds effectively served as a monthly bribe for continued recognition of China, particularly in the form of votes within the United Nations. Most recipients of these funds used the money to supplement their own income, to buy votes at home, or as a general slush fund.

Parliamentarians in many South Pacific islands already received the highest salaries in the public sector, equivalent to about US $10,000 per year. The grassroots initiatives represented an enormous boon, a lump sum of $54,000 per member, per year.

A handful of Sur Merian parliamentarians had long despised Koyl for prohibiting their access to these funding sources. Even moderate politicians had started to appreciate the wisdom of amassing personal fortunes in the face of growing uncertainty; their potential relocation, where their hold on power and privilege might be less assured, swayed their vote.

Only a handful of Grey Hairs and parliamentarians remained loyal to President Koyl's doctrine of unconditional sovereignty. Full independence seemed increasingly like a romantic ideal, and not everyone had supported the idea of national sovereignty. From the very beginning there had been Sur Merians who thought their country unprepared for freedom. Some believed their colonial masters hadn't been all bad. Those old enough to remember recalled better opportunities for migration under the French regime, and that the country had been better governed and better resourced than it was now.

Independence had brought with it a dependence on foreign aid. For some, this was not true sovereignty, just reliance of a different kind. Then there had been Malhoun's followers, the devout, for whom faith mattered more than all else. Many believed God would deliver them from suffering, in this life or the next. There was little point worrying about anything beyond tomorrow.

Malhoun had promised to change everything. His plans needed money, and he saw no dignity, no valor in letting opportunity pass him by. As President, he would agree to recognize China. Koyl was his only obstacle. It was time the world discovered the father of this nation was no more than a meddling con man. Koyl's deceit was in the coffee-bean and mango plantations that lay half-buried under brackish yellow swamps; his lies were hidden inside cocoa and sugar-cane refineries that existed only on paper; in the plans for an eco-friendly palm-oil plantation that would never see the light of day; it was in the millions of carbon offset credits linked to environmental projects that didn't and never would exist.

The no-confidence motion against the President had been unanimous in the Sur Merian parliament. Koyl hadn't stood a chance. There was no way he could win a general election. Not now. Maybe later, if given more time. Maybe then he could turn things around. But his people were impatient. He knew his time was over. He had been swept away.

"Please. You must allow me to change. I cannot go out like this," said Koyl, gesturing to his terry-cloth bathrobe.

The officer nodded. "Make it quick, Sir."

"Thank you."

Koyl went into the bedroom.

He stood with his back against the wall. He wiped sweat from his brow and the top of his lip. He searched the ceiling of the room for … what? An air vent? His eyes followed the line of the ceiling. Four walls caged him in. He swallowed.

A siren, muted by the double-pane glass, wailed below.

"Mr Koyl," said a muffled voice through the wall. "We're going to have to wrap things up here, Sir."

"One moment. Please. I'm in the toilet." Koyl leaned his head back, bumping it against the wall repeatedly. Tears welled up.

He peeled himself from the wall. He took a few slow, quiet steps towards the balcony.

"Two minutes," said the voice behind the wall.

Koyl didn't answer. He nodded, sweated, focused on the twinkling lights of the buildings just ahead, at the horizon beyond. He closed his eyes and opened the balcony door.

It had been forty-eight hours since the Gaia website had been shut down. The office phone rang out and Stephen had received no correspondence from the company, not even an email. It didn't feel right. It never had, really.

Stephen often felt less anxious if he masturbated. Orgasm seemed to complement, reinforce or diminish whatever emotion had preceded it. It soothed him when he felt lonely, emboldened him when he felt insubstantial, and offered a focal point for his anger, culminating in a sense of release.

He hadn't downloaded any porn while surfing the net on Gaia's time. He was sure it was exactly the kind of thing Gaia would have wanted him to do, so the company could get a better sense of where their target audience hid on the net. Of course Gaia knew porn was popular. Who didn't? But Gaia wanted to know what porn, what sites, what specific perversions they could add to their consumer profiles. They wanted to own the data sets. Stephen hadn't wanted to help Gaia do that. He'd wanted some things to be private. Even now, even in this brave new world of permanent disclosure and hyper transparency, he wanted some things to remain just for himself.

With the Gaia website down, he felt better about scrolling down a list of familiar filenames, and considered each one like an item on a menu: blonde, brunette, big butt, teen, cougar, threesome, bisexual. He chose a group-sex video, and shifted his attention to the various acts performed by couples and groups in the scene. Where was this video shot? It looked to be someone's personal residence. There was a pool table being put to good use and some miscellaneous gym equipment on which couples bent and arched themselves. It all looked very boring and suburban, the mismatched furniture and little framed pictures hanging on the peach-colored wall. The people looked American or northern European. They looked healthy and well fed. The guys looked solid, but not fat; the women were round and smooth. One woman wore sunglasses. Why was that? Did she think it stylish? Or did she imagine the glasses offered her a measure of anonymity? Did she really think that those black frames would shield her from a future lover's reproach at seeing his girlfriend aggressively swallowing a dick in some suburban basement recreation room? Fuck her. Either she was a slut or she wasn't. She couldn't have it both ways …

Early Christmas shoppers buoy retail recovery—Woman dies in train collision—Oil Baron Charged With Fraud—click to view video—Paradise Lost: End of Island Nation?—

Stephen came downstairs to find Gracie sitting on the living room sofa in her bathrobe. She was eating a bowl of muesli.

"No class today?" he asked.

Gracie shook her head. She had made a little nest out of the throw cushions, a little sanctuary in the cold expanse of the living room.

"Hey, can you drive me to the mall?"

Gracie peered at him over her shoulder. "Seriously?" She slid a spoonful of muesli into her mouth to demonstrate that she had better things to do.

"Come on, you're supposed to be here helping me out," said Stephen. "You're just sitting around here anyway."

Gracie had been a brat about offering him rides ever since she got her driver's license. Stephen knew his sister didn't like driving and had almost failed the test, but at least she could legally take him places. Stephen didn't have the nerve to take any of the cars out by himself, so he had to rely on Gracie or his mother to get him around, especially on weekends when the bus system virtually shut down, turning what should have been a fifteen-minute car ride into an odyssey.

"I am helping you out by not taking you to the mall, believe me," said Gracie.

Stephen knew this was all bravado and that Gracie would cave if he persisted.

"Why do you want to go to the mall anyway?" she said, as if the proposition had been ludicrous.

"I don't know … hang out, look at stuff, buy something maybe."

Gracie just sat there, dipping her spoon into the muesli, pulling the yoghurt up into little strands that drizzled off the end of her spoon.

"Come on," said Stephen. "I haven't asked you for anything in, like, two days."

The timing was delicate here. Stephen knew that if he badgered Gracie too much, she would feel cornered and refuse him on principle. But if he let the silence linger a bit, if he let his neediness float in the space between them, she would eventually relent.

Gracie continued to sit, stirring the contents of her bowl.

Stephen watched her; he knew Gracie had a thing about people watching her eat.

"Urgh. Fine." She dismantled her ring of pillows. "One hour, though. I'm not hanging out there for ages."

Westgate Mall's Christmas decorations were up. Red and green garlands were strung from the ceiling and an enormous Christmas tree stood in the three-story mezzanine right beside Santa's village, where children would soon line up to have their pictures taken. While Santa himself would not arrive for another week or so, his padded throne lay in wait for his arrival, and, with it, the official start of another season of joy.

Gracie walked around with her hands folded across her tummy as if to shield herself from the surroundings. Stephen had always enjoyed the spectacle of Christmas. It was a nice ritual to dig boxes out from the dark places where they were kept for most of the year and rediscover their contents, reliving the past moments enjoyed in their company. All of these baubles and ribbons and bows were part of the chain of remembrance that added to each Christmas.

It was familiar and comfortable, and he felt deep down that Gracie must have felt the same way. Not just about Christmas, but about everything. But she pushed it all aside, and worked so hard to find fault with everything. It must be tiring for her, he thought. She must work hard to avoid being sentimental.

Stephen was on a mission. He was going to buy an outfit for the house party. Tal had invited Dean, who had invited Natalie, and Natalie had invited Sara. Stephen couldn't believe that Sara was actually coming to his house. Just imagining her walking around his home made Stephen tingle with excitement.

Now he had to tell Gracie about the party. Stephen didn't want to. He preferred to let the idea linger in his mind, unopposed, but he knew he had to broach the subject eventually. Now seemed as good an opportunity as ever.

"A party," said Gracie. "Why?"

"I don't know. It'll be fun," said Stephen. He always knew he would have to fight this battle, but he resented it all the same.

"What, so, like, you and friends can get drunk and be idiots together?"

"It's what people do, you know. Most people like to have fun. Not everyone wants to be a saint."

"You're an idiot."

"Whatever. I'm having it anyway. It's not like I'm asking your permission. I'm just telling you, that's all."

They walked on through the mall. The cheerful holiday melodies wafting out of the shops amplified the awkward silence between them.

The fight with her brother had been stupid. Gracie felt bad about it. She didn't feel like hanging out in her room anymore and had been moping around the basement for a change of scenery. There was a studio apartment down there that had probably served someone else as a nanny's retreat, but no one from the Van Dooren family really went in anymore. It was full of boxes, bags and containers piled high on the bed, almost to the ceiling, and spilled out of the open closet. Gracie peered inside one of the glossy, colored bags. Clothes were bunched up at the bottom. She pulled out a pair of dress pants and a red polka-dot skirt with the price tag still attached. The receipt fell to the floor as she unfolded the skirt. Gracie retrieved the paper; the ink was fading but she could make out the total at the bottom: $835. She put the receipt and the clothes back in the bag then picked up another and another—$300, $700, $55, $2,300. Gracie tore open sealed cardboard boxes and pulled the lids off plastic storage tubs. Out came skirts and shawls, cashmere cardigans and a sateen vest trimmed with embroidered lace. She pulled out blouses and blouses and blouses in linen and cotton and silk.

Gracie dug out three curling irons, two hand mixers, a stack of frying pans and a tower of baking trays. There was a food processor, a pearl necklace and four pairs of fur-lined leather gloves. There were travel cases and overnight bags in zebra and leopard print, handbags adorned with rhinestones and peacock feathers. There were trays of Christmas decorations with baubles made of hand-blown glass. There were face creams and hand creams, and jars of vitamins and mineral extracts. It made Gracie sick to see all of this stuff hiding away in the bottom of the house. How could they have so much while others had so little? How could her mother be so weak? A slave? How could God have let that happen? But if God, in all his glory, created everything, then how could the world and all the people in it be so imperfect? The world now seemed a more dangerous and lonely place than it had only a moment ago. There was nothing and no one she could entirely trust. She slumped into the pile of opened boxes and cried.

Jesus had been pierced for our transgressions. His wounds had healed us. Had it been enough? Could he do it again? *Could personal sacrifice still save the world?*

Chapter Thirty

Stephen wandered around the house trying to imagine what and where someone's drunk curiosity might lead them, what it might break and what trouble it might cause. In preparation for the party, he had pushed furniture against the wall of the living room and removed the glass coffee table. He locked the door to the basement wine cellar, as well as the doors of the dining room, in which he had piled a few antique chairs, a gilded mirror, two paintings that he knew nothing about except that they were valuable, and his laptop computer. He didn't much like the idea of people prowling around the house, spilling things, but it would all be worth it if the party drew Sara here. It was enough just to imagine her wandering around the place, as if her experiencing his natural habitat, his day-to-day environment would somehow bring them closer together. He made the bed in his upstairs room, arranged throw cushions at the head of the bed and closed the door behind him.

Carol's station wagon lurched up the circular driveway. Tal leaned out the passenger window.

"Yaoooooow." He jumped out of the car before it stopped moving.

"Home sweet home," he said, putting Stephen in a headlock.

Carol lit up a cigarette and stretched her back.

"Not bad," she said, taking in her surrounds. "Not bad.

You got an older brother or anything?" She laughed at her own joke, got out and fiddled with the latch of the trunk. She pulled it open.

"Tal, remember what I told you about this stuff."

"Coming." Tal made his way to the trunk, carrying Stephen along, still in a headlock. Five cases of beer and a bottle of vodka were packed in the back of the hatch.

"Bee-her," said Tal, showing Stephen his stash.

"Now, Tal," said Carol. "Seriously. Just for a sec. I don't mind you guys blowing off a little steam, okay. But remember what I said. No driving after this."

"Yes, ma'am."

"Tal."

Tal straightened himself.

"I'm serious. No fucking around. I don't mind you having some fun but you are not getting behind the wheel of a vehicle. I don't care if it's a lawn mower. No driving. Got it?"

"Yes."

"Okay then. And I don't want to be getting any calls from the cops, either."

"Yes, Mom."

"Pinkie swear."

"Mom."

"Ah, I'm not leaving until you pinkie swear it." Carol held out her pinkie finger, tilting her head to keep the smoke from getting in her eyes. Tal wrapped his pinkie finger around Carol's.

"Swear it," she said.

"I swear I won't drink and drive," said Tal.

"Okay. Cool," said Carol, satisfied.

"You, too. Come on." She held out her long, veiny arms to Stephen, her pinkie a dagger on the end of her hand.

Stephen wrapped his pinkie finger around Carol's. She had a firm grip.

"Okay," said Carol, getting back in the station wagon. "Have fun." She started the engine. The car wheezed and sputtered to life. Carol worked hard to turn the wheel, cigarette still between her teeth. She waved through the windshield and made her way down the driveway, leaving an oil stain and eerie quiet.

Tal cracked two beers immediately after his mother left and handed one to Stephen. "Here, get that into ya."

Stephen hoisted the can to his mouth. It was nice and cold, and relaxing, and it helped him to embrace the spirit of the event.

The two of them hauled the rest of the booze into the kitchen. Stephen had cleared the countertop of the espresso machine and the blown-glass fruit bowl. The emptiness of the place emphasized its clean, straight lines. It felt good to just stand there now, beer in hand, as if drinking it crowned an accomplishment, as if everything was right with the world. Then Gracie sulked through the door.

She was wearing black leggings and a long, button-down shirt that hung almost to her knees. The sleeves were too long and the cuffs almost covered her hands. Jiggling her wrist, she freed her hand and reached into the refrigerator to get some orange juice.

"Hey, Grace," said Tal.

Gracie took a long drink of juice from the bottle before answering. "Hey," she said, lowering the bottle. "So, big party tonight, eh?" She lifted her shoulders to her ears in mock excitement.

Stephen took a drink from his beer.

Tal put his can down on the counter behind him. "Thanks for letting us have a few people over, Gracie. It's really cool of you. My place is too small. Mom doesn't have a lot of money, being a single parent and all. We'll try not to make too much noise for you, okay," said Tal. "They'll all be gone by midnight. Promise."

Tal smiled as he stood there, hands at his side. Tal could do that, just stand there with his hands out of his pockets, not even with his arms crossed or anything, but just let them dangle at his side like it was the most natural thing in the world.

"Thanks," said Gracie, and lifted the bottle of orange juice back up to her lips.

"Did you want a drink, Gracie?" asked Tal, gesturing to the bottle of vodka. Gracie shook her head.

"Okay, well it's here if you want any. It's good with orange juice."

With a mouthful of juice, Gracie forced a smile and left the kitchen.

When she was gone, Tal picked up his beer can and looked at Stephen. The two of them shared a smirk, clinked cans and drank their beers, savoring their freedom.

Tal plugged a hard-drive into the stereo. The loud music emphasized the emptiness of the room. Stephen thought it possible that no one would show. This thought briefly calmed him.

"Sweet," said Tal turning the volume up. "What's the point of having these kick-ass speakers if you never use them." He put his beer on the window ledge, freeing up both arms to drum the air, which he did until he was red faced and out of breath. Tal downed the rest of his beer in panting slurps. Stephen self-consciously took a big sip of his own can, still half full. The beer inside had warmed and the liquid now felt thicker and heavier going down, altogether less pleasurable than those first cold sips they had shared on the driveway.

For a while it had seemed no one would show for the party, but they began to arrive in groups of three and five and ten, piling out of station wagons and SUVs with kids in the trunk and stacked three-high on each other's laps. The front doors of the Van Dooren house stayed open, despite the wintery chill. Inside was a jumble of legs and arms and feet, girls dressed in crop tops and mini-skirts. They breathed mist from their mouths as they stood at the door, waiting to come in. Soon they were indoors, rubbing their bare arms with their hands, their high heels clomping like hooves on the kitchen's tile floor while their boyfriends rummaged in tubs of ice to find them something to drink.

Stephen searched each new wave of arrivals, but Sara was nowhere to be seen. He wandered the house, half looking for her, half checking to make sure people stayed out of the forbidden zones. The dining-room doors were still locked, the contents safely stored inside. The basement door also remained closed. It was an out-of-the-way door anyway, hard to find if you didn't know what you were looking for. He looked outside at the pool house, which now looked dark and derelict. How much easier this evening would have been in the summer, when the pool could be the focal point of the party.

When the house was full of people, Stephen walked down the hallway to the eastern wing. He'd had a few beers and felt a bit unsteady. His head was spinning. It was a strange sensation to be wandering around a space he knew so well yet have it seem unfamiliar, its proportions distorted by the alcohol. Absurdly, he opened a cupboard door on his way down the hallway, half expecting to find something other than the linen and board games stored in there. He closed the door and headed down the long hallway to his father's study. There was a light on that might attract attention.

Stephen turned off the light and closed the door. His limbs felt heavy and the whole party suddenly angered him. He wanted everyone gone. Sara hadn't come. What did he expect? It's not like Sara was his girlfriend. Rationally he had always known Sara would remain a fantasy, and yet there had been something comforting about that, too, something liberating in thinking about a strange twist of fate that might bring them together. His job, this party, he had done it all for her. There was no real plan to it. He didn't expect to achieve anything. Maybe he had been trying to impress Sara. Or maybe the idea of her had just compelled him to mold himself into a slightly better version, someone worthy of her attention. It all felt pretty stupid. She wasn't even here. What was she doing tonight?

As he walked from room to room his thoughts grew thick and murky. It dulled his anger and made him want another beer. In the kitchen he dug around in the ice tub to find another one of Tal's beers. People had been adding their drinks to the tub for a while and the ice was jammed with cans and bottles. There were bottles of cider, rum coolers, wine spritzers, and cans of rum and coke. His hand grew numb from the cold as he searched for one of the cans that Tal had brought. He couldn't find them and was growing impatient. He noticed a bottle from which the label had peeled away. Whatever, it was his party. He opened it and drank it urgently.

The living room was a nightclub. The music was deafening, and the glass of the bay window shook with each thump of the bass. Kids danced and giggled and playfully swiped at each other between slurps from their plastic cups. No longer able to contain his or her exuberance, someone occasionally yelped or screamed. One girl climbed up on her friend's shoulders and jousted with another who had done the same. Stephen could see their G-strings climbing out above their pants from across the living room. That was the point.

He wasn't the only one who noticed. Guys gathered on couches, on chairs and ottomans and on the floor, swaying to the music from their seated positions, hoping to catch a glimpse of flesh.

Stephen needed some quiet. On his way out the front door, he passed the entrance hall under the stairs and noticed a group of guys leaning against the top of the bannister, near Gracie's room. Tal was up there, too, almost propping himself up with the railing. As Stephen went up the stairs he could see that Tal was wobbly and glassy-eyed, and part of a loose circle of guys taking exaggerated puffs off what smelled like a joint.

"Hey, guys." Stephen wanted to act cool and avoid assuming authority. "This is my parents' place so do you guys mind, like, smoking that outside." He looked over at Tal, who seemed to look right through him.

One of the guys nodded as he took a long pull off the joint, leaning his whole body back into the draw. He was a tall, wiry guy with a long, bushy soul patch under his chin and thick, rubbery veins on his arms. The guy held his breath.

"It's almost out, Boss," he said, without expelling the smoke from his lungs.

He wet his fingers with his tongue and snuffed the joint by pinching the smoldering end.

"See, it's out." He released the smoke that had been swirling inside him then held up the joint. He had a self-satisfied smirk on his face. Of the others, one guy was wearing a ball cap that was pulled down so low that he was mostly chin, the rest of him hidden beneath the brim. They all looked a bit older, these guys, and Stephen wasn't even sure they went to the same school. They were Tal's friends, guys he worked with at Motel 6. Tal had said nothing about inviting them.

Gracie's door opened and a broad guy with a shaved head stepped out. He covered his look of surprise at seeing Stephen with a broad smile, overly friendly.

"Hey, man," he said to Stephen.

Tal glanced at the group of guys assembled in the hallway, then back at Stephen.

"What's going on?" asked Stephen. The guy with the big chin stuffed his hands deep into his trouser pockets.

"Just trying to have a good time, man." The guy stepped a little closer.

"My sister in there?" said Stephen, glancing at the closed door behind the guy's shoulder.

The guy sighed. "She's pretty fucked up, dude. I think she just needs to sleep it off."

Stephen looked at him. Imagined the darkened room beyond the door. "You're an asshole."

The guy cocked his head. "What did you say?"

"You heard me," said Stephen.

"Don't be a loser," he said.

Two others squared up behind Stephen. Tal stayed propped on the bannister, looking down at the ground. The lanky guy crossed his wiry arms and the guy with the sharp chin looked up from under the brim of his cap. Stephen felt a rush of hatred for these guys. He imagined running his full weight into them like a bowling ball, knocking them over the bannister, their broken bodies heaped on the parquetry floor below.

"You should probably go," said Stephen to the guys, but speaking to Tal.

"Hey, man, fuck off. This isn't what you think," said the guy with the shaved head.

"Oh, it's not?" Stephen looked at him. He had a thick neck and a swollen, jowly face. Stephen looked at Tal, searching his face for reassurance, solidarity, something, anything that would help him disbelieve what he felt was going on here. Tal's face was blank.

The jowly guy had moved in really close, head cocked almost entirely to the side, revealing the thick veins of his neck and the stubble on his face. Stephen stared back, resisting the urge to swallow hard. The guy was now cheek to cheek with Stephen. He slowly turned his head and whispered in Stephen's ear. "She didn't do anything she didn't want to do." He exhaled with hot breath that smelled of beer and sweat and stale cigarettes. Stephen felt goose bumps at the nape of his neck, the shiver interrupted as the guy inserted his tongue into Stephen's ear and lapped his earlobe with a slurping sound. Stephen pushed him away hard.

"Oooh," said the guy. "Feisty."

"You're an asshole."

"Whatever, man," said the guy.

He turned to leave but Stephen grabbed his arm. They stared at each other. Without turning his head the guy addressed his crew from Motel 6, "Come on guys, let's get out of here."

At the foot of the stairs, he whipped back towards Stephen with his fist drawn back over his head. Stephen crouched down, held up his arms and turned his head to the side, flinching. He waited for the punch, for the thump, the flash of pain. But felt nothing. Stephen opened his eyes and saw him still standing there, his balled-up fist hovering. He moved in closer and started grinding up against Stephen in simulated sexual thrusts.

"Just what I thought, man. You're just a little bitch." He turned and shepherded his posse down the stairs.

Stephen kneeled on the floor, the ghost imprint of dick and balls still fresh in his side. He stared at the back of that shaved head with its barcode tattoo. Stephen's eyes widened.

"You're lucky we don't fuck you up, man," said the guy with

the soul patch, pointing at Stephen and spilling beer on the carpet on his way down the stairs.

Stephen's heart raced. He clenched his fists. *Now. While they're at the top of the stairs.* He charged, swinging at anything that got in his way. He missed the tattoo and caught the guy's shoulder. More slap than punch, Stephen's hand ricocheted off something sharp and bony. The guy turned and grabbed Stephen by both wrists. Hard. So much power in those hands. The thumbs dug into Stephen's wrists, squeezing the life out of his hands, his arms, his knees. Stephen's legs gave out and he crumpled to the floor.

"Take him out, man," heard Stephen. "Fuck him up."

With a crack his head jerked to the left. A fire on his cheek. He looked up. The guy stood over him, a silhouette in the hallway of his parents' house.

"You get a bitch slap," said the guy. "A bitch slap for a bitch."

The posse laughed and headed down the hallway. Tal went with them, bowing his head as he trudged down the stairs.

Stephen managed to work up enough saliva to swallow past the lump in his throat. It took all of his concentration not to cry. He got to his feet, eyes watering, cheek hot. He rubbed the side of his face, his jaw. He brought his hand down and inspected his fingertips. *No blood.*

In Gracie's room the air was heavy. Sticky and sweet with the odor of vomit and orange juice. Gracie was crumpled on the bed with her face burrowed in the quilt cover. As he approached, Stephen saw she'd been sick all over the bed. It had pooled on the white bedspread and collected in the valleys of the ruffled duvet. Creeping closer, he asked if she was okay. She didn't move. He got close. She was breathing. He stood there for a moment, by the side of the bed, trying to edge her legs around to sit her up. She swatted the air in front of him. She'd soiled herself. He dry-retched as the smell caught in his nostrils.

"Don't," she said.

"I'm just trying to sit you up."

Gracie curled up in a tight ball on the bed. "Go away."

Stephen didn't know what to do. He walked into the en-suite bathroom and stopped at his own reflection in the mirror, saw the stupid outfit he was wearing, the ledge of fat that hung over the front of his pants. His face was flushed, his cheek red.

"Motherfuck!" he said and paced the narrow space between the sink and the bathtub. He was welling up.

He punched the bathroom wall, which jiggled his chubby arms and jostled the fat on his back. Feeling that extra weight, that extra skin, that blubber hang off him like raw dough, filled him with rage. He hit the tiles again and again until he heard one of them crack.

He stopped. He was panting. Stephen's hands trembled and his knuckles were bleeding. The cracked tile stared back at him. The outburst had calmed him a bit. It always felt better to bleed. Now he could gather his thoughts.

He had to fix this situation. Time to focus. He ran a bath and poured in some soap bubbles, if only to mask the odor of vomit that clung to him and to everything else in the room. Vomit seemed to permeate the rising steam that now fogged the bathroom mirror. The bass beat rumbled through the floorboards from downstairs. It was 11:00pm. The party was in full swing. Gracie sobbed in the other room. She gagged, drew breath, and threw up again with a liquid squirt.

Stephen went to the foot of her bed and put his hand on Gracie's foot. He let it sit there for a moment, just resting it, cautious, the way he might have approached a stray dog or a wounded animal. It felt better to at least touch her. It somehow helped him feel like he was managing the situation.

"Grace. I just want to get you to the bathroom. Okay? Do you think you can make it in there?"

Gracie shook her head. She was crying and burping. Some of her vomit was clinging to one of the neatly formed curls of her hair. Stephen knew he had to do something. He had to take her somewhere. Take her to the bathroom, take her downstairs, to the hospital, but none of that could happen in the state she was in.

He wanted to call his mother but she would freak out. There was no way around it; he had to get Gracie into the bath and into fresh clothes. Maybe that would help her.

He pushed his arms under Gracie's back. She squirmed, but he managed to lift her off the mattress. He lowered her into the bath. The water overflowed onto the tiles. His hand stung in the soapy water. His knuckles were still bleeding. Gracie sat up with her eyes half-closed and leaned her head back against the tiles. Stephen undid the buttons on Gracie's blouse and pulled it off. She resisted, tucking her hands under her armpits. She was crying. Then she stopped crying and began to convulse. Stephen knew he needed help.

Alma's phone buzzed inside her purse. She felt the vibration before she actually heard the ring. She finished her drink in one gulp and went cold when she saw it was Stephen. "What's going on, what's happening?"

Stephen was instantly unsure if he had done the right thing calling Alma. Maybe he *could* handle this on his own. Maybe he could just make up some other reason why he'd called. Surely she would hear the music in the background. He had already been silent for too long now.

"Stephen. What's going on?"

He hadn't really thought about what he might say. Where would he begin?

"Mom, uh, hey."

"Stephen."

"Umm, Gracie's … not okay," he said.

"What do you mean? What's happened?"

"I think she's had a lot to drink or something. She's throwing up and she can't walk, and I don't really know what to do."

Silence from the other end. And then: "Where is she now?"

"She's in the tub."

"What? Why is she in the tub?"

"I wanted to clean her off."

Alma took a deep breath. "Stephen. What is going on?"

Stephen's mouth trembled. His face contorted, gripped from the inside by an inner sadness that would not let go. He fought to control it. He swallowed.

"Stephen!"

The tears came. They rolled down his cheeks, warm and salty. "I don't know, Mom. I don't know what to do." He cried, his mouth opening and closing silently between slurping, snotty breaths. "I don't know what to do."

"Stephen."

"Yeah?"

"I need you to listen to me now, okay?"

Stephen nodded and wiped his eyes. "Okay."

Alma breathed deeply. "I need you to call an ambulance."

"Seriously?"

"Seriously."

"You call me when you get to the hospital, do you understand? We are on our way."

"How are you guys going to get up here?"

"I don't know, Stephen! Just get your sister to the hospital."

Alma hung up and looked at her phone. Her fingers were trembling. She went to the closet and pulled out her suitcase. She put it on the bed.

"What's going on?" said Peter.

Alma threw her clothes into her suitcase. "I have to go."

"What's going on?"

"I don't know."

"Well what was that phone call?"

"There's some kind of trouble at the house. Gracie's sick or done something—I don't know." Alma went to the closet and got her coat.

"Well is there anything seriously wrong?"

Alma zipped up her suitcase.

"Alma."

"I don't know! Okay. I'm not there." Alma stood there, a crumpled nightgown in her hands, suitcase on the bed. "I've got to go." She turned to leave.

Peter grabbed her arm. "Alma, wait. This is crazy, leaving in the middle of the night. Why don't you wait? We'll leave in the morning."

Alma shook out of Peter's grasp.

The hotel phone rang. Peter turned away from Alma towards the flashing red light that lit up the dark corner of the bedside table.

"You do what you want, Peter. I'm going home."

Alma zipped up her coat and opened the heavy door. The hotel phone trilled and flashed on the nightstand.

"Alma. Wait."

The ambulance pulled up on the street outside, lights flashing, no siren. Stephen had imagined the paramedics would rush in and take charge. He thought they would order people around and quickly move about their business of setting things right. But the man and woman moved slowly. They ambled up the stairs, carrying their collapsible gurney past the family portraits and into Gracie's bedroom. They had arrived at the same time as the police, who were responding to a number of complaints about noise and a fight that had started out on the front lawn.

Gracie was still in the tub, her head was slumped to the side. She was unresponsive. Only now did Stephen think about the risk of putting Gracie in the tub in the state she was in. What if she drowned? One of the paramedics turned to Stephen. "Is she on anything?"

Now that other people were here with him, here in the bathroom, things seemed more serious. The paramedics were leaving muddy footprints all over the wet tile floor. Absurdly, those footprints worried him, adding to the chaos of the situation and making the whole thing more real. There was no more denying that things had got fucked up.

"I think she drank a lot," he said.

The paramedic paused and searched Stephen's face.

"What happened to your hand?" asked the male paramedic.

"Punched a wall," said Stephen automatically.

"Are you her boyfriend?" asked the female paramedic. The question seemed to have some significance for her.

"No, I'm her brother," he said.

This seemed to reassure her. She softened. "You sure she didn't take anything else?"

Stephen shook his head. The paramedic persisted.

"No drugs? No pills?"

Stephen shook his head again. "Yes. I mean, no." He collected himself. "I'm pretty sure she's just been drinking but … I don't know. I don't know."

The paramedics lifted Gracie out of the tub and onto the stretcher. They covered her with a blanket, strapped her down with seatbelt buckles and carried her down the stairs and to the waiting ambulance.

A few people cheered as the stretcher made its way down the driveway, as if casualties lifted the party's status. Clumps of kids were now scattered on the lawn as the police set about emptying the house of revelers. Girls sat barefoot on the snowy sidewalk while their guys shouted obscenities into the night, if only to hear themselves speak. Some were still drinking and carrying on, determined to keep the party going, despite the cops and the lights, and the neighbors in their bathrobes peering from behind half-opened drapes. Others had decided this party had come to an end, and made their way, in groups, down the street, up over the crest of the hill and past the cul de sacs to find the next big thing.

It was almost dawn when Stephen and Alma sat on gray chairs in the waiting room of St Vincent's Hospital. Stephen watched the lights twinkle on a miniature Christmas tree that was wrapped with too much tinsel. The gaudy colors of those lights projected out, casting long, dark shadows on the lime-green wall.

Alma wore a puffy down jacket over a black cocktail dress. She was twirling one of the straps of her coat around her finger and staring at an eye chart that was fixed to the wall.

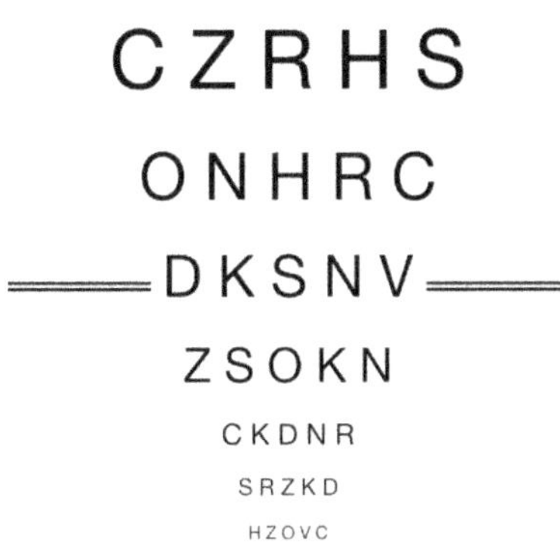

It was soothing, meditative, to lose herself in those letters. Alma had almost drowned once when she was seven. She had gone out too far, beyond the place where she could stand, had got caught in a current that pulled her out to sea. Alma was a good swimmer, but no matter how much she struggled, how much she had wanted to reach the shore, the current was stronger; it wanted her more. It had gripped her and would not let go. She had grown exhausted and gone under.

She remembered the feeling of when her head sank beneath the waves. At first she had panicked, and fought to get back to the surface, desperate to break through that thin line where the light rippled on top of the water. Where she could breathe.

Then she had stopped. She had stopped kicking, stopped fighting, stopped demanding to be anywhere else. She had become aware of a vast quiet surrounding her. She felt it again now, that impossible quiet. But there was no one there to help her this time, no one there to reach in and hoist her out of the water, no one there to pull her up from all of that weight and pressure piling on top of her as she sank deeper and darker than she had ever been.

An external door opened and Peter walked in, his shoulders dusted with fresh snow. Stephen looked up at his father. He felt that inner sadness tug at his mouth. Alma looked at Peter, her eyes puffy and raw. She half smiled. Peter approached his family. He put his arms around Stephen and Alma, who stayed seated in the gray, plastic hospital chairs. Their arms folded around Peter. They stayed there like that, the three of them, collapsed onto each other.

Peter turned and looked out the window. At the snow. The drift was heavy—dense but slow. He watched as each downy flake glowed pink for a moment as it caught the light of the emergency ward's red neon sign. It had probably been snowing for hours. Peter had forgotten how beautiful snow could be. It was as if the world had been covered in white lace, briefly making it cleaner, purer than it really was. There was beauty in the world. You had to learn to see it. He remembered when Gracie was little and how she used to sit in the little hollow space between his crossed legs, and how his body had enveloped hers, protecting her little limbs from the world beyond. How he wished he could always keep her as safe as she had been then. Peter held out his hand. Alma took it and held it to her cheek. They had come so close to losing everything.

"Alma," said Peter.

Alma turned, but didn't look at him. "There's nothing more we can do here tonight. Why don't we go back home?"

"I'm staying," said Alma, still looking at the wall.

Peter leaned in and touched Alma's knee. He let his hand sit there a moment. "We can come back in the morning," he said. "She's resting." Peter leaned in, searched Alma's face. *Look at me.* "Don't you think—"

"I'm staying!"

Peter took his hand off Alma's knee. He rubbed his own, leaned back in his chair and looked up at the clock. It would be dawn soon. He stood up.

"Stephen." His son snapped out of a daze. It'd been a long night. "Want to go back to the house, maybe get a few things and bring them back?"

Stephen looked at the Christmas tree. Its lights glowed red, then blue, then white.

"I'm going to stay here with Mom."

Peter looked out the window. Everything seemed to move slowly, more slowly than it had before—no faster than snow could fall. They would be all right now, the four of them. Things would somehow be okay. In the distance, an ambulance wailed.

"Okay," said Peter. "I'll stay too."

L'Eden Sur Mer peeked over the still ocean that licked its shores. Dawn broke on the horizon, and the morning sun gently warmed the sheltered places where life had survived another night. The routine had endured for millennia. But the island remained a lonely place, not favored by the currents, which had, for centuries, swept the great happenings of the world past its rocky shores to land somewhere else instead. It was, after all, but a pinprick in a constellation of islands that spread across the great blue waters of the Pacific. Like the stars above them, these worlds were born, they sparkled and they died, leaving only traces, hints, to say they too had once been there.

Acknowledgments

Thank you to Charmaine Rodrigues from the United Nations' Bureau for Crisis Prevention and Recovery for putting me in touch with various representatives of Pacific Island states, particularly Katy Le Roy in Nauru and Winifereti Nainoca in Fiji, whose advice, perspectives and personal experiences were invaluable in the preparation of this book.

Thanks also to Dr Michael O'Keefe at La Trobe University in Melbourne, Australia, for helping me to better appreciate the history and geopolitics of the South Pacific. I am no expert, so it was helpful to be able to lean on one.

Thank you to Writers Victoria for the support and occasional teaching work and to my mentor, Clare Allan-Kamil, whose tough love helped to make this a better book and me a better writer.

I am grateful to my wife, Suzie, for her precious insights, and for taking care of everything and everyone when I disappeared on mornings, evenings, weekends and holidays to write this novel. You taught me to go after my dreams.

Thank you to Tim Leurs of Zero21 for designing my book cover. You turned a thought bubble into a dramatic work of art. Equally, I am grateful to Tauseef Ahmed for your beautiful illustrations. You plucked the images from my mind.

Thank you to Caroline Duyvestyn for your encouragement in reading early drafts of this novel, back when it was about different people and set somewhere else.

I'm also grateful to Faber & Faber for permission to quote from Philip Larkin's poem, 'This Be the Verse' in Chapter One.

Thank you to Brad Wallace at www.bradwallaceimaging.com for generously offering me the use of the crest that appears at the top of the Presidential letterhead from L'Eden Sur Mer.

A variety of Pacific island states informed the fictitious cultural, political and historical landscape of L'Eden Sur Mer. Influences include: Fiji, Kiribati, Tuvalu, Nauru, Samoa, the Maldives, Papua New Guinea and Hawaii. At the risk of being culturally reductive, the idea of the book was to imagine a pan-Pacific nation, rather than draw on the specific experiences of any one island-microstate or its leaders past and present.

The concept of the floating island was inspired by various existing designs for buoyant infrastructure, particularly the work of Dutch Docklands, an independent company operating out of the Netherlands and Dubai. An existing joint venture between Dutch Docklands and the Government of the Maldives plans out the construction of more than 800 hectares / 80 million square feet of water with floating developments.

In 2012, the Kiribati Cabinet agreed to purchase approximately 6,000 acres of land on Viti Levu, the largest of Fiji's islands. Kiribati President Anote Tong underscored that the initiative was in consideration of a younger generation, for whom an exodus will be a "matter of survival", and that Kiribati may become uninhabitable by the 2050s due to rising sea levels and salination provoked by climate change.

President Koyl's speech to the United Nations draws largely upon statements made by His Excellency Mr Apisai Lelemia, Minister for Foreign Affairs, Trade, Tourism, Environment and Labour of Tuvalu, and His Excellency Mr Tuila'epa Fatialofa Lupesoliai Sailele Malielegaoi, Prime Minister of Samoa, at the United Nations Framework Convention on Climate Change held in Doha, Qatar, in December of 2012.

About the Author

Yannick Thoraval is a professional communications adviser and university lecturer.

Best known as an essayist, Thoraval has published widely for both academic and general audiences.

He formally studied film, philosophy and American political history, attaining a Master's degree from the University of Melbourne before leaving academia to pursue commercial writing interests. He worked as a copywriter and associate editor in marketing and communications, as well as a speechwriter for the State Government.

Thoraval's fiction has received critical acclaim. His first screenplay Kleftiko was a finalist in the International Showcase Screenwriting Awards. Judges of the prestigious Victorian Premier's Literary Awards, Australia, highly commended his first novel, The Current.

The novel draws from Thoraval's personal and professional experiences of working in the Victorian State Government, particularly his work in international development, including with the nation of Timor-Leste.

He is a career migrant and has lived in the Netherlands, France, Cyprus, Canada and Australia. Moving internationally from a young age has left him feeling culturally stateless, despite holding three passports.

Thoraval is a quiet advocate for refugees and asylum seekers. He is a founding member of the World Writings Group, which helps refugees write about their experiences of forced migration.

He has pledged to donate a portion of the proceeds of his book to assist the settlement of refugees and asylum seekers.

He currently lives in Melbourne, Australia, where he teaches professional writing and editing. He is working on his second novel.